T0129528

The Derived and The Deprived

and The

Deprived

Eniola F. Fagbemi

authorHOUSE®

AuthorHouse™
1663 Liberty Drive
Bloomington, IN 47403
www.authorhouse.com
Phone: 833-262-8899

Published by AuthorHouse 03/30/2021

ISBN: 978-1-7283-5751-5 (sc)
ISBN: 978-1-7283-5750-8 (hc)
ISBN: 978-1-7283-5749-2 (e)

Library of Congress Control Number: 2020905722

Print information available on the last page.

Dedicated to all deprived Africans.

It's all fiction

Contents

Chapter 1: Ruqayah 1

Chapter 2: Nana 40

Chapter 3: Do thi Ngoc 73

Chapter 4: Dafina 94

Chapter 5: Senami 123

Chapter 6: Kenosi 149

Chapter 7: Zinyoro 201

Glossary 235

1

Ruqayah

*…giving a child a skill is worth more than a
thousand pieces of gold.*

At age fourteen, still in my highest junior secondary class, I was
always compulsively agonized about my parents' plot to consent my
marriage to Alhaji Harun: one of the richest brokers in my country.
He wasn't only rich and influential; he was also blessed with thirty-
two children and thirteen wives. In all, my royal pain was the
presence of his numerous children who were either my exact age or
older. He staked a claim to his other wives at precisely my age or even
younger. According to the tradition, as I was told, it all depends on
menarche-when a girl's first period is detected. The monthly course
means readiness for marriage and productivity. The youngest wife
he ever got, Ramatu, began her period just at the age of ten and had
no reason to remain with her parents anymore. She was married off
the same week.

The signal was considered too late for me. The groom- to -be
continuously mounted resistance on my parents' slow up to hand me
over to him. It was so sad that they had no say over me again. They
only pleaded each time he popped in for confirmation. But, overall,

what caught me by surprise was the verity that my suitor was my father's best friend.

Yes, I knew him from childhood. I knew him as just my father's friend when he would call in on our polygamous home with a lot of gifts for everyone. I looked upon him as my father. And it never crossed my mind then, that they had something up their sleeve- something that would cast a cloud over my life. A subject more death-defying than just offering me as a sacrificial lamb for all his solicitude to my family. Astonishingly, none of my parents asked my approval before my head is shaven.

Their plan wasn't revealed to me until the day I overheard the argy- bargy between the two friends, on my arrival from school, one day.

'No, listen to me! No! That is not the issue', Harun retorted, his accent heavily interfering with his spoken English. He tossed impatiently in his vast traditional attire, shrouding his enormous body and feet as he occupied a sofa in my father's living room. Each time he spoke persuasively, he flashed an orangey set of teeth, tastefully furnished with kolanut -and eyes as red as spleen. He's, undeniably, too ugly, unsettling.

'I'm not disputing it, Alhaji –*na iya bayanna mini cewa*', my teeny-weeny father interrupted him, his long hand-woven cap fitting to his small head like the crest on a cock. He appeared undismayed by his great deal of badgering after he was mollified and quieted like a propitiated god. He smiled erratically and pleaded with noticeably poor effort. I am not important to him.

'We have agreed to give her a chance to finish her secondary education before she is handed to you ', Baba managed to conclude drowsily. And that was the first time I was able to gather from their whole conversation that, it was all about me. He wanted to marry me off to his friend. My heart thudded heavily in my chest. I felt depressed, anxious, and obviously tired. I forced my entire being on my shaky and shivering feet to eavesdrop on the rest of their evil plan, know my inexorable fate.

'*Haba*, Alhaji Tahir- Ruqah is mine. I raised her from childhood to teen age. Besides, I have paid and over paid her dowry', he managed to wear a smile and continued. 'That alone, gives me the right to take my wife. Please, let me finish. *Ina zuwa*', he waved his judgment aside as he opened his mouth to talk.

'It is good to follow an agreement. Is it because we are friends or what? Traditionally, her mother, Nasreen, has informed me that the signal emerged last month. So, what are you telling me?' he furrowed his brows, already tired of his needless protraction of the rites. Did he do the same to marry his own wives? Verily, he got my mother the same way. Still at the same spot, I clasped my hands above my head and bit my finger sadly, having heard my mother's contributory plan. So far, I wasn't satisfied. I wanted to hear more, hear all. I blinked my eyes and looked through the split in the half-opened door to catch a glimpse of my father's expression. He appeared soberer than when the dialogue just began. His sense of guilt had set in.

The suitor had paid him more than my bride price when I was just three months old. He had always been supportive to my brood of brothers and sisters – to everyone. Even if he wanted to back off from the deal, he wouldn't have enough money to return, at least, a quarter of his payment. Should he remember to pay for just his provision of food items? Or bear in mind his return for all he paid for our wears, school fees, and other necessities –most of which he cannot remember? He had, indeed, been the backbone of the family when my father's farming business wasn't worthwhile to meet our needs. He was constantly having unbeatable rivalries from the neighboring villages, with lower prices for their farm products. After a bewildering turn of events, he didn't have enough to provide for our needs.

The look on his face was not one sided. He was grieving over his consent to give out his only jewel: I was his only jewel, his pride. Of all his seventeen children, I was the most intelligent, the bravest and the most unwavering. I was not just prepared to pursue my studies up to Master's degree but to bring fame and fortune to my family expeditiously. This was very quick to materialize as I never faltered in representing my school anywhere in the entire nation. I always took the lead. Baba himself could not dispute having a feel of the high regard. He was continually respected in my school and in the community except for the financial gain it was not yielding yet. Was he prepared to lose these? Was he about to entreat me to abandon my esteemed future and marry an ignominious illiterate? I thought dismally.

'Humph-', my father heaved a sigh and shook his head. He removed his cap absently, his bald head at a slight tilt.

'You kept saying school-school-school. *Haba*! *Me ne wannan*? She's a girl. What does a girl do with education? She only needs to produce babies for me and- ', he was interrupted by Baba's anguished reaction. He couldn't go through the pain any longer.

'Give me time to think about this. We had an agreement that she should, at least, have secondary education', he looked at him squarely, an overwhelming despair fixed on his face.

'O-kay, when will you decide? She's all mine. A restless foot walks into a snake pit', he stretched out his hands from the *Agbada* for the first time, since he sat in the sofa. I almost thought he had a problem there. Who cares?

'Why not just leave her to finish her secondary education? She's still yours, nothing changes that'.

'Alhaji Tahir. Why? You should know by now that this education opens a woman's mind. It's an eye opener. Once she's exposed to things she should not know, she won't marry me again! I need my wife now, right now', he laughed from ear to ear in desperation. Rich black bastard. From where I stood, I looked at him despondently. Nothing would make me escape his pro-active desire if my parents connived with him, but I knew miracle could set me free.

'No - education doesn't do that. It will help prepare her for the future. It will also make her a better wife- and a caring mother too. Please-am pleading with you. I know she belongs to you but-please, give her this one chance. This only one chance to finish her secondary education. May almighty Allah bless you and your family', Baba squatted in front of him apologetically, traditionally. Again, I shook my head at this. Greed had thrown him under the shadow of fear and had overly turned Harun his god. This is the persuasive power of poverty.

'Okay, okay, it's alright, get up - get up. *Da ita*. Just tell me when she will finish this her secondary education and I will arrange for the rite', he said ignorantly, a fiery look on his face.

'In three years' time. Just three years and she will be all yours'.

'Three years! Three whole years? That's too long. Can't she continue in my house?'

'No, she can't. She can't concentrate in your house. Besides, when she's pregnant, she will be out of school', he beseeched on my behalf.

'Give me time to think about this. I don't think this is good. You want me to lose her to civilization, I'm afraid. Educated women are too wise. *Khai!*'

'I'm sorry please, my good friend. She's yours, all yours. I want to give you the best wife you've ever had', Baba said smiling but he was quick to refute his plans.

'I think you have tried enough. What else do you want to give? I don't even think she's enjoying herself here anymore. I have enough money to look after her in my home', anger flickered in his eyes.

'We just want her to be special to you, nothing more', he cleared his throat, stood up and spat a gob of phlegm through a glass window. I grimaced. Heaven knows how much he sickened me with this.

'*Yuowa*, but you know it's not safe to leave her in the system for long. I think you know that. Education is a fast eye-opener. Only a fool tests the depth of a river with both feet. She's looking more matured and beautiful every year', he pointed out on a more serious note, craned his neck, glared around for a while and turned back to Baba.

'Please, can you get her for me? I want to see her'.

'It's alright- I'll get her for you', he rose to his feet and sauntered away from the large living room, calling out my name. I quickly withdrew from the spot, hurried out through the back door and into the backyard where two of my step sisters were busy preparing the corn- meal for dinner. Altogether, we were five girls and twelve boys, but my mother had only three of us. I was her only girl and the oldest of the girls. We lived together happily as one would hardly tell our real mothers apart. They loved us equally.

'Ha, Ruqayah, we were arguing about something before you came', Alimah, my first step sister of twelve years, snitched on her sister.

'What is that?' I asked disinterestedly. I had a bothersome issue on my mind. I hurriedly bent over the corn- meal they were preparing, started assisting them to avoid being taken to the mischief maker in the living room. Each time, I looked over my shoulder, expecting my father's arrival.

'Kabirah said that it's not proper to share the same room with your parents that-that', she laughed again, sneaking a look at her.

'That what?! Are you crazy or something is wrong with you? I don't want trouble oh', Kabirah removed her hand from the meal and yelled at her, their noise biting my ears. If only they could be silent and allow my thought to flow. I wasn't just in the mood.

'Yes! You said that you saw Baba and Ajia last night', she pushed her veiled head, sniggered at her.

'You saw what?!' Baba asked surprised, as he appeared behind us. 'Repeat what you just said now, or I will pull these ears away from your body', he twisted Alimah's ears cruelly. She groaned with pain and knelt in front of him. He did not unfasten his grip. He pressed on to get the truth from her. Matters of discipline were always his priority. I washed my hands, folded them behind me then stepped aside sullenly. He wasn't there for them, anyway; he was there for me. And the reflection of his plan to entwine my future with the miscreant really upset me. I gave him a bad shot from behind. If my eyes were bullets, he would have dropped dead.

'You! Didn't you hear me calling you?' he pointed a finger at me ferociously, his eyes burning with fury. I wasn't shaken by his overreaction. I shook my head and looked away.

'No', I muttered.

'Alright, go in now and see Alhaji. He asked of you', he instructed.

'What for?'

'Go in now and see him and- stop asking me cock and bull questions', he lunged forward for my arm and pushed me into the corridor weightily. Baba already forgot that you can force a horse to the river but cannot drive it to drink. I yielded with reluctance and perceived his anger as a mere transfer of aggression. What he just heard infuriated him, maybe.

I stomped into the room, recalling how I treated him with courtesy when his intention wasn't disclosed. Sometimes, either Baba or my mother would engage me in a chat with him for hours. But, he never revealed his true feelings. He just fished for information about my relationship with the people I knew, especially the opposite sex.

I caught him relaxed and busy biting off his finger nails like a kid when I walked in. This should be a habit he's accustomed to from childhood because he usually did it most time he visited. When he saw me approaching, he quickly dropped his arm, sat up on the sofa, and smiled seductively. He wasn't, at all, manageable.

'Ruqayah, my darling girl, how are you?' he reached out to draw me closer to him. I refused, taking a step backward. I just couldn't imagine myself loving at that age. He disgusted me, I hated him. But only when you have crossed the river, can you say a crocodile has a lump on his snout.

'I will stay here, I'm okay here. Anything the matter? I'm busy right now. Please, be quick to tell me what you want', I retorted.

'No, you can't be okay there. Come and sit here with me', he touched the arm of the sofa, the nearest position to him, an aura of love on his face.

'Why?' I asked scowling.

'Okay-o-kay, I understand. Someone has offended you. No problem-but you are not always like this. Do you need anything they didn't give you? Come- come to me- come and tell me and I will get it for you right now', he stood up from his seat, flung out an arm to wrap me closer to him with his *Agbada*. He'd always done this but at that point in time, it seemed crazy and weird to me. I smelt incense all over me, felt nauseated. Before he took further steps, I walked out on him, scourged by his unending advances.

'Baba! Baba!!' he called my father. He was, undeniably, agonized by my unanticipated reaction.

'Alhaji, have you spoken to her?' he burst out from one of the eight rooms aligned in the corridor, leading to the living room.

'No- no. What happened to her? She looked very angry. Does she know anything about our plans?'

'No, was she angry?'

'Very angry'.

'I only pushed her into the corridor. Don't mind the silly girl. Ruqayah! Ruqayah!' Baba shouted my name, also correlating my misdemeanor with the way he treated me earlier on. I kept to my room inflexibly. I didn't answer him.

'Leave her alone. I'll be leaving now, and I'll return to see her next week. Please, help me give this to her. I got this gift from Dubai three days ago', he slipped a golden watch in my father's hand.

'*Khai*, Alhaji', he received it, gaping. 'Is this not too much for her? She's just a little girl', he admired it constantly. It wasn't the first time he would present such a precious gift to me. I didn't understand why he marveled at that. Everything he did disgusted me.

'No, it's nothing. I want her enriched before she comes home to me. She's a very beautiful girl. She deserves everything', he sank his hand into his pocket and pulled out a thick wad of currencies.

'This is for the family and my wife too', he spoke in whispers.

'Ah, Alhaji, this is too much. Thank you so much. You have been so helpful to this family. *Na go de, Na go de.* May almighty Allah continue to repay all your compassion'.

'*Amin.* Don't worry. It's alright', he peered at the corridor bemusedly then broke into a gleeful laughter. 'I'll be going. I'm still going to inspect an ongoing project in my factory', he slipped on the shoes he left on the threshold.

'Alright-yes, that's necessary', Baba followed him.

'My greetings to Nasreen when she returns and remember to pamper Ruqah for me', he smiled, walking out of the house.

I still couldn't get my eyes off this sixty-five- year -old man who didn't only help nurture me but continuously asked my parents for my hands in marriage. What a haphazard mode of proposal! Why did they deem me irrelevant in matters concerning my own life? I went berserk, slammed the door to my room and brooded over my predicament.

Destiny, sometimes, will determine a human's decision: if considered traditionally. My decision and determination grew into my destiny. My willpower to acquire a higher education already created an air of detachment from either early marriage or whatever would create paucity in my drive. My parents didn't care about this. If only they were learned enough like some erudite parents I met in my school, no awful fate would have been designed in the name of tradition. An open secret is no longer hidden. All through the weekend, I kept to myself, ruminating over the perplexity of my situation. Each time I ran into either of them in the house, I felt an overpowering heat running through me, implanting my heart with perilous hatred.

I hate them so much and they became so intolerable to me. What I needed mostly, at that time, was someone to talk to, possibly a confidant.

In my moment of turbulence, I turned insomniac, rejected my meals and cried at all times. I was distressed. I finally made up my mind to disclose the problem to my best friend in school, Fatimah. She was, at that time, my only ally in the college but was three years ahead of me. She was insightful and uninhibited by any family or domestic force of circumstances like me, in so far as I knew her. Her parents, Mr. and Mrs. Abdullahi were both highly educated and had earlier exposed their children, Fatimah and Fatiu, to an atmosphere of peaceful and understanding domesticity. They were both given unflagging love in all their endeavors. I considered them too lucky; not as unfortunate as I was. In my case, I identified with illiterates, lived in a polygamous home and even risked my integrity.

'Fatimah' I called after her as she made her way to the assembly ground with a book under her robust arm.

'Hello-friend', I walked up to her excitedly, anxiously. I saw freedom standing next to her and I wished I was her.

'Hey, Ruqy', she broke into her usual friendly smile and waited for me to cover the space between us. 'How is everything? I didn't see you at the Literary and Debating society last Friday. What happened?' she helped me remove the speck of dust in my eye with her handkerchief and continued. 'That was unusual, what happened?'

'It's a very long story. Can we sit somewhere to talk about something?' I looked around for a quiet environment. It was still break- time and the students were busy moving around in groups.

'Alright, I was just going to return this book to the Physics teacher-but I can do that after break. Let's go to the vacant class behind the Chemistry laboratory', she held my wrist and drew me along cordially. I smiled as I followed her. Whatever advice she gave might not be worthwhile but deep within me; I felt relieved discussing it with someone and unburdening my heavy heart.

We didn't come across anyone that would distract her, and our destination was peaceful, so, we met to discuss the matter secretly: my life matters.

'What?! They want to do what? They want to do what?! Why do they want to do that to you? Why?' she exclaimed bitterly, having heard the whole story with keen interest and giving it a serious thought.

'I don't know oh. I don't know why Baba wants to hand me over to his mate oh'. I folded my arms across my chest and shook my legs in anguish, profoundly affected by the predicament. I sighed and explained on.

'I was heading to the hall to present my own view on the topic we debated in the literary and debating society when I saw Baba looking around for me in the school. Imagine! My mindless father came here to inform me that a suitor was waiting to see me at age fourteen. I already told him that the principal didn't allow me, not knowing his intention', I swallowed then added, 'but they didn't know I was later permitted to leave and was right inside the house, listening to all their plans. Can you see how desperate my father is?' tears streamed down my face.

'No-no, you don't need to cry. Crying is not the solution. We just have to act fast before you're forced into that marriage'.

'What do I do now? That's why I've come to you. Please, help me out of this problem and God will help you too. I don't want this. That is not my dream. Please -help me', I begged amidst sob.

My devastated friend looked at me pitifully, an expression of despair written on her face. For a moment, she was mesmerized. What advice was she able to give me? What would she tell a girl whose parents are willing to give her out in marriage to a man of their choice? Following the tradition, no one had the volition to do this except my parents, so, what was she to say or do? She only reached for me and wiped off my tears with her handkerchief.

'What do I do?' I repeated the question, still crying.

'Oh God, Ruqy-please, let me go home and discuss this with my mum. I don't know what to say or do right now. I'm only a teenager like you. Don't bother your mind so much about this problem. I understand how much it's affecting you, but you have to take it easy. Wait for my mum to intercede please'.

'Yes, that's what you will say and that's what your mum may say too because- you think they have made the right choice for me. Marriage is not what I want now. I want my education. I need my education as you need yours.' fresh tear filled my eyes. I cried convulsively.

'Yes, you need your education, I know but this matter should be resolved sensitively if you must break free from early marriage. *Muka fahinita da'.*

'Uhn-uhn', I nodded, wept on. I asked her to return to her classroom and leave me alone when the bell rang to end the break time. I wanted to be alone-all alone to think about my life. But she refused. She was also worried. She never saw me in that terrible mood since we were friends. I was good at persevering hunger, challenging work and pains, not early marriage I knew nothing about.

'*Haba* Ruqy, don't be like this. Just bear with them. I mean, we still have three whole years to plan against their decision. Thank God, we know their plans now. What if you knew nothing?'

'Yes, uhn-uhn'.

'Don't worry; no one will marry you now. Not until you become a medical doctor. Hmmn-hmmn?' she tickled me, smiling. I stiffened but managed to smile. It isn't a joking matter at all.

'Look at me Ruqy. Every reasonable person knows that you don't deserve that kind of life. Maybe someone like Sinatou'. She drew my attention to the dullest girl in our class. At that time, she was unintelligent but always appeared with well ironed uniform and lot of unread recommended books. She would sit emptily at the back of the classroom and listen to the teacher with rapt attention and also jot points in the process of learning. What she made of all the points and her concentration remains a mystery to everyone. Of course, she couldn't recollect everything again, even with the aid of all her jotted points and textbooks. Call back all the teachers to reiterate every lesson over and over again, Sinatou will still not assimilate. Does someone like that deserve deferment of marriage? She ought to be ushered into matrimony, not me. I thought of this regretfully then shifted my mind to Baba again.

'*Wallahi*, Baba is too greedy and wicked. I didn't know Harun is not just his friend but a suitor. Uhn? God will punish all of them and my mother too'.

'This is unfair, except that we respect the tradition. I'm just lucky my parents are enlightened. That's why my education must continue. If not, I would be in your shoes,' she corrected my wrong impression about them.

'I will never marry that man. He can't sell me to feed those chickens he calls children. I will disappoint all of them. You- wait and see ahn?' I stamped my feet in all seriousness, folded my pleated uniform between my legs and blinked back the tears emerging in my eyes. I realized that, my parents are like a pest in a nut that does nothing to refresh but anything to destroy.

'Don't worry; I will invite you to my house next week Friday to seek for my mummy's advice. She will be off duty on Friday. Let's return to our classes. The break is over now'. She rose to her feet and led the way. And that was all I got from my friend on that day. Assurance. She didn't react to the matter as I really expected her to- or give the slightest idea of what to do. I pulled myself together and prepared to see Mrs. Abdullahi- my new hope.

Back at home, where I felt too unsecured, I was often offended by the pretentious looks on my parents' faces. I don't care if my mother's mates already knew about this. What interested me was her plan for my future. Did she really want this for me? Heaven knows how much I hated that unserious smile profoundly rooted on her face. From my childhood, I always marveled at the way she kept smiling. To me, it's a face of deception, greed and despair. If not, she wouldn't be smiling, even in her deep sleep. The most surprising of all was when Habu, my brother, had an accident and the news was divulged to her. Mama maintained the smile on her face. When Baba brought two new wives to join her in the house, the smile never departed from her face. I came to realization that there's only one thing that will wipe it off forever. My disappearance. Maybe when I bolted, and they had to return all they took from the suitor, either by hook or crook.

'Ehn? Ruqah, why do you keep indoors and read only book-book-book?' she walked into my room and sat beside me on my bed. Her appearance joggled me because I was actually not reading the book. My mind had travelled far away from the room and the book. Sadly, I dropped the notebook and sighed.

'Ajia, please, I want to read for my examination and I don't want anyone to disturb me. If you'll please- excuse me'.

'Exam *ko*? Anyway, Alhaji Harun said I should give you this money to do your shopping for Salah, most importantly, your hair. You have to look good, you know? He also bought the two rams in the compound for the celebration', she slapped the crisp notes on the bed, smiling from ear to ear.

'Hmmn', I felt sadness clutching at my heart as I stared down at the money beside me. I watched my mother's happy mood for a minute and realized we don't feel the same way. We are not the same. She wasn't feeling my pain and she had no idea what I was going through. Then, and only then, I thought, was the right time to have a conversation with her.

'Keep the money before Baba comes in. He doesn't know that I collected that for you after Harun has settled all of us.' She gathered the notes and pushed them to me.

'Ajia! Ajia!!' I yelled at her, unable to control my mental state any longer. 'Why is this man giving me money and gift every time? Why not Kabirah or Alimah? Why me?' I tried to keep my voice down. Only discourteous children rant at their parents, but the condition had pushed me on the border of insolence. I was resolutely prepared to fight.

'*Haba*-Ruqah is there a crime in giving? The man cares for you more than anyone else in this house and showers you with money and gift. Is that a crime? Don't you appreciate his kind gesture? *Haba*!' she looked away from me. I didn't concede; I wanted to hear more from her-the simple truth. I wasn't prepared to give up easily. I looked straight at her face.

'Ajia, does this man want something from me? Hun? A man like that doesn't just give a girl something for nothing. Mama, say the truth. He has a motive for giving precious gifts and money. He definitely wants something in return and I'm begging you to tell me what it is he wants from me', I knelt in front of her courteously, my wobbly voice loaded with remarkable spirits. The feelings I never conveyed before. She closed her eyes for a moment, against my persistence, ran her veined fingers over her head and pulled her veil to get some air.

She felt so uncomfortable with the question I just asked. She was not inclined to let the cat out of the bag until the night I would be taken away for nut-breaking -the discovery of my virginity. Yet, she said nothing. She merely dropped her head, her full lips pursed for the first time and there was no smile.

'Ajia, tell me what Harun wants from me', I fixed her with a malevolent stare and she began to fan herself with the veil. What was she waiting for?

'Nothing. He wants nothing from you. He only cares for you as a father, nothing else', she lied, her dark illusive eyes attesting to this. I hated her more for lying to me and never willing to break their traditional rules. Initially, she wanted to say yes, to spit it out but she did not. They had planned it well, all too well to ruin my life.

I stood up like greased lightning and said 'look, Ajia, if there is more to what you've just said, I will simply disown you and Baba. Allah! That's exactly what I will do. *Shikenah*', I swore bitterly and walked out on her. My message, whether rude or not, was at least, to the point. I was determined to do worse than that to them, albeit she tried to gain my attention after the discussion. I did not pretend not to have known their secret plans.

It was a Friday morning, the day I had to see Mrs. Abdullahi. I had admitted to myself, finally, that I would leave without informing anyone after my parents did not consent to my outing. They both changed their approach towards me suddenly. Baba became more desirous of my movement while Ajia turned more vigilant than before. And I had to see Mrs. Abdullahi as planned.

'Where are you off to this early morning? Are you running away to somewhere?' Baba's angry voice stalked me as I reached for the gate, a little exercise book rolled in one hand. I sighed tiredly, turning around to face him. An aura of despair crept over me.

'Baba', my voice trembled with emotions, but he didn't want to listen to me.

'Keep quiet there! Have I not warned you not to go anywhere except your school? You are allowed to leave this house only from Monday to Friday, so where are you going?!'

'Baba, eh-today is Friday and we are having a debating competition in school. I will be back in three hours' time. I promise you', I pleaded almost crying.

'Today is the Independence day celebration. Even your teachers are on holiday. You think I am not aware of that? Get back into the house now! You are not allowed to go anywhere today!' he pointed in direction of the house, standing twenty six feet away from us.

'Baba, I have all their points written in this book and I have to give it to them. If I don't do that, they will report me to the principal and that will land me in a serious trouble'.

'I don't care. What matters to me now, anyway? I don't care! Get back inside now. We are expecting Alhaji Harun today and you must be present. Get inside now before I lose my temper', he lashed out at me angrily. He removed his rosary from his *Jalabia*. It was what he used to flog Kabirah two days ago. Lumpy chain of beads formed on her shoulder. I quickly withdrew from the gate, burst into tears and clomped into the house.

'Stupid girl. Debate-debate every time. Are you the president?' he locked his gate properly and walked into the living room. I continued my movement into my room, still crying. I felt Ajia's presence in her room but ignored her. She merely coughed derisively then called out to my younger brother for attention. I knew she had the mastery to incite Baba to restrain my outing. This embittered me more and I allowed more tears to stream down my face. It was obvious they wanted to delay me for Harun.

'Ruqayah, *mini ni*? Why are you crying?' Rihanna, my mother's mate, the second wife and Baba's favorite wife burst into my room as usual. Being the clumsiest of all in the family, she pissed me off- only that she was set to assist me on that day.

'Come, come with me', she dragged me to him after listening to my story. We met him resting in the living room. When he saw us coming, he puckered his brow saying, 'that girl is not going anywhere today'.

'*Haba*, Baba-let her go and give this book to the owner and return to the house', she pleaded, holding up my exercise book. There was, sincerely, no point in the book. It was just a rough mathematics calculation none of them can read or understand.

They were both not learned.

'Just that? Are you sure? Are you sure she will not go and sit in the school or elsewhere? You know we are expecting an important visitor and she has to be there.'

'I know', she turned to me to give the final consent. 'Ruqayah, hurry up and return right now. *Kanji ko*?' she drew her ear warningly.

I quickly collected the jotter and rushed out of the house. I breathed an air of freedom when I walked in the street. I knew that one day; I would finally have that chance to make selections, without divergence of my choices. Although young at that age, I was matured enough to know what was virtuous for me. Marriage was never the right supposition. Not in the next ten years of my life- when I would be only twenty-four years old. At least, the drive I have from within was enough reason for me to wait. Yes- that drive from the inside surpasses all. Good things always begin from the inside. If an egg is broken from the outside, life ends but if broken from the inside, life continues. What emboldens me is my innate capability.

By the time I arrived at my destination, I was exhausted, both physically and mentally. I trekked a far distance when I had no money to pay for my fare. The time I wasted trekking alone was enough to trigger more trouble for me back at home. I didn't care. I was interested, particularly, in my future matter and ready to face the consequence. After all, it wasn't the first time he would flog me.

'Ah, Ruqy', Fatimah called from their balcony elatedly. She had sat there for over two hours, expecting my arrival. She almost told her mum I wouldn't visit anymore because of my father. But when she spotted me from afar, she broke into a broad smile and rushed down the stairs to welcome me. She was just my heavenly sister.

I sped up when I saw her coming 'I trekked. I didn't have money for the transport fare, so I-',

'I understand. You should have told me yesterday in school. I had some money with me', she closed the space between us and embraced me.

'You look too worried'.

'Ahn? They didn't want me to go anywhere today. I think Ajia has told him all I said', I removed my veil, tucked it under my armpit wearily.

'Let's go inside. Mummy has been waiting for you. And Fatiu too. He refused to go out today because of you'.

'Don't mind him. He just wants to trouble me, a little', I thought briefly of his unconcealed interest in me anytime I was there.

Mrs. Abdullahi breezed into the living room, beaming at me, her bright eyes sparkling behind a clean pair of spectacles. She looked beautifully robust and more attractive than Fatimah. She was a medical doctor in a general hospital in Kebbi. The only time she was unoccupied was when she was off duty and had an entire day to rest. Just like that Friday I was there.

'How are you, Ruqayah? I've never met you in my house before, but my daughter always tells me about you. And Fatiu says a lot about you too', she sat on the sofa opposite me, still smiling.

'Yes ma, good morning ma', I greeted her reverently, stole a glance at their wall clock. It was already twelve noon. I prayed Baba never suggested sending someone to find me in the school. I became so nervous and uneasy.

'What? Are you still going somewhere?' Mrs. Abdullahi was quick to read my sudden change of mood.

'No ma, it's my father. I mustn't keep long here. My suitor-no the man he wants me to marry is visiting our house today. He didn't want me to come initially when- '.

'Ruqayah-', she cut in. 'I've heard the whole story from your friend and I feel so sorry for you. You are such a beautiful girl, I must confess'.

'Thank you, ma, - '.

'I won't take much of your time. I will only hit the nail on the head. I'll tell you what you should know about this and what I'll do to help. Child marriage violates a girl's rights to health, education, equality, and employment. It causes a huge deprivation and often leads to domestic violence, exploitation, and emotional abuse. A lot of organizations like the Convention on the Rights of a Child (CRC), Convention on the Elimination of all forms of Discrimination Against Women (CEDAW), United Nations International Children's Emergency Fund (UNICEF), and other International Human Right Standards have all worked against this', she paused, looked seriously at me and persisted. 'I repeat- it's a monstrous deprivation. Lest I forget, how old is the man?'

'Sixty-five. I think he's sixty-five because my father is sixty-nine now. He once said that he's four years older than him'.

'It's all nonsense. Absolute nonsense. Even if he's younger than that, you shouldn't be compelled to marry him'. Her eyes wandered to the clock at about the same time with me and she quickly added, 'to save your time, this is what we're going to do. My friend is a human right activist. I'm going to call her today and discuss the issue with her. I think she's going to help us. You know it's difficult to fight tradition, but she will assist us', she stood up and reached for her purse on top of the sofa next to her. 'You have to leave now', she gave a crisp note for my fare.

'Thank you, ma,' I knelt gratefully. And for the first time after two months, I felt a great weight off my mind. I was happy to restore my confidence in her.

'Hey, Ruqy', Fatiu called from the dining room. He had moved in stealthily to pick up on all our conversation. I looked at him and forced a smile.

'Hi Fatiu, bye. Thank you, ma,' I hurried out of the living room, my face burning with shame.

'Don't worry, just go home. Everything will soon be settled', Mrs. Abdullahi followed me to the door.

'Wait, let me see you off', Fatimah shouted after me as I rushed down the stairs.

'Don't worry. My steps will be too fast for you. You can't catch up with me', I closed the gate behind me and continued my journey home.

It wasn't long before I arrived home, transporting with the money I was given. I walked into our living room, precisely at 12.30pm still holding the exercise book I used to fool them. Altogether, I spent four hours away. There was no one around, everywhere was quiet. What happened? I proceeded into the corridor and heard whispers. This was so strange. I expected to meet Baba at the gate, waiting to flog me with a whip in his hand or his *Tesbiy*. Or his friend, Harun, bordered by his guards, also waiting to see me. No one was there, except for the murmurs. I stood at the door, trying to make something out of the dialogue. It was impossible.

'Ruqayah', Kabirah walked in from the backyard. She was carrying a large bag.

'What is this? Where is Baba?' I inquired, my eyes never leaving her face and the bag.

'He followed his friend to see some people'.

'And Ajia?'

'She's the one talking to my mum in her room', she walked past me with the bag and continued to the end of the corridor.

'Wait!' I grabbed her waist desperately, her *hijab* swept my face.

'What is in this bag?'

'Ahn? I don't know. Alhaji Harun brought it and- '.

'Bring in that bag right now!' Ajia instructed from inside her room where the secret discussion was on-going. She overheard all we said. She knew I was back but didn't care about anything except the bag. I stood and watched Kabira carry the bag into her room.

'You-Ruqah, why did you keep too long in your school?' Rihannah, who I realized had been the one in the room with her, questioned my late arrival. I didn't answer her. I went back into my room and shut the door stubbornly.

It was obvious they just collected another gift from Harun with unflagging mindset to give me in return. As I laid my exhausted body on my bed that afternoon, I pondered on what I would transform into if I followed their lead. I pictured the opposite of myself, poorly dressed, looking older than my exact age, nursing a brood of male and female kids with a year or two birth gaps-about five or six of them. In my imperfection of motherhood, they would be inadequately clothed too, their large tummies sticking out of them like a large *pito* pot. Crying occasionally for attention and gripping my apparel, they would all surround me as ants gather round sugar. What becomes of me? I would stand in dilemma, absorbed in several domestic works, also waiting around for me. No self- esteem, no education, no future anymore. I snapped my fingers across my head and quickly travelled back to the world of reality- the real life I wanted for myself.

Conversely, I was determined never to allow that happen to me. Never, no matter what they did to me. I wouldn't become a victim. Enwrapped in a deep thought, it wasn't long before I slept off.

'Ajia', I marveled at the big cow I saw at the back of the house two months after. Salah was over. No one had a living cow or ram still tied in his yard. The arrangement was for Salah and it was over so, what was a cow doing in our lawn?

'What are we celebrating?' I shunned asking who presented it though I knew it came from Harun. Who else?

'What? Oh! That's for em-er-your grandmother's remembrance. Baba wants to remember his mother after twenty-five years she died', she deflected in a smart manner and continued stirring the stew she had on the stove. I looked at her searchingly, my face grim. I didn't believe her. She also sneaked a look at me and resumed her work.

'Ajia, my grandmother died in February, why do you want to remember her in October?'

'Well, that's not my business. The deceased's son wishes to remember his mother now that he's capable of doing it. So- ', she snapped, not looking at me. I was too insightful for her.

With that, I left her quietly, feeling her eyes on me as I looked round the house. Again, I saw two bags of rice leaning on the wall of the corridor and three gallons of vegetable oil aligned with two brand-new suitcases. I sighed and gazed around wonderingly. What sort of remembrance is this? Are they sending wears to the dead too? It's utterly against the tradition. I walked past them then looked for Kabirah or Alimah. At least, someone should give the right information I needed. I finally met Kabirah slicing vegetables in the second kitchen, our modern kitchen.

'Hey, Kabirah, what's going on in this house? What are we celebrating tomorrow?' I carried a wooden chair and sat next to her.

'Hun?' she continued slicing a juicy onion, smiling. She drew her runny nose, squinted to see me clearly. I hate slicing onions. I turned away a little, when I started having the same sensation.

'What is that?'

'For that, you are going to wear the best cloth tomorrow and that cow will die for you tonight. Just- '.

'Kabirah! Come over here right now!' Ajia yelled from the kitchen where she had been snooping on our discussion. Kabirah obeyed right away. I stood for a while and walked back to my room sadly. I forced myself to concentrate on other important things I had to do: my assignment on Mathematics and English and fetching water from a well in our backyard. I remembered it was my turn to fill the two large drums we used to store water for the family. I put on my flip-flop again and plodded into the terrace.

For few minutes, I stood there, peering around for the little pail we used to draw water out from the well but I couldn't find it. Someone must have taken it because it was always there. I went to ask my mother for it.

'Don't worry about water. Just go and rest, we have ordered for water', she had finished frying her stew and was busy slicing vegetables. Kabirah sat beside her in the kitchen, now slicing the onions, seriously. She didn't look at me.

'O-kay, can I help you do something here?' I said worriedly, my rambling eyes on other chores scattered around the kitchen.

'Maybe I should slice the tomatoes,' I made for the fresh, big and red tomatoes in a large plastic bowl.

'No, like I said, just go in and rest. You have a lot to do for us tomorrow'.

'What? Me?' my mouth hanged open in total disbelief. What would they want from me at a remembrance ceremony? A poem or a drama? Those were the stuff I could do very well. What else?

'Ajia, tell me what you want me to do. Do you need a poem to entertain our guests?' I said with humor, my mind registered on something else. On the other hand, I was excited to have that privilege- in an organized event- inside our house. Such had never happened since I was born. It wasn't long before she drew my attention to something totally different.

'What? What poem? What do you mean poem?' she hissed and continued slicing.

'Is that the only thing you can do? How many of our visitors will understand your poem? Don't you know there are other very important things you can do as a female?'

'Like what else can I do?' I looked from her to Kabirah. She didn't smile after she'd been hauled over the coal. She merely concentrated on her work.

'I don't know, you will get to know soon'

Again, all the exhilaration I felt when I got there vanished. I was obviously affected by her tasteless remark. I became nervous.

'And look oh- Baba said that you must not step out of this house till he gets back from the mosque. He went to invite some friends to the ceremony', she added as I stepped out of the kitchen.

'O- kay', I replied drearily and got back to my room.

I realized I was drenched with sweat, so I pulled my veil to get some fresh air. It wasn't enough on that sweltering day. I threw the window wide -open, tied the curtain to ventilate the room. I sat on my bed emptily and reflected on Ajia's statement. If truly there was something else I could do for them, what was it? I considered it a dozen times before I concluded that the next day could be the day they scheduled for my wedding. They must have changed their strategy without informing me.

I stood up instantly and strode across the room, my blood pumping with rage. It's only a goat you can walk to a market and exchange for money without its consent; not a human like me. Not in this digital age should my parents force me into marriage. I folded my arms and cried from within – cried for fairness- cried for help. I needed to take a step immediately. I wanted to inform Mrs. Abdullahi before I got enslaved by the unfeeling tradition.

'Ruqayah, Ruqah', Baba called me as soon as he entered the house. He sensed my intents faster than I expected. He was also watchful.

'Ruqah!' he called again, his voice drawing nearer. I hurriedly threw myself on my bed and pretended I was asleep.

'Ruqah', he saw me sleeping but didn't relent. He woke me from sleep.

'Ruqah! What kind of life is this? Why are you sleeping at this time? Get up!' he slapped my arm and shook me awake.

'Hmm?' I stretched my body, dawdled after him in deception.

'What is the time now? *Na wa ne*?' we both looked at the clock.

'Five thirty p.m.', I looked at him discontentedly.

'Go back to your room'.

Taking a leisurely stroll back to my room, I wondered why he asked just that question and dismissed me. What were they going to do to me? Were they about to arrange for the event? I knew that I meant nothing to them. I felt so unhappy and regretted being a member of such a family. If only I had a chance, I would have run away or denied them before I was deprived. Immediately I entered my room, I locked the door to have a little chance to decide. I needed not be told that they were planning for me; not my grandma. They made all the arrangement for me; not the unfortunate deceased that died in penury. I looked around my room for where to creep out but there was really no opening. Not any. My heart thudded when I finally returned to my bed and blinked back the tears in my eyes. I wished God could send an angel down to fly me out of the house; no way. I wanted a magic to disappear from the room, re appear in a safe place. No way. Nothing I dreamt of was possible. Then, I began to cry. I cried my eyes out.

'Ruqah!' Ajia came again to knock the door. I didn't answer her. I only sat, stared blindly into space. I was engrossed with the new unwelcomed life they were about to usher me into.

'Is she sleeping at this time? Ruqah!' she banged the door harder, but I didn't utter a word, my back merely turned to the door.

'Ruqah- Kabirah, call Baba for me,' she requested Baba's attention. I didn't budge. A couple of seconds after, Baba arrived with them. He hit the door violently. I must open the door to their desire. If not, they wouldn't let me be. But Baba's attempt also didn't make a difference. I merely stared, perhaps, unconsciously.

'Did you tell her anything?' Baba inquired with a tone harsh enough to quake the earth.

'No-ehn, I only said she will perform at grandma's remembrance ceremony tomorrow. Just that, nothing again,' Ajia explained apologetically. She moved away to avoid a startling slap.

'You are a stupid woman. Very stupid woman. What burial were you talking about? Eh? Answer me!'

'Kabira said she has the best cloth and –'.

'Uhn? No oh, she was asking about the cow and', Kabira distant herself from him too.

'Both of you get out of here now!' he moved back and set to break the door with all his might. He succeeded. There, he met me sitting like a dreary statue: stonehearted, straight-faced.

'Ruqah, what is it?' he wasn't, at all, angry with me. He merely dashed to me and forced me on my feet.

'Come; come with me to the living room. *Da ni*. We need to talk'.

'No, Baba -leave me alone. I'm not going anywhere with you'. I cried, withdrawing my wrist from his grip.

'Why? I am your father, come with me',

'No, Baba- leave me alone. I won't marry anybody. I will not marry your friend. I dragged him back, leaning backward. I had to break free from him- break free from his diversion.

'*Khai*, who told you -you will marry my friend? Who did that? Tell me -'.

'I heard you myself. I heard you discussing with him. I heard everything you told Alhaji Harun. I will rather die than marry him. You will see. I will die right now! You can give my corpse to him', I turned violent too. I screamed and knocked myself on the ground. He rushed to put the situation under control. Without hesitating, he swept me up into his arm effortlessly and sat me on a chair. He couldn't flog or scold me like he used to do, knowing how wrong it would be. He shook his head in disbelief. How did I know about their plans before the celebration day? He didn't belief that completely.

When he hanged his head and said nothing, I seized the opportunity to ask him hard questions amidst sobs- questions he couldn't answer.

'Haba –Baba, why? Why do you want to give me to him? Why do you want to push me away? Are you tired of me in this house? Am I eating too much of your food? Can't you care for me anymore? Am I a bad child? Don't you like me anymore? Baba, this is not fair. This is not good', I bit my finger in sheer bitterness. He looked at me feelingly, stretched out his arm and drew me closer.

'It's alright Ruqah, it's okay, come with me. Come to my room.

I will explain everything to you'. He forced me up and took me to his room. Other members of the family gathered and watched with mixed feelings.

'*Khai*, Ruqah is leaving tomorrow. When will someone come for Alimah?' Aliyu, my younger brother of twelve, giggled and whispered to my half-brother, Salau.

'She's no man's choice. No man will marry trouble', he rejoined inconsiderately. They laughed, knocking heads together.

'Both of you- go and kneel down in my room right now!' Ajia punished them out of infuriation. My reluctance had affected her. She wished I could just accept Harun like she accepted my father even when she was younger than I was. She wished I could give no worry and all our family financial problems would be solved forever. To her, marrying a rich man offered a shortcut away from hardship. If just that would stop her from peddling groundnut to raise numerous children, she was willing to let go.

On my supposed wedding day, I was woken up with the warmest smiles and the most hospitable treatment I never received in my entire life: from the women of the house. They were female family and friends required to make preparations. The males had turned up at the mosque to play their parts. They each arrived one after another while I was asleep. By the time I was awakened, about thirty two women were waiting for the event to commence. I blinked awake to get conscious of my surrounding. I had slept with eyes misted the previous night, in my father's room. It was my first time there. I only used to serve his meal sometimes he wished to dine within the confine of his room. My head hurt as I recollected what led me to the room and my unusual sleep.

'What is it? What do you want from me?' I shot the women a revolting stare when they proceeded towards me to grab my hands and take me away.

'Don't you dare touch me!' I warned seriously but no one listened to me.

'Calm down, Ruqah, calm down! It's all in your interest', Asana, my aunt, who I had not seen for almost six years, appeared, brushing the other women aside. She lived in Abidjan and never had time to visit due to her *Kente* business and her expensive family accountabilities. She lost her husband eighteen years after marriage and had since then been responsible for the upkeep of her family, being the eldest and the most industrious of all his eight widows.

'Ruqah, calm down. You are the reason I am here today. It's the tradition we're following today. Yes, you have to get married today. You should be married one day like we all did. It's her turn now, isn't it?' she turned to the women for an answer and they all echoed, 'yes'. They fell about with laughter. Asana reached for me and dragged me out of the room. I couldn't believe my eyes, couldn't believe it was happening. That I was going to become one of Harun's wives on that unfortunate day, share the same bed with him and become a woman at fourteen. Mrs. Abdullahi hadn't enough time to talk them out of their strategies.

'No! I'm not marrying anyone. No, leave me alone', I pushed Asana out of my way then cried inconsolably.

'*Haba*, Ruqah, you're overstraining yourself. How do you want to look in the video? Like a wet witch? The camera is coming oh', Rihannah chipped in, wiping the tears off my face. I pushed her hand away too. I wanted to be left alone.

'Come on, be happy. You'll be discovered a real woman tonight and afterwards, no problem again. Marriage is good', Naomi, my father's youngest wife, and the laziest in the household counseled frivolously. What matters to her when she also married Baba at fifteen?

'Marriage my foot! *Wallahi*, this is how you will all gather to mourn me tomorrow', I swore acrimoniously.

'Hmmn? Are you mad? Are you out of your mind? Why are you cursing? Do you want to die in poverty?' Ajia slapped my mouth, shoved me into her room.

'No more lamenting, no more begging. *Mun ki yarda da*! It's time to get dressed for the occasion. You must agree right now or I'll kill you myself', she followed me inside straight away. The other women tagged along after her, chuckling and mumbling.

I cried for hours; hit myself on the floor a couple of times, kicked and cursed. I wished all the guests were dismissed and the wedding cancelled. Impossible. Nothing worked. I only made a clown of myself and turned a show, prompting more uproar and belly laughter. All my struggle broke off when no one came to my rescue. And I gave in to their wishes, finally.

'Maimunah-come and make her up! It's about time. I've cleansed her'. My mother shouted over my troubled head, checking the time, craning her neck to find her from the group. I never minded, I just sat like a sculpture and allowed them to do all they wanted.

'She doesn't need much make-up. She has a beautiful face. Let me see', she admired my face and I did too- in the large mirror sitting in front of me. I saw myself: my shapely forehead, thick brows, long lashes and a pointed nose, looking over my small beautiful lips. I had always seen these but never attracted to it or distracted by it. What lies within me, if they could all see and value it, is more saleable than mere outward beauty they traded for money. It's powerful. It procures money, fame and exaltation.

'Lower your head, please', Asana came around my neck with a lovely jewelry adorned with pure gold. I did not know the value of those ornaments then but later understood their worth. Some are kept away and used for special events while others were borrowed from the richest women in the group. Nevertheless, Harun bought all I needed to appear for the wedding.

'You're such a lucky bride. All of these will become yours soon after the wedding. I borrowed everything I used for my wedding, including my undies. Most unfortunate ladies fall in the hands of a church rat', Asana wrapped another bangle around my wrist, her eyes never departing from the stunning set. She flipped another box of gold open and began to unseal a new set. Other women drew closer to admire its beauty.

'You are right. My sister married a kola-nut hawker who was already married to six wives. They were all seventeen in the family. She suffered a lot when the kola-nut wasn't vendible anymore. It soon turned their meal in their household when they had nothing to eat', Asante, the funniest of the women, amused everyone and it was a relief for me. I also smiled briefly, for the first time since the arrangement began.

'My daughter, don't think twice about seizing this opportunity. Alhaji Harun is a caring husband. He will take proper care of you', Asana adjusted my rather too large ear rings. I felt like a tree was hanging down my ears. I felt uncomfortable.

'If you see the house you are going to live in, you will bless your parents for preparing this glorious day for you. It's a paradise,' Naomi, who had stood all the while, just watching, added.

'Listen, we have a good reason for this tradition. It's to protect our girls from the danger of pre-marital sex or being a victim of unserious sexual affairs several times before marriage. A lot of those boys out there are never prepared for marriage. They use our girls and abort pregnancies a couple of times before they finally meet a serious man. Do you still call that a good wife? 'Ajia expressed her opinion after listening to the women.

'Humph. Most men are very wicked. The funniest thing is that they won't show to the girl that they don't like her until she rots away like onion. Do they consider the man she will end up with?' Asana wondered.

'That is if he himself has never been bad to any girl before. What goes around comes around. Thank God we have a good tradition to preserve our girls for only their husbands; not the public', Ajia concluded, picking all the items used for beatification. As far as she was concerned, she had said it all, made me understand why she took that position. To protect me for only Harun, but then I should have chosen by myself when I was ready. I thought drearily and Asante drew my attention back to the scene.

'Besides, a girl that marries with no virginity is like a bottle without a crown. If she gets opened before marriage, she will become vulnerable to men. Anyone can enter a house without a door.'

'Asante! You are more than a lecturer', Rihannah teased.

I pulled a long breath and nodded as I listened to all their jokes.

They were pleased I did so –it meant acceptance. And it was finalized that there wasn't a thing to worry about again.

Few minutes after I was prepared for my presentation, Asana brought out a red bridal veil that matches my outfit from my suitcase and covered my face. I sighed, my eyes filled with tears. I was walked to the biggest *Nikkai* hall in the neighborhood- just a stone's throw away. Seventeen women surrounded me, sang jubilantly. They showed all sort of stunts to make it a special one. It was Alhaji Harun's wedding.

Immediately we got to the entrance, eager voices drifted nearer. Some rites were performed and I was accompanied to my seat, next to the anxiously waiting bride groom. I peeped under my veil to see the number of people waiting to witness the event. There were hundreds of them. They were all smiling; nobody had a sad face like me. Harun himself wore the same pattern of lace as me. He was all smiles. He was, indeed, the man of the day. I wished I had a knife to stab him and run away from the crazy scene.

It wasn't long when the reading of the Holy Quran for the ceremony began. The *Mallams* went on busily with this for hours, reading from verse to verse, chapter to chapter. I got sick and tired and almost passed out. Have I ever sat for this long in such an uncomfortable outfit before? No. What's more? I wasn't comfortable sitting next to the twist of my fate.

Just like my mood was being studied, the recitation ended and the bridegroom was asked to unveil his bride. It was the moment everyone was waiting for. Necks lengthened to catch a glimpse of us. Again, I was sick, my head throbbed, my heart pounded. I was about to crack- up but he felt different. He felt so happy to have me at last.

'Oh my queen, you look so beautiful', he removed the veil carefully.

'Hmmn?' I gave him a similar shot I gave Baba three weeks ago. All I wanted was the end of the madness and my freedom. I didn't want any marriage.

'Come here, come to me', he hugged and wrapped me with his vast *Agbada*, almost choking me. The smell of his incense churned my tummy. I gasped for air and turned away sharply as he leaned forward to kiss me.

'Look, it's okay- it's okay. Thank you', I collected my veil from him, wiped my face and pursed my lips. I turned away from the attendants, I didn't look up.

'Alright', he got back to his seat, unaffected by my rudeness and the event continued.

By 5pm, it was time to move me to my matrimonial home. I had two suitcases already loaded with the best of wrappers from my suitor. I had to leave all my old clothes in my house and prepare for motherhood, matrimony. That was no problem but there was a thing I wouldn't forget in the house. I hurried back inside and searched for the purse Baba bought for me when I took the first position in a national competition.

'Welcome, *al –marya*. Please, enter gently', the driver Harun got for me alighted from one of his fleet of cars, then threw the boot open.

'Hmmn?' I breathed. I wasn't interested in anything. Not the driver, the car, the suitor, or the marriage. I wanted freedom. I wanted my education.

Three women swiftly packed my belongings in the boot, their expressive eyes stuck to my sad face. At the same time, Asana opened the back seat for me. 'Get inside. Your sister-in-law, Sekinah is waiting for you'.

I crawled into the car, not looking at the woman in her late fifties. She had been introduced to me earlier at the *Nikkai* ceremony, as one of Harun's younger sisters. I didn't like her at first sight. She was too pompous and unruly. She neither welcomed me nor said a word.

'Farewell oh. We wish you a happy married life and the best of luck', Asana shouted with excitement.

'I will come and see you tomorrow evening. Be a nice girl', Umu began to cry whilst the ignition of the car started. Umu! First, she seized the moral high ground, and then she wants to be a sight for sore eyes. This amazed me; I doubted if she would miss me after her participation in the untimely nuptial. I guessed it was a pretense.

'Hmmn', I breathed again, still ignoring all their gestures.

'Goodnight'. Sekinah stole a glance at me and motioned the driver to the car.

'Anidu, let's go'. She had enough of their sickening noises.

Our ten minutes journey began at 7:30 pm. Anidu cut through a park into the slum with hordes of people hawking, fighting and playing loud music: our ghetto I was about to miss. He automatically rolled up the glass and set the air conditioner to work. And it was just us- in a refreshing world.

There was a little snarl-up as he went southward- to the general residential area -where only the rich live. He made a sharp turn into a quiet neighborhood - an avenue. He drove for four miles. He then turned perfectly into a driveway and finally halted in front of a lovely edifice. That was the most adorable house I ever saw in my whole life time, all four stories of it. With its mansard roof, it looks so elegant.

'Where is the gate man?' Sekinah reacted to Anidu's hassle on the horn, her face a symbol of infuriation. She had kept mute all through the journey merely sight-seeing and not looking in my way. I didn't care. All I wanted was my freedom, not jumping from frying pan to fire.

Two minutes after we waited in the car, the gate slithered open and a beautiful woman stepped aside for him to drive in. That was Aisha, my immediate mate in the house. She wasn't as old as I thought she would be. She was about twenty years of age and a mother of two. I later learnt that she was handed to Harun when she was only sixteen. She had spent the whole day moping about the arrival of a new and more beautiful wife.

'Get out of the car', Sekinah instructed me crudely. She got off the car, slammed the door.

'Welcome mah', Aisha greeted her courteously, collecting her hand bag from her.

'Where is that useless gateman? *Ina ya ke*?' she looked around for him-from angle to angle.

'He is praying in his room. He was busy cutting the grass in the afternoon', Aisha explained spying at me as I dismounted the car quietly.

'What is wrong with Sanusi? So, it is prayer first now, not his master. All his prayers for the past five years he got here fetched him nothing. He's still a poor man. Can't he see? It's not working for him. Who gets him paid at the end of the month? His master or that prayer. I think he has found a new job elsewhere because he will soon lose this job. He will! You will see'. She hissed and turned to me for the first time since our journey began.

Anidu hurried to the boot to set off my belongings one after the other, on the interlocked concrete floor. I stood still beside him, waiting for the witch to give the next order. Aisha stood next to her like ear to the head; like a maid to a mistress.

'Madam?' Anidu asked for her consent when she was just staring at the guard's office and the gate. She disregarded him and continued cursing the man.

'*Wallahi*, God will punish Sanusi for wasting his time on prayer. Shouldn't he come out here by now? You show no respect for your master now.'

Everyone was obviously tired of her insistence on him. Anidu dropped his hands from the boot tiredly. Seeing this, she yelled at him.

'Take her to her room! *Mini ni*? Aisha- that is your new mate, Ruqayah. Anidu, leave the black suitcase for her. Let her carry something too', she eyed me.

'You are welcome', Aisha greeted me and also carried one of the bags.

'Thanks.'

As we climbed up the stairs to the second floor of the building, she followed me closely, her eyes never wandering from my body for a moment. She had always been the best of all the wives and never imagined someone would fill her boots anytime soon.

'Drop that bag and leave', she instructed Anidu then focused on me.

'This is your room, mine is downstairs. There are only two wives here. Just you and I. The older and the oldest wives- thirteen more of us, are everywhere in other houses. In the north, south, outside the country and-', she turned the key to unlock my room. Us? Was I one of them already?

'I know. It's alright-it's okay', I removed my veil and used it to wipe my face uneasily. I didn't need her nauseating introduction. Rather, I needed privacy to remove all the heavy ornaments hanging down my ears and neck like fruits on a tree. I needed to undress and take a cool shower. It's been a hectic day for me. I was emotionally and physically disturbed.

She led me into a well decorated room with flowers, neat and fluffy rug, well laid standard bed, nice closets and a lovely dressing mirror sheltering all sort of cosmetics to enhance my beauty. There was absolutely nothing there to remind me of my education. It was entirely a new world of matrimony. Though, she saw me staring around the room, admiring its beauty but couldn't enter my mind to tell precisely what I felt or wanted. The whole of a dog's dream remains in its belly.

'Sekinah told our husband to bring you here instead of other houses where there is always war between the women and their children. Those women are too tough. You are lucky to be here', she leaned on the door, also preparing to leave. She was quick to read my unreceptive mood.

'Hmmn-that will never happen to me. Is there a bathroom here?' I changed the topic disinterestedly. I wanted her to leave the room; leave me to my fate. I will never be one of his numerous wives or compete with anyone.

'Yes, every room here has a bathroom. Our husband spent a lot on this building. You can get anything you want from here. There's even a pool at the backyard. You will really enjoy living here. But do you truly love our husband?' she spoke her mind at last. I forced a smile and nodded 'yes, I do. I don't mind if you will please- excuse me now. I want to take a shower. I will get back to you'.

'Alright, I will be back tomorrow with my kids and the maid. We have a maid and-', she sighed and concluded 'have a wonderful night'.

'You too. Goodnight', I smiled and locked the door the instant she left. She seemed nice and accommodating with all her kind gestures.

Someone in her position wouldn't have been happy seeing a new bride. But that did not matter to me.

I spent almost twenty minutes in the bath merely standing under the showerhead, enjoying its warm stream, ruminating over my next line of action. When a thought crossed my mind ultimately, I stepped out of the bathtub and grabbed one of the clean towels arranged on the towel rod.

I pondered on different moves while I slipped into my night wear. Should I jump down the stairs? Peering down at an outlying floor of great altitude, I shifted a long drapery shielding the window. Without delay, I dropped the self-destructive thought. I chose to stay alive. After that, a lot of damaging plans occurred to me; nonetheless I finally resigned myself to my previous strategy. I hurried to one of my suitcases and pulled out the purse I brought from home.

Harun did not return in a rush. He took his time to celebrate with my parents. It was, indeed, a happy landing for them getting their loveliest and most intelligent damsel to quit her aspiration for marriage. He risked his health condition with much undertaking in addition to unusual intake of his routine drugs. He began to feel flashes of heat in the evening and demanded to take his leave.

'I have to return home now. Thank you very much my in-law', he stood up to leave. My greedy parents followed him to his car. When he opened the back door to take a seat, his phone began to ring.

'Yes, what? She did what?!' his condition worsened from the moment he received the bad news.

I overdosed myself with thirteen pills of a sedative drug I bought from a pharmacy two weeks before the wedding, each representing his old wives. No one knew I hid it in my purse that night I was driven into the deplorable wedlock. I laid unconsciously on the floor, foaming profusely in my mouth. My eyes drifted into a close and I wasn't aware of the happenings around me. Was I dead? I didn't know but my intention was to fulfill my promise to them that I would marry Harun over my dead body.

I wanted them to gather again and regret their thoughtlessness. But, fortunately for them or for me, my restless mate returned to the room with my meal. She met the door locked then peeped through the opening at the bottom of the door curiously.

'Ajia! Ajia!!' I could still hear her distress call as she raced down the stairs for help.

Two hours later, ten of my family members, also in attendant at the vainly wedding, emerged at the hospital in total disbelief and confusion. They peered at me lying supine on one of the emergency beds in the casualty ward, half dressed, being oxygenated.

'Ehi! I just went to her room to serve her dinner when I saw her lifeless body on the floor and she was foaming in the mouth. She almost killed herself because she locked herself inside the room. *Subhanallahi*!' Aisha explained breathlessly. She was taken aback by the unexpected and deadly situation. She didn't understand why I did that after I confessed to her that I love Harun.

'I'm not surprised at all', Ajia declared soberly. 'She said she would do it and I almost lost her. I've warned Baba after she discovered our plans but he wouldn't listen to me. Look at what just happened. Look at her now'. Umu wept bitterly.

'We should thank God that she didn't use the rat poison Aisha found in that same purse. She had that too. *Wallahi*, Ruqah is a stubborn girl. Stubborn and wicked', Asana shook her head, full of pity. She refused to sit in the reception hall like the other people there. She stood, leaning her back on the wall, waiting on the doctor's report. All she hoped for was my fast recovery. A moment after, Baba rushed in with Sekinah and Harun.

'How is she doing now?' Baba inquired, looking from face to face.

'The doctor hasn't returned to say anything. He just covered her nose with a cup. What is that thing?' Asante asked Asana but she gave no answer to her ridiculous question. Must she joke with everything? All illiterates there knew it was an oxygen mask meant to oxygenate and revive me. And she thought she knew that too. No matter what happens, the joke is inevitable.

'What is that thing? Is it a cup?' she asked again, shaking her arm for a forceful reply.

'Leave me alone?! It's a cup, go and use it to drink'. She left the hall in anger.

'It's not a cup, it is called oxygen mask. The doctor is giving her air with that. If only Harun had listened to me, this wouldn't have happened. As for me, Ruqayah is not the kind of girl for him', Sekinah exploded, hatred filling her voice. Her sudden reaction saddened my family and they reacted to this.

'Come- Sekinah or whatever your name is. What did you just say, eh?' Rihannah confronted her first, 'don't you have human feelings or is it not blood- that is running in your vein? Tell me Sekinah. Do you not have your own children?'

She didn't utter a word. She merely puckered her face, turned her back at her.

'Remember? This was what you did at the *Nikkai* ceremony', Asana walked back into the hall, giving a further remark. She overheard their rant from outside the hospital. 'It's all in the video. How you turned your back at the camera and avoided everyone. You are such a wicked woman. A great enemy of happiness'.

'What else? She has ruined it all. No wedding again. We can't let her die in our house. *Alekia eh!*' she reacted to Asana's vicious attack.

'Oh shut up, Sekinah. Shut your mouth! Don't talk here again. Don't you have regard for me, the father of the girl? Or you don't know I am her father? She's still lying unconscious on the bed and you're talking like this, *abah!*' Baba fired back at her, his eyes bulging with irritation.

'What is this about?' Harun spoke to the surprise of everyone. The problem had bowed him down since he walked into the hall. His health had also worsened. If his in- laws could read the sullenness in his heart, they would just keep mute.

'You can't gather here and beat my sister, can you? Your daughter is wicked! I haven't married this kind of wife in my life. *Wallahi*, all my women are well behaved. *Abah!* Marriage in the morning, hospital at night. Not to deliver a baby but to save a stubborn bride. What do you call this? Self-denial or self-destruction?' He rose from his seat and looked around in confusion. No one had the gut to answer him, especially Baba who was praying that he shouldn't demand for his prices.

That wasn't important to Harun anymore. He needed his life to look after his family. And no one could predict what I would do if I recovered and returned to his house. He knew I did not want him; no matter what he did. He put two and two together and said to Baba 'look, Alhaji, the marriage is over. No more. Take good care of your daughter and your family. Take her back to your house when she recovers. I will ask my driver to return her suitcases immediately', he waited for a while- for my father or someone to say anything but nobody spoke. He tapped his sister's shoulder shouting, 'Sekinah, let's go-where is Aishatu? Aisha!'

'Alhaji, I'm here. I'm right here', she walked up to him cheerfully. She was the happiest of them all. Of course, her dream had finally come true. No wife, no more rival in the beautiful house as far as she was concerned. She remained the most beautiful wife. God knew how much she blessed me that night.

All the three of them walked out of the hospital that same night, expressing their different opinions about me.

'Her father planned it with her and they should pay back all they took from us. They want to get their daughter back after eating all your money. Sekinah followed her brother closely as they walked to his car. Yet, Harun had nothing to say. He slammed the door of his car, drove off without checking out on the other two with him. He drove roughly, unsteadily and unconscionably out of my life.

At the hospital, Sekinah was everyone's subject of discussion. Nobody liked her.

'Sekinah is too harsh and wicked. Who knows if she led Ruqayah into suicide', Asana said, stretching her neck to be sure she was gone. She didn't have the power to contend such a woman.

'What is she doing in her brother's house? Doesn't she have a home?

'She just lost her husband'.

'Must she kill someone for that?'

The doctor emerged with a report for my family. They all stood up at once and walked up to him.

'How is my daughter? I am her mother', Ajia informed the wiry man impatiently. His eyes fell on the sheet of paper in his hand, and then he looked from face to face.

'It's a good news. She has recovered', his face cracked into a smile.

'Ehi, *Al hamdulilah- Alhamdulillah*', Ajia went on her knees in gratitude to God. Others also showed their happiness in one way or the other.

'But she will be on admission for the next three days before we discharge her from the hospital. Thank you and congratulations'.

The doctor returned to his office, marveling at my bravery. I sincerely made my decision to determine my inexorable destiny.

Today, I'm a competent medical doctor. I studied Medicine in Danladi University Teaching Hospital (DUTH) with the sponsorship I got from Mrs. Abdullahi. Fatimah and I graduated the same year and I'm happily married to Fatiu, her brother. Fatiu studied Engineering in London. We love each other and we are happy together. My skill is worth more than a thousand pieces of gold.

2

Nana

...a wise cripple hardly falls prey to enemy's attack.

Anytime Akwasi was crossed with his wife, everything about him changed. He wore a monstrous look. The real size of his eyes transformed, bulged like a full moon. When all was well, he had no obvious vein on his temple but in a mood swing, six of them appeared like a thunder bolt. He surged out his chest in fury and exploded hysterically.

'Please. Don't hit me. I will say the truth. Please-' Nana fell back on a chair in the room as she tried to escape. The twenty-seven-year-old furniture he inherited from his great grandfather cracked with pain. Its spring rang off in unsettled poor condition.

'Where is my money?!' he yelled at her, gripping her arm effortlessly. It felt very different. It wasn't a grip of love or desire but hatred and vengeance.

'Please, it's there', she shivered with trepidation.

'Where?!' he looked around at a loss, did not know where precisely she was pointing at. When he shook her body with much more effort, she realized she had to speak up or he would wring her life for nothing serious.

'There-', she pointed with a whole arm, shot her mouth at an old cabinet in the room.

'Take me there right now!' he pushed her to the spot - just three steps away from them. 'Bring it out, right now! You are a trained thief!' he pushed her against the cabinet.

'I will- I will. I'm sorry', she threw the first box open to release the note. He snatched it from her.

'You should be ashamed of yourself. *Wa ami awu!*' he pushed the cabinet close and all the empty toiletries they used for mere decoration fell off, declaring their bareness with much scrunching noises. There was no money to buy new items and flaunt them like the first time. They'd all stood emptily for the past four years, only for beautification.

Nana stood staring at him menacingly. There was, indeed, no true love between them- she knows. A beloved wife a man holds in high esteem wouldn't be subjected to threat over just three cedes. It kept ringing in her head. She had slipped the note into her wrapper and later transferred it into the safe when he asked her to wash his clothes. And it wasn't the first time she would pilfer from him after he prevaricated that he had nothing. Why didn't he just say the truth instead? Why did he have to lie every time- that he had nothing when they were hungry? After all, with honesty, she knew she wouldn't steal from him.

'Why did you lie to me that you didn't take the money? Don't try it next time oh. It may cost you your life. Thieves are given jungle justice. I can murder you for stealing my money. You miserable thief'.

'Hmmn-Hmmn', she mumbled and reserved every punishable comment within herself. Her gut ignited his anger.

'That is why your kids are also stealing. You are just a liability. You are dependent on me every time. Am I in this world for you?' he proceeded to the door, murmuring. 'That was how I lost all my money last week. My whole pocket was empty. Why not marry a president and finish him? Why me? I'm only managing', he slammed the door and persisted- in the long corridor of their leased single room- in a defaced bungalow of twenty rooms.

'*Adjei*! *Kabako- kabako*. I'm in trouble oh, God help me. God, where is your face?! God!' Nana clapped her hands over her head miserably. She shot her face in the corridor to check if no occupant listened to all he said. She was wrong. She caught three of them twittering and nattering about them at the same time Akwasi walked out of the house.

Everything about that bungalow often disinterested her. It had twenty single rooms in all with only one toilet and bathroom detached behind it for every occupant to use.

There are other houses built in that same fashion around the street but theirs appeared the noisiest and filthiest, for the number of dwellers. In some rooms, there were ten people living together as a family. In theirs, they were four altogether- Nana herself, Akwasi, and their two sons. Badu's family of room 12 had the largest occupants. They were thirteen in number. And such was very common in urban areas.

She reached for their broken door, pulled it close then strode back to the same fatigued chair. She dropped her head in memoirs of how Akwasi occurred in her life. It was a fairly good starting when she had their first child, Kobena, out of wedlock. Her step mother, Mrs. Awurama, who she was helping to hawk *Adua bie* in Kumasi, at that time, wasn't supportive anymore. She had been her backbone since she lost her parents in an auto accident many years back. She felt utmost dissatisfaction when she was impregnated by Akwasi: the worst of all the men she ever knew. She gave her mind to her last comment about being her own worst enemy for introducing a devil into her life. And she never took it seriously till it dawned on her. Given that all her pleas for forgiveness fell on deaf ears, she ended up in his room unfortunately. She admitted that her fate led her to the squalor and impelled their unwelcomed second child, Kojo. Akwasi wasn't really embittered about his coming when he knew quite well that he was going to have a fair share of their penury -as the first child. And Nana would be the one who suffered the pain of seeing her kids put up with much more pain than she bargained for. Before her eyes, her children would be enslaved by poverty- as she experienced in her childhood; not him. He was right.

Nana closed her eyes in distress, her head leaning on the chair as she thought of the boys. They suffered almost every day. There wasn't, precisely, a day she could recollect giving them three square meals or a day they wore new clothes and looked better than other kids in their locality. What was the need to have them when they were deprived of all the basic necessities of living? Why did they have to identify with them, the impecunious church rat, when there were thousands of the rich out there craving for babies? They have virtually all they need to raise a good child. Why them? What do those kids stand to derive from their own kind of family: wretched folks? She sighed and straightened up to her feet. Her hands trembled with hopelessness, uncertainty and obvious desolation. She drew their tattered curtain quietly to look around for them.

They hadn't taken any food that morning, before darting into the street with filthy panties, baring their jumbled buttocks. When she finally clapped her eyes on them, they were busy rolling worn out tyres in the street, with their peers. They appeared the most unsightly of the kids in the group. They had hair as kinky as that of a vanished loony and were simply an excellent portrait of starvation.

'Ekow! Ekow!! What are you doing with those infected kids?'

One of her most complicated neighbors approached the kids darkly, her face like rumbling thunder. Scuttling back into the house, Ekow hurriedly threw his tyre away.

'Let me see you with them next time. You will see what I will do to you! Can't you play with just Amma and Kwame? Why those two ugly boys?' she snapped her fingers bitterly, turned around to give them a belligerent look.

It wasn't the first time they would be treated like smuts each time they played with their children. Nevertheless, they were just innocent kids whose hearts hadn't been trained to hate or avoid: to hate the ones that hate them or reciprocate evil for evil. They were only kids.

'Kobena! Kojo! Kojo!!' Nana called out to her sons, having seen all that transpired. Her heart sank. As more and more problems came her way, she became more overwhelmed than before. What a wicked world! She felt like committing suicide to end the whole sad story even though it was impossible, considering the suffering kids. If people pointed cluttered fingers in their faces and threw dirt at them while she's still alive and watching them, how much more would happen when she isn't there for them? They would, possibly, ostracize them from their expanse.

Nana broke into a dull smile at the cogitation of the poor and their eccentric segregation. It is intriguing when a fellow poor still squeezes into a class in the poor social strata. They had the poor-poor, the poorer-poor, and the poorest-poor. Nonetheless, they were all poor but theirs was the worst rank of all. They lived in inflexible shame and turned the most deprived and unacceptable in the society. Their own forest provides food for the hunter after he is bitterly exhausted. It was like God never remembered that they existed.

'Mum, did you call us?' Kojo, her seven-year-old son, asked her, raising their window curtain from outside the room and sticking his little head inside for enquiry. He pursed his lips as Nana nodded sadly.

'What are we coming there to do? You told us to go and run errand for people- to get our breakfast. Do you want to starve us this morning again?' Kobena, her first child of nine, pushed against the rattling window nervously, his tummy stinging from late feeding. He blinked back the film of tears in his eyes.

'Are you mad? Are you now controlling yourself? I told you to come inside right now!' she bawled at them, also restraining the tears in her eyes. She admitted that her attentive neighbors must have heard all they said. The boys exchanged glances, dropped the tyres behind the window and snaked through the house to the front yard despairingly. What was she up to? Was she going to starve them to death? If not, did she have anything to offer them to eat? They pondered as they entered the house one after the other.

As soon as they crossed the threshold, she stole a glance at the wall clock, and then sighed again. It was 11:30 am. She didn't know what to do or how to do to save them from the troubles in the environs.

The neighborhood in and of itself, was an immense trouble, hunger was a more serious affliction and life was unavoidably disappointing. What she considered necessary, at that point in time, was filling the boys' tummies with something, even if it wasn't nutritious. They had to eat something. She had stolen from Akwasi because of them but it didn't work. What next was she going to do? She stood staring at them, wordlessly.

'Mum, I was waiting for Ma Super to call me to fetch some water for her. She gave me the money I used for my breakfast yesterday', Kojo said pointedly, his belly standing out of him like a matured pregnancy.

'Me too, I helped Pa Yaw to wash his dirty bandages yesterday and I got some money to eat', Kobena added.

'What bandages?'

'They were from his wound'.

'Wounds?' she sighed then broke into a sad smile. What choice does she have? Would she dictate to them what her kids would do to have their money? She only knew Ma Super, the bread-seller at Makola market, not Pa Yaw or his wound.

She had no option than to break them free to fend for themselves, no matter what they experienced in the street.

'Both of you will go back out- there- and find what you'll eat. Your father has disappointed us this morning but-', she leaned forward and assured them, 'I promise to get something for you this evening. I will also dress up and go out to find a job to do'.

She drew them closer and fondled their ring -worm infested hair. She knew the right thing to do but money is the key to everything achievable. Cutting their hair and treating the ring worm, she calculated, would cost her what she needed to feed them for, at least, five days. It's partly one of the reasons mothers don't want their kids near them.

'Please, stay away from their kids. You are two, you can play together, can't you?' she advised.

'I heard Ekow's mother is organizing a birthday party for her daughter tomorrow. We will gather some food from there and eat from morning till in the night!' Kojo announced excitedly. He began to dance, humming a tune, crouching then rising back in a slow motion.

'Why are you going there? ', Nana marveled at how indifferent children can be. It was the same woman that affronted them while playing. 'Don't you dare go there! That woman hates you. Don't you understand?' she warned.

'Why? We didn't do anything, we were just playing'.

'She doesn't like you'.

'Why?' Kojo pestered for an answer, his arms folded across his chest stubbornly. He wanted to know why they would be hated for no reason. Nana drew a long breath and looked away in quest of the right response he deserved. And at last, she said 'she thinks you are not good enough'.

'How?' he asked

'I don't know but am sure that, if you go back there, she's going to kill you. Steer clear! Don't you understand? Abah!' she cautioned breathlessly.

She took nothing to bed the previous night and there she stood straining herself to correct a demanding kid. She realized she also had to leave quickly to fill her stomach. She brought out her bag and rummaged through it to find something to wear, leaving them to decide on their own: to choose to stay and starve throughout the day or leave to fend for themselves.

'O-kay, we shall see you in the evening. I have to run before Ma Super runs the errand by herself', Kojo threw the door open and ran out of the house, walking zigzag, drawing a circle, playfully in the narrow corridor. Kobena followed closely, although heading for a different location.

Again, she was left alone in the house and her search for a befitting wear continues for the next thirty minutes. She couldn't make a choice from her collection of rags and faded clothing- from friends and well-wishers. She pulled out a long, striped, tasteless maternity gown, looked at it closely and slipped it on. A stale smell filled the room. It was barely adaptable; not satisfactory. She bent over it, smoothed out the creases busily. Am I ready to go? She questioned herself as her finger ran into an unnoticed hole in the sleeve. Rat! She drew a long exasperated breath then began to hunt for her tired and scratchy sweater. At first, she couldn't find it; she had to empty the whole bag for a painstaking search. Yes, she found it and wore it on the gown. A cockroach slipped through; however its stench infused the air. There was a sudden rise of temperature within and around her. She didn't feel much of the day's hotness initially until she set her whole being on fire. A rivulet of sweat formed on her forehead, meandered from her armpit to her waist. She closed her eyes against the agony of being deprived of food, clothing and good shelter. What a life! Why was she always bedeviled by all life's essentials?

She hauled off everything at once, the sweat towing the gown along. She returned all the wears on the ground back in the bag, crying. When she was done, she sat on the edge of the bed and wept her eyes out. Poverty has, undeniably, taken a heavy toll on her. In her moment of bitterness, she understood that only someone in her situation can tell what she felt and how tough it is to live without the basic needs to survive. The spoilt and over pampered rich cannot feel or tell a thing about this. A lot of people in her shoes can tell how it feels to be estranged from happiness, stay hungry for a whole day and even trek barefooted. They understand the atmosphere of losing her voice when she should speak up or dress in rags and turn to an object of mockery. Victims alone can comprehend deprivation better, she admitted.

Every man thinks of a solution to his problem. What ends misery is the success a human derives from striving. How would she talk of success when there was no opportunity for them? God had never crowned her husband's effort with success. They kept running from pillar to post but she was sure it would all end one day. Things would look up and they would have enough to live on. As for her, it wasn't over yet. The struggle just began.

Four more years of hardship rolled by in the squalor and it wasn't over yet. No one volunteered to help the couple secure, at least, a job that would earn them a better living. Everything remained same as ever -the same sad old story.

Nana sat back in the chair listening to uproars from the street on restoration of electricity.

'Heii!' adults and children screamed and ran around the house in delight. Electricity had ceased for two whole months, with no hope of early restoration when their transformer suddenly exploded and burnt some vital parts beyond repair. Residents almost gave up hope to utilize power supply that year except the poor-poor class that could afford to buy quality generators, purchase fuel constantly and live off the grid. Machines were set to work with unbearable noises for nine to ten hours every night. Angry neighbors had no choice than to tolerate the disruption till the bitter end: the minute the owner would willingly turn it off and give a moment of silence. No one had the nerve to complain as they would do anything for a quiet life. What should they say to the one that had enough to live a healthier life unlike them, the poorest, that lived from hand to mouth?

She reached for a switch and put off the blinding bulb in their room. It was of no use: only widened its eyes and served no purpose all day. She sneaked a look at the wall clock when she remembered her children. They were attending a free government school. Thanks to the new administration, making provision for unrestricted child-education from primary to secondary school level, coupled with free supply of books, uniforms and instructional material needed to impart all-encompassing knowledge. This helped revamp the sickening child abuse and denial of the poor masses of high-quality education. For Nana, it was a far-reaching achievement. She needn't worry about how to finance the boys' education as she burdened her mind with their feeding. On that day, they took only the *Abolo* she got from her neighbor to school. In as much as she helped them with that, abundance of food in your neighbor's house will not satisfy your hunger. It wasn't enough.

A close television blasted away, dropped in on her. Lot of housewives hanged around the house: engaged in home chores, cooking, gossiping and expecting their children's arrival from school.

Later in the evening, their hubbies arrived with goodies for them. Who made these rules? This is it. He chose a woman who would lumber with home chores, prepare his meals, look after his children and wash his clothing. At the end of the day, she's compensated with whatever he can afford. That completes the role of an abiding, primitive African woman. Education has nothing to do with this. Majority of them are highly educated and still compliant except for women that are accustomed to higher wages and aspire for more in life. Such women get themselves employed, in one way or another, to support their men. Nana had no work, no expectation from a husband and no food to cook.

She cracked a smile as she overheard a laughable talk show being aired on the same television. She stood up, shook off the sand on a fatigued bed and spread a clean sheet on it. Time to sleep. Since there was no television to watch, no radio to listen to, or a fan to cool off her burning emotion, she conceded that it was time to sleep. She rolled a window curtain, their only curtain, into a ponytail for ventilation and stretched herself on the bed, her eyes fixed on the ceiling in deep thought. Was she still physically attractive or older than her twenty eight years on earth? She wondered raising a leg up and caressing it amorously. There were official women that offer men services to earn a living but does she have the look? It would have materialized before she met Akwasi, when she was averagely pretty: a dark-skinned damsel of 5.5 feet and passably attractive facial features. She was neither pretty nor ugly. Now, her middling look had made an exit for only money, upholds a good appearance. She quickly broke her mind from the idea and forced herself to sleep.

By 2:15pm, she was woken with the ruckus of children arriving from school. At school closure, they often turned up in groups, fighting and cursing. Her kids identified with such groups. Wasteful hours were spent wandering in the scorching sun, distinct from a responsible kid who would have long arrived home to rest and prepare for the next school day.

'Mum-', Kojo called immediately he entered the room. He had turned completely dark and dirty all over.

'This is very good of you. Very- very- good. You know what? There is no soap to wash your uniform today and that's how you will wear it to school tomorrow', Nana said sitting up on the bed. *'Akuaba'.*

'No, my teacher will beat me. I know how to get soap, don't worry,' he guaranteed. He dropped his old school bag, began to pull his school uniform.

'How will you get soap if I don't buy it for you? Do you have money to buy it yourself?'

'Mum-don't worry. I will get the soap from Ma Emma's cupboard. She has a whole packet there and she doesn't lock it', he smiled broadly. At first, she wanted to discourage him from stealing but when she remembered the corporal punishment he will suffer in school on the next day, she had no option than to be quiet. After a moment, she rather diverted,

'Where is Kobena?'

'He helped the primary- two teacher to sell groundnut today and- ,' he swallowed and concluded 'she said her money is not complete, that one groundnut is missing ', he spread his little arms vaguely.

'So, where is my son?' Nana rose from the bed nonplussed.

'He is on his knees in her classroom and she has flogged him several times- everywhere - on his - head and buttocks, even his face.'

'I have to go to your school right now. Is the teacher insane? Is he in the school to sell groundnut? Ahn?' she looked around for her slippers and scarf. Her hair looked so untidy. She hasn't made it for days.

'Mum, the teacher is very wicked. She can flog very well. She called Kobena a thief. And everybody was watching. She said you taught him to steal'.

'Where is my scarf?!' she raised the mattress to find it, losing patience with injustice, unable to bear more insult. She longed to appear before her and get even with her, at once. Kojo joined her in the search tiredly. All he wanted was food and rest, not the trouble his mother was giving him. Had he known that it would result in that, he would have kept his lips sealed. He wished he had nothing to do at all.

'Mum, *Maa a-*', Kobena entered, looking so exhausted and unhappy.

'What happened between you and the teacher?' Nana asked eagerly, her eyes shifting around Kobena's face and body for a cane mark.

'Nothing oh. *Me ho ye. Kwa taa*', he shrugged.

'Nothing? Did you not help her sell groundnut and-?'

'Okay, that one. I ate her groundnut and removed twenty cedes from her money when-when I was hungry', he pulled his uniform, looking less concerned or affected by the price he got from his teacher.

'Is that all you did?'

'Yes ma'.

'No problem. Next time, don't sell anything for her. She's so ungrateful. She supposed to give you something after helping her to sell'.

'She's so stingy. She has never given me anything in return. She always says thank you –thank you and that's all'.

'Don't sell for her again, alright?' she returned her slippers under the bed and sat down on the chair with a happy face -happy for the poetic justice. She had heard stories about tightfisted teachers mistreating innocent kids in their school. However, with their status of living, she wasn't against such errands if there was a worthy return.

'Mum, look – *Akosombo*! I told you last night that we will soon use electricity again', Kofi shouted enthusiastically. He had changed into a faded yellow pair of knickers.

'Yes, you have to go and fetch some water from the well and have a bath. You can't stay like that. And – remember, you have to wash your dirty uniform', she turned to Kobena, her eyes fixed on a spot. He had a slanting cane line on his face. She swallowed hard at the sight of this.

'Mum, after washing, we will go and watch the t.v in Pa Yaw's room', Kofi said again.

'No, just wash and return here', anger flicked on her face when she revived the memory of how they were treated the last time they visited there.

'Mum, we promise to be good', Kofi pleaded.

'No, you were accused of farting in their room every time you went there. Stay away from them. Don't you understand?'

'No, only Kobena farts there -not me', he pointed at his brother, who seemed uninterested in their discussion. It was a black day for him. He only stayed focused on his search for what to wear from a pile of filthy clothes.

'Whether you'll fart or not, I don't want you there! Why are you so stubborn? You are just like your father, ahn?' she scolded him.

'Mum? Any food at home?' Kobena asked finally and Nana hissed. She looked around for a while like someone suffering from loss of memory then replied, 'what did you do with the money you stole?'

'The money? I've eaten candy with it.'

'What candy? With the whole of twenty cedes?' Nana marveled at his foolhardiness. He used what he stole and suffered for to buy ordinary candy with no nutrition value. What he needed to feed himself!

'I was hungry', he leaned forward explicitly, his face wrapping up in anger. He looked like a bubble about to explode.

'Did candy fill your tummy? *Chale* - as you can see, we have nothing left at home. Go to Pa Yaw and help him to do some works'.

'Pa Yaw is dead. Didn't you hear?' Kobena announced, wiping what appeared to be tears in his eyes. Nana wasn't sure. She looked at him steadily to observe his red eyes. Was he crying for his friend or food? She still wasn't sure. She rubbed her blurry sight after recovering from the shock. She couldn't help but ask again.

'He died?'

'Yes, the wound killed him', Kofi explained further.

'It's okay, you don't have- to cry. Everything will be fine. I will go and fetch water for Ma Super now and get some money for our dinner and breakfast', she looked from one face to the other and read the same feeling. As for Kobena, he was affected by the memory of his dead friend but she had much troubles clashing in her head already.

She hadn't time to sit and lament the death of a man she never met till he died. On the other hand, both of them weren't pleased living on the smell of an oily rag, even though they were accustomed to it. Father always unavailable and mother available for nothing but to sit in a broken chair and give instructions. Kobena stormed off the room and slammed the door. Kofi still stood grumbling.

'You are a stubborn boy. Your brother is more understanding than you are. You are Akwasi's true blood. Get away from here before I open my eyes', she warded him off, closing an eye, the other partly watching him. He uttered no word again. He also left angrily, the spring of the door ringing out from his furious hammering. Nana didn't mind, so long as he was gone.

She heaved a sigh of relief as they both concurred and left her alone. The way the wind is blowing, her biggest prayer every day is to break through all the problems before they became matured to enter the street and commit crimes. They would be guilt- ridden if they grew up and accused them of all their failures in life or become lawbreakers in their quest for money. The whole blame would be on them that drove the boys in the world with nothing to raise them in the path of God. Nana exhaled loudly, closing her eyes in pain.

At about 8:30pm, in the night, the boys had each returned home, at different times, tired out. They sat in their room in front of a burning candle they lit by themselves. As usual, there was power outage- a lifestyle everyone had familiarized with. It meant nothing to them. Meanwhile, they both dropped on the floor, sharing their experiences about the people in the street: with the good, bad, ugly, wicked, and nice, in quest for survival. In all, nobody showed enough care. They were regarded as pests on a plant looking for favor. Despite that, they forced their way into their cruelty and survived every day.

'Mum is still fetching water for Ma Super since in the afternoon', Kobena remarked drowsily. He yawned and leaned on his brother.

'Watch the candle, don't burn somebody's house ', he cautioned, pushing him away. He was still very hungry. He wasn't as fortunate as him. He roamed the street and got food from his friend's family. In his case, he went from house to house but no one needed his service. He later got three bean cakes from the mosque three hours ago.

'Which house are you protecting? This one? This old house with bad windows', Kofi pressed the neck of the candle, molded it into a triangle.

'Burn it, burn it and live outside. Why is mum still outside? Kobena checked the time and stood up apprehensively.

'Where are you going?'

'I want to go and find her. It's too late now.'

'Late? What about your dad? You don't ask of him, do you?' he played with the hot wax dripping from the candle, his little face transfigured by the light.

'Hmmn? Who knows where he is? I care for my mum, not him', he looked through the window, into the pitch dark street. Only the voices of their neighbors were heard: their chatter and exuberant joke. He saw mosquitoes resting on the window net and began to squash them on the spot. He'd learnt this habit from his mum. His attention drifted to a torn part of the window, their main entrance into the room and he tried to fix it. He pressed the ends together with his fingers.

'I saw him last night', Kofi's voice broke the long silence. He wasn't interested in the candle anymore. He had shifted to the broken chair he always wanted to fix its joint.

'Who did you see?' Kobena stopped and paid attention to him.

'Who else? Your daddy. He was drunk and couldn't recognize me in the crowd. He leaked all our secrets and people laughed. I was ashamed of myself'.

'Hun! Bad father. He's disgracing us every day. I wish he was dead', he curled up his lips in sheer hatred for him.

'Ahn? *Ayekoo*!' Nana barged into the room. She had stood at the entrance for a couple of minutes, listening to the boys. She heard all they said about Akwasi. What saddened her truly was Kobena's bad wish for him.

'*Akuaba*, mum.' They welcomed Nana in unison but she didn't answer anyone. She was crossed with both of them.

'You, where did you see him? And you, why do you want him dead?' she demanded successively, yet waited for only Kofi's answer. She needed no answer from Kobena, no matter what he had to say.

She was upset. They both spoke at the same time however, Kofi's voice was heard. Guilty already, Kobena didn't fight for prominence like he used to. He knew he was wrong to hope for his father's death.

'He was on Jones Street. His cloth was dirty and he had several children singing and dancing with him. And I didn't like what I saw so, I don't like him again'.

'Keep shut! What do you mean you don't like him again? He remains your father, no matter what. You better watch your mouth because no one knows tomorrow. I know he will be a better man tomorrow, so don't judge him', she retorted, almost crying, Kojo kept quiet, looked at Kobena's face. He expected him to say something but he didn't. He just swept the portion he would sleep on with his shirt and slowly rested his head on his palm, legs crossed.

'Are you sure you saw him there?' Nana needed more information and certainty before going to look for him. For five consecutive nights, her husband hadn't returned home to sleep. He would come home to change his cloth without saying a word to anyone, including his children. Each time she tried to talk to him, he would curse her or ignore her.

'Yes- mummy. I saw him with my two eyes. I can take you there tomorrow if you want to see him. He is there, drinking and dancing for the children', Kofi clarified noisily.

'Please, bring down your voice, no one should hear about this. It's okay. Have you eaten?' she changed the topic. She opened her bag and brought out the *Kenke* and fried fish she bought for them. Kobena sat up, crept closer to the food.

'You! You want to come and eat under the roof of the man you want dead. Is that how it works?' Nana shot him an angry stare.

'It's not his house. Its-'.

'Shut up there! Who is paying the rent?'

'I - I am sorry ma,' he apologized, finally. But deep within him, he wanted him gone. He felt he was a disturbance to all of them.

'It's okay, eat your food and go to sleep', Nana dished out the food, her mind occupied with Akwasi's problem. Will he ever change?

For ten years, after the birth of Kofi, he toughed out abstinence from alcoholism. He wasn't completely responsive to all his obligations as a father and husband but was always available to participate in the upkeep of their children. He was also more caring before he suddenly revisited drinking. Whatever led him back to the rough patch could be the psychological problem he suffered in next to no time. What was she to do to end it all? Was she going to stalk him and grab the bottle from him everywhere he went? Impossible. Akwasi, ordinarily, was a very violent man, how more sadistic would he be in his drunken state? She shook her head against the idea, and began to plan another approach out.

By 9:30pm, the boys had dropped asleep on the floor without spreading their mat. She remembered she went to spread it in the sun early in the morning, to relieve it from bugs feasting on them. She stood up quickly to fetch it from the backyard. There, she overheard two of her *lasi lasi* neighbors engrossed with her own family issues, mostly her husband's drunkenness: the way he liquored up on locally made gin all night.

'Where does he get the money to drink like a fish and his children are suffering that way? *Chale*, that man is so senseless', said one of the women.

'Do you blame him? I blame Nana for subjecting herself to this kind of living. If only a stove knew what it would suffer in the hands of its buyer, it wouldn't follow her home. I mean, look at the way she is-like a destitute beside the road', replied the other, laughing. The second woman joined in and they laughed their heads off.

But for the need of that mat, Nana almost returned to her room, sheepishly. She counted two steps backward then decided to pass quietly, to at least, accomplish her mission.

'*Maa dwo*', she greeted vehemently, passed without waiting for their response. They exchanged glances, stopped laughing, their legs shrinking back in their seats.

'Nana-*Yaa nua*. How are your children?'

Sure enough, one of the women called her attention to what she just saw by the time she returned with the mat.

'Nana please, I want to ask you a question', she moved closer to her, a great concern all over her.

'Yes?' she pretended not to have heard them'.

'We were actually discussing you and your husband', she declared, drawing nearer. 'What are you doing about his matter? He now drinks and disgraces himself in different neighborhoods. Last night, I saw him with some kids clapping and singing for him and he was all messed up. Humph. This is bad. I will advise you not to fold your arms and just watch because he is your husband', she waited for her response, her arms folded behind her casually.

'The lord will do it. Thanks for your advice', Nana replied, unfazed by her great concern. She marched back to her room, obviously displeased with her advice. The only reason she approached her was because she was caught in the act. She should have related the story to her friend alone, other than making a fuss about it.

When she returned to her room, she felt different, became nauseated by all around her. She didn't know what to do to end the disgraceful act immediately, stop neighbors from snooping into every corner of her life. She paced around the room, still holding the tattered mat with grim determination to end it all for good. She clenched her fist, bit her lower lip painfully. No money, no food, no future, no morality. What a life! Why did Akwasi choose to disgrace them despite all they had been through? She dropped the mat with a start and ignored the children on the floor. Why? Why didn't she wait for the right man to walk into her life? Patience is the mother of a beautiful child. If she waited, maybe that special man that was meant for them would have emerged. Why Akwasi? Why didn't she listen to her aunt? She regretted, crying.

For the umpteenth time, she had attempted suicide for her unrewarding existence. That night again, she considered swallowing the rat poison she bought few weeks back with the money she got from her laundry service. As she proceeded towards the bottle, her conscience set to work effusively: she began to think more about her helpless children at the same time. If she killed herself, who would look after them? She was the only one they had, not Akwasi. She did everything to straighten herself out, and disentangle from self-destructive considerations. She decided, however that Akwasi should be her focus at the moment.

Since sleep eluded her, she decided to evade it too. Her mind toured miles away from the house to a strange land where she wanted to be with the young boys. Where there is all they needed to survive and be respected. A world free from victimization: a world of love and satisfaction, freedom and peace.

Her gaze shifted to them in their sleep. They curled up together, Kofi's head in Kobena's arm. The weather was still very hot, so they were sweating copiously on the bare floor. She wept on. For all intents and purposes, like she intended to deprive them of a pleasant sleep, but it wasn't so. Her exasperation centered on the whole situation. She hissed loudly then flung the mat away.

Few minutes after she sat staring blindly into space, she began to hear noises from outside the house.

'Nana oh, Nana is a witch! Yes, she is and I'm going to finish her today. I swear, I'll finish her soon-sooner- soonest. You'll hear from me soon, I swear. Nana will be in a serious trouble', Akwasi's unabashed drunken expression filled the entire street in the dead of night. He still had some children with him- the wayward ones that may not return home to sleep. They clapped and sang enthusiastically and he danced for them. Nana raised herself from the ground, cocking her head to pay attention to the ongoing hue and cry. She then believed that, eyes are not for the prevention or acceptance of genuine shame or honor. Akwasi's eyes were wide open, yet he showed no honor. Noisy children gathered around him as a swarm of flies on a wound.

'Ah! This Akwasi, oh my God- I'm in serious soup', she threw her trembling hands above her head dismally and proceeded to the window to have a view. She saw Akwasi, in filthy clothing and barefooted, dancing in the midst of euphoric children. He had vomited on his body, fallen in naked ditches and stagnant water on his way before heading home that night to rest on his oars. For that night alone, he had held free shows in different locations. He wouldn't sleep out as usual; he was dancing home either for a continuous performance or a good night rest in Nana's arms.

Nana bit her finger and pulled away from the window half-heartedly. What was she going to do? Bring him back into the room and clean him up? Or stick with him outside there all through the night - and be beaten like Kampala?

He already spoke his mind: he wanted her dead. Most people, including her, believed that alcohol fortifies a frail mind. In such a moment, he acts oddly and articulates all his intentions: either good or bad. Yes, Akwasi wanted her dead, out of his way. She realized, only for once, that he had seen her as the inevitable problem in his life. A preceding war suits a wise cripple since war itself has no eyes. Nana got prepared.

'Nana, open the door now before I reach there!' Akwasi screeched from the little window. Nana got up speedily and bolted the door. No way. She preferred to lock him out there. He wasn't going to enter and beat her to a pulp or hold her in contempt.

'Get up! Hurry up! And help me with the door. Your shameless father wants to break in and beat us all. Look! He's forcing the door open', Nana shook Kobena awake. He rubbed his eyes sleepily, forcing himself on his feet. Whatever kept him awake that night was an unforgiving mugger of peace. He needed that sleep badly, more than anyone else; after all he'd been through in the day.

'Mum, what's wrong?' he blinked in confusion as he regained consciousness. He didn't hear all she just said.

'Your father is-', she carried the broken chair quickly and leaned it on the door to keep it firmly shut. She looked around for other heavy things to use, set her eyes on her baggage and lugged it there.

'Oh, it's my father again', Kobena drawled. He watched Kofi also rising from sleep, wondering what was transpiring around him.

'What is it?'

'It's your daddy again. He has taken his *Akpate-shie* and *akuffo*. He wants to break the door and kill us all-', Nana explained uneasily.

'Why? We didn't do anything', Kofi remarked.

'Do we always do anything? He won't come inside here tonight',

Kobena cried, also helping his mother to move objects to the door with might and main. Akwasi didn't relent. He continued hitting the door, abusing Nana verbally. Neighbors, passersby stood to watch him but didn't cut in on his crazy demonstration.

'Nana tonight is your funeral. Let's bet it, if I don't kill you tonight-if I don't kill you soon-hmmn. Me Akwasi Edward-you locked me outside my house. You are doomed. You are in a serious trouble. I will not stop until I see your end'. He took a few steps backward in the corridor, sped to the door and pounced on it. The brave entrance shook, felt its onslaught but didn't fall or open. It saved his target.

'Hey! Don't kill yourself for nothing. You will just kill yourself for nothing', Nana stood akimbo, her eyes glued to the door in preparation to defend herself once he fought his way through. When Kofi peeked from end to end, he saw his contemptuous look and formed a different opinion.

'Mum, let's allow him to come in and clean up. He's looking very dirty',

'You must be mad', Nana struck his buttocks with great belligerence. 'How on earth do you think that's possible? I should bring him and be battered like a broken vehicle eh! *Ya –min -pengu.* Hold the door for me right now!' she untied her wrapper and changed into a pair of knickers and camisole.

'Tonight, he will not enter here. I'm prepared for him. He doesn't care for any of us, does he? He wants hunger to kill us', Nana's eyes turned red hot, Akwasi didn't give up.

'Oh! The same hunger that killed your parents in Tema. You have chosen the same destiny with those two bastards with you', he started singing again.

'Did you hear that? And you called him your father. You want to clean him up. Shouldn't you wish him death?!'

Kobena sneaked a glance at his mother. She had suddenly formed the same opinion with him. That such a man deserved not to live and make life miserable for them.

When it was about 1:00am, all the singing children returned home, some of their neighbors also returned to their rooms. Nana became more hardened, especially when her children gave her the basic support she needed. Nonetheless, everyone was wakeful, including children. They all kept to their rooms and cursed the upsetting family for wasting a whole night of peaceful sleep.

'Push it harder, push it! He has no place to rest his filthy head tonight. Not here', Nana directed her tired children. They wished the drama was over, regretted having them as parents.

'Mum, this side is open, it is broken. See', Kobena showed his mother the part of the door Akwasi had successfully broken. It was the hinge of the door he had been hitting with a stone. She observed the spot, looking exhausted. If he should break through and enter, she would be in severe trouble as he already said. And what about the boys she involved in the distress? He would do anything possible to punish them. Nana reflected for a minute then assured them.

'Don't worry, he won't enter', she encouraged them, her back still on the door. They concurred and made more efforts even when they knew they had failed.

'Nana, I swear, I must kill you today', Akwasi continued breaking the door. The wood had fragmented and about to fall apart. He seemed to have recovered from his drunkenness as everything he said afterwards was serious and accurate. Now, Nana had to pay considerable attention to him.

'Ever since you came into my life, I've been deprived of every good thing. You brought ill-luck into my life. Why? Why? Who sent you on this evil mission? Why?' he paused and pressed on 'look at me now, I can't enter the room I am paying for. I'm all messed up and I can't enter my room to clean up. I swear those two boys will cry for you soon', he grabbed the stone and continued breaking the door.

'Never! You can't do anything. You were the one that brought problems into our lives and deprived us of every good thing in life', Nana fired back at him, her head breathing like a giant heart. The boys withdrew from the door when all they used to hold it fell on them and got them injured. They both stood in fear, watching their dauntless mother fighting to avert his invasion. Were they about to lose her in the battle?

'You- just- watch what will happen to you now. I'll waste you, you are so useless', he made his way through the door, stretched an arm into the room and reached for Nana's neck to throttle her. He pressed so hard that she began to struggle for survival. For a moment, it was like he was about to accomplish his mission. She lost her voice but managed to make a croaky shout for help. No one rolled up to help. Her boys couldn't approach her. Out of fear, they both burst into a thunderous cry: in their fragile minds, they were about to lose her.

'Eh-ehn? Why do you want to murder someone in my house? Why are you destroying my house? Is it a crime to let a debtor be?', the owner of the house, Mr. Aato Samuel, whose second house was just two streets away from them, rushed into the corridor unpredictably. He grabbed Akwasi's waist, forced his arm out of the door and pushed him away. One of his tenants had called to inform him of the ordeal. At first, he didn't care, didn't take the matter seriously until he was called again that someone's life was at stake.

'You don't want to turn a new leaf. Are you the only one in this house? Are you not ashamed of yourself? For the past nineteen months, you haven't paid me and now, you're destroying my property. What do you want from me? You want to deprive me like you?' He regretted letting the room when he appeared more responsible fourteen years ago.

Someone should have prophesied then that he would be the demolisher of what took him years to build with his low income. After the government had staked a claim to his cocoa plantation, the house became his only source of income. He had no other expectation. He used the money he realized from lease to raise his large family so, what was Akwasi up to?

'Are you drunk or insane? I want you out of this house tomorrow. No apology is required or accepted. Just get the hell out of my house', he sat on a bench outside his house to watch him before leaving. He had called his police friend before, and was ready for him. He saw him pacing around the corridor then persisted.

'You are a wretched drunkard. You don't have any means of livelihood so; you want to wreck me- to be like you. Be gone with your family tomorrow', he shot a vengeful stare at him. He won't want his feats crumbled by his own debtor.

Akwasi left Nana alone for a while, having seen another challenger to confront. He lifted up his head, with his chin jutting out and said, 'Tomorrow? Did you say tomorrow? Won't I be happy to leave now? Do you call this a house or poultry?' He laughed his head off.

'Excuse me please', the same man that called the lessor walked past him. He was only there for their landlord, not Akwasi he hated so much.

'Did you hear what this beggar just said? He called my house poultry', he reported to Mr. Adjua.

'Good morning sir'.

'This is a very bad morning. This devil here doesn't want anyone to sleep. What kind of trouble is this?'

Another occupant came out and joined them, followed by another one until everyone was outside except a family.

'They must all leave the room for me tomorrow. No one should beg me to spare them. Their wretchedness is now obviously affecting every one of us. Useless family', the landlord stamps his feet frantically. He wished he had a chance to evict them straight away but it doesn't operate that way. They all supported this; they wanted Akwasi's family out of the house.

Akwasi didn't respond to all their prattling. He only stood and blinked. He had actually made up his mind to face only Nana, the heart of the matter, before the issue took a new turn. If it metamorphosed, he knew he didn't have the potency to handle all of them.

Nana, indoors with her kids, was restless. She overheard the eviction threat and began to twitch. A wood already touched by fire is not hard to set alight. He had wanted to evict them before. Where would she go with her children? To where exactly? She paced around the room, musing about what was about to befall them. The landowner would, possibly, return with his aged boys to toss their mucky stuffs in the street with fury. He worsened it all by tagging his house a poultry. People would definitely gather to watch their shame and mock them. And what next? She would have to roam the street and sleep under bridges like the down-and-out. It was the beginning of another purposeless life for them. She grabbed her head and fell, crying. Her boys rushed to her in solace.

At the end of the whole show, the drunkard fell asleep, on the bare floor, in the corridor, at about 3:45 am. The landlord returned to his house to sleep while all lodgers returned to their rooms, one after the other. They were full of pity for Nana but no one could approach her for the fear of her desires at the moment. They had neither food nor shelter to offer her or her children since they were also managing to live a pleasant life. She was left alone to her fate.

The richest lodger in the house, Mr. Kwame, was a merchant in Makola market and was married to four wives. He rented a room there for his second wife, Fouwa and her children. He scarcely visited except he needed her attention. His first encounter with Akwasi's family was their endless need for money. Nana had secretly begged for his financial assistance several times when no lodger was around to sneer at her or discourage him from helping her. He always marveled at her saddening lifestyle and the troubled children.

That night, he was there during their usual obnoxious display. He kept to his room with his family, minded his own business. Having listened to his heart's content, he laid his head on his bed looking so unhappy, and affected as he continually thought about the victim. Someone should have, at least, intervened to shut Akwasi up or end the disreputable show. But no one did. He glanced towards his wife, sitting beside her daughters, fanning them with a piece of paper – her expression one of sobriety. All residents, except one with stony heart, were sorry for Nana.

'I think I should go outside now and start the generator for these children. They are sweating and you're restless', he looked around for his singlet.

'No-no, please, I think the neighborhood has been through a lot of distractions', she stood up and blocked him from going out.

'I think we shouldn't disturb with our generator again or what do you think?' she added. He sighed and turned back inside the room.

'It's okay if that's what you want. Fine', he perched on a settee in the room, folded his arm on his belly distressingly. He wasn't pleased Akwasi was laying his glitch on everyone, including his family. In the other apartments he rented for his third and fourth wife, and their children, the like of Akwasi didn't exist. The houses were so peaceful.

'But, I still don't understand what that man's problem is', he broke the long stillness in the room after a couple of minutes.

'Who? Akwasi?' Fouwa stopped fanning her children and looked up.

'Yes! I don't care whatever his name is. I don't know how such a gentle woman met a devil like Akwasi'.

'Well, we all meet someone somewhere, somehow- he's just a worthless man'.

'Worthless, hun?' he arched a brow at her and finally suggested, 'I think- what do you think we can do to help that woman and her kids? They will be evicted from that room tomorrow. The landowner has been looking for a way to quit them since they didn't pay him. I feel so sorry for them', he pictured Nana in his mind. He saw her frustration, desolation and stream of tears.

'What will you do? Hun? Listen to me- my husband. Except you want to assist her secretly, people will soon conclude that you want to make her your fifth wife. And-'.

'Is that what you think? You are mistaken my dear. I told you that I don't want any wife again. Fatima is my last wife and that's all. I only want to help Nana and that's all', he gazed in awe as she allowed sentiments to pervert her sensibility. He turned his back at her.

'My husband, are you angry? I'm only talking as a woman with true feelings'.

'What do you mean by that? That woman needs help right away. Put yourself in her shoes and feel what she's feeling. Imagine how hopeless you would be- in such a penniless life', he stood up and continued thoughtfully.

'I'm going to assist her tomorrow, no- today, no matter what anybody says'. He peered at a wall clock in the dim light. It was 5:00am.

'Yes, when it is 5:10 am, we will know what we're going to do,' he sat down on the bed.

'O-kay', Foowa nodded disparagingly. With that kind of gesture, he knew how much she detested polygamy, however she had no choice. She wanted it to end with just the four of them, no more anywhere. Only his first wife, Efua, enjoyed his own house and the rest of them are in rented apartment, suffering from the woes of a cursed neighbor. If all he wanted to do was to help Nana out of her sad situation, then she was willing to give her support. If otherwise, no way.

At about 5am Nana needed to use their restroom. She looked round the room for their improvised potty, made with a paint bucket. It wasn't there. She agreed she must have forgotten it when she picked the mat. At first, she was scared. She had to verify that Akwasi was truly asleep before she ventured the step she was about to take. She sighed miserably, looked around her again. Her sons were fast asleep on their disarrayed stuffs in the room. She had been busy packing some of them together; nonetheless everything was still here and there. What was she going to do? She hadn't the slightest chance to escape. If Akwasi should overpower her and enter the room, he will beat her to a pulp and scatter all she had suffered to put together for her exit. Again, people would gather and scrutinize their indignity. She thought deeply about her intentions, sighed once more then returned to her preparation, ignoring her drive to take a leak. She took her time to arrange all their needed belongings properly and hurriedly. No one had to see them leave. When she was almost done, she felt a sharper pain in her abdomen and sooner realized she was dancing to call of nature.

She peered through the door only once, opened it gently and hurried out of the room. Akwasi wasn't, at all, asleep. He pretended to have his way and he succeeded.

'No-no-no-help! Somebody help me! Akwasi is going to-kill me. My head ah-my head. *Adjei! Yah- yah- yah'*, Nana squirmed on the ground after getting a whack from a chunky twig he picked from the spot.

'Yes, when I said I will kill you today, you thought I was joking? You've made me homeless, haven't you? I will finish you today', he battered her up vengefully, tore at her wears. Once again, everybody awoke to Nana's distressful cry. They stayed away still, looking forward to the next day they would be thrown out of the house for peace to reign.

'Where are you going?' Foowa rushed after her worried husband.

'Where do you think? To help the woman of course.' He threw the door open and made to leave.

'No-no, my husband. Akwasi is a drunkard in temporary madness, don't challenge him. He's a dangerous man', she warned him to steer clear, just like other lodgers who thought they were matured enough to settle their differences.

'Should we all fold our arms and watch him murder her? What about her kids? Get out of my way now!'

'Hun,' she accepted.

It was too late when seven lodgers eventually came out from their rooms to rescue her. Nana ran naked in the street.

'You! You must be dead today. You- wait and see', Akwasi chased her around breathlessly.

'Please, help me- help!'

All of a sudden, three people were spectated chasing one another instead of two. Who was the third person and what was he up to? They gaped as he struggled to catch up with the second runner. It didn't take him long to succeed. Kwame thrust out his arm and grabbed Akwasi from behind. He lifted him with a little effort and flung him on the ground.

'Why do you want to kill your wife? What do you want from her? Uhn? Stay there and stop struggling', he pinned him to the ground, his eyes red hot and full of hatred.

'What concerns you, ahn? Is she not my wife? Get away from me. It's not your concern', Akwasi struggled to break free from him.

'No way, this is where you'll be till you are arrested. We can't leave you to murder her'. At the same time, a man brought out his phone and called back the landowner. Bystanders cursed Akwasi for tormenting his family. Only the oldest man in the house, Pa Mensah, had a different outlook.

'What lesson do they want to teach him now? Is he not her husband? Before a wound turns to a disease, won't you find its cure?' he told one of the women at the scene quietly.

'Hmmn-', she breathed in annoyance but did not respond to his indefinite statement. He glared at her, sighed and said again 'women are bad. Look at what she turned her husband to'.

'What does that mean? Won't you stop now? Nobody answered you, considering your sixty-five years on earth, yet you want someone to disrespect you. Respect yourself', Maami Ekow answered him finally and walked off the spot.

'Do you mind him? You are the bad one. No woman is bad; you were the bad one that deserted your family for a very long time. We women deserve better than that. Watch your mouth', Kakuwa, the most undaunted, retorted. She had listened to Pa Mensah's story: about how his wife left with his four kids. She didn't believe him. To her, it was a fabricated lie to dissuade people from fretting him about them. The truth should be that he abandoned them to break away from his obligations. No work would have brought him there for twenty nine years.

'I did not desert my wife. She ran away with my kids after she ruined my life,' he managed to defend himself. That was a history he wouldn't tell anyone. Verily, he ran away from them and that was the truth.

'You too- shouldn't you have gone back to find them after donkey years? You're comfortable without them. You bring out your little pot and prepare only your meal every day. Ehn? No one to ask you for school fees, no wife to search your pocket, no baby to mess your clean shirt! We shall see how you'll end up in this house', Maami Ekow returned to express her anger. She was scourged by his disrespect for the women at all time.

'Dat one dem talk now na true. You no do well. You come close eyes leave them like that', Kodjo, a bus driver, also living there, chipped in on his arrival from an overnight transportation. He was attracted by the chaos three streets away.

'Look, today is not for my matter oh. Face what's happening now. Face Nana and Akwasi. I'm warning you', he walked away from them and a scornful laughter followed him.

'He doesn't like the truth', Kodzo watched him shut his door.

'Do you mind him? He should get out of here. Liar', Kukuwa saw the big crowd around Akwasi and Kwame, shook her head and walked back inside her room. Whatever she saw on that day wasn't new to her. She had seen a lot of eyesore around the congested street, since she moved in. As long as the noise was driven out of the house, she had to sleep.

A few minutes after, Mr. Aato returned with three police men in a van to arrest Akwasi. He was hand cuffed and taken away before the onlookers. He amazed them with the way he just stared like a lost cow and followed obediently. There was a mixed feeling about him. Some believed he deserved to be punished for maltreating the woman while others felt pity for him. They imagined a poor man in police custody.

'Where is Nana?' Foowa pushed the broken door open and stood agape. The room was empty, only a baggage stood behind the door and pieces of rags thrown around. Did she sneak away? She hurried to the room adjacent her to gather some information.

Nana continued her journey down the street with her children. They were with all the useful items they could carry, including an old stove, wears, buckets, and a saggy mattress. Some needed items like mats, and potty were forgotten in a rush. What really mattered was getting out of the street alive before daybreak and also avoiding scandal mongers that saw her nudity.

What more? They had all seen what made her proud, what made her a woman, both old and young. Before then, she was disregarded and looked down upon. How much more when they saw everything? For her, it was over in the street. No more Akwasi, no more worries. All she derived from their relationship, after fourteen years, was bitterness, uncertainty, unrest, shame, poverty and hopelessness. She had been deprived over the years with her kids. She then believed that marriage is like a nut. You crack it to see what is inside.

Fresh tears streamed down her face when she stopped at a train station to get some rest before their journey to an unknown destination continued. It's their fate, maybe. She could recollect her parents talking about fate before their demise. They once said that our fate was designed by us at the onset of our journey to earth. Why she would wish that for herself was still a mystery.

It was 7:30am. Pedestrians and bystanders stopped and stared at them and their possessions. Who are they? Are they refugees? They edged by, asking themselves. It was odd how they appeared in the day, looking so dejected, depressed. Nana sat on a bare floor flanked by her children. She thought of where to go from there but no place occurred to her, precisely. She had no relation, no friend or in-law.

'Mum, stop crying. God will help us', Kobena also began to cry.

'It's okay, mum. We will soon be big to look after you', Kojo assured her, wiping the tears on her face.

'Thank you, it's alright, it's okay', she collected the rest of the load from them and put them together in the same place like garbage piled up in waste bags. She threw the bed on the ground for them to sit on and be comfortable. Her heart skipped when she realized that they were not far away from the house. She relaxed again when she remembered that Akwasi had fallen in the hands of law.

'Ahn-ahn? Nana', Kwame's voice jolted her, broke into her deep thought. She looked over her shoulder astounded. She saw him advancing towards them, his wife closely behind him, her baby strapped to her back.

'My husband said we must find you that you've not gone too far. We expected you to leave at noon', Foowa explained excitedly.

'Eh-oh, thank you so much. God bless you', Nana rose to her feet and knelt down before them, still crying. Throughout her whole lifetime, she chose never to forget these great people that remembered her in her time of grief.

'It's okay. I came with my car and I want us to leave before anyone sees us. Let's take your stuffs in the car before they start looking around for you. Do you understand?' Kwame patted the boys and led them in the car.

'We don't have any place we're going to. We're just-', she wept on.

'Nana, I'm taking you to my own house in Tema. I have a storey building there. You'll manage there with my wife till I get your apartment for you', he started to lift their properties to his car, beginning with the bed. Kobena and Kojo exchanged glances, smiling.

'Thank you sir. Eh-oh. God will always bless you and your family. May you not fall in the trap of your enemies. You will never be deprived in Jesus name. Poverty in any form or any class will not enslave you'.

'Nana, let us go away from here before the gossipers locate you and spread rumors', Foowa interrupted, also carrying one of their items.

When everything was set and they were ready to leave, Kwame turned to her and said 'Nana, not all men are bad. Akwasi just chose to be wicked for one reason or another. I don't know. That should be between both of you. I'm also a man. I take proper care of all my four wives and their children. It's who I choose to be. As there are bad men, there are bad women, I think you know that?' Nana nodded sadly and he added, 'I will assist you and your kids because you have no one to help you', he started the ignition and began to drive them out of deprivation and poverty. Nana's face cracked into a smile. She reached for her children and nestled them closer to her head in joy. It was finally over.

Kwame was, indeed, their guardian angel. He gave them a lovely apartment in his four- storey building and some money to kick off her first business ever. With the trade of food items, her life changed completely. She enrolled her boys in a nice private school, took proper care of herself.

In no time, the leaking mattress was emptied in a trash with all the rubbish that followed them to the house.

Her sorrowful stories became a history. And her real beauty

emerged. She, unbelievably, turned a laudable black beauty. At long, at last, Nana became wise and empowered. One who causes others misfortune teaches them wisdom. No one can deprive her again. Not anymore.

3

Do thi Ngoc

...however long the night, the dawn will break.

The lecture was held in the school's main lecture theater, delivered by the most eloquent lecturer, attended by multitude and enjoyed by all except a mournful being. She occupied the fifth row, straight faced, obsessed by her predicament and oblivious of the exhilarating moments around her. What lounged in her was heavy, nerve-wracking. It haunted her like a ghost, occurred to her everywhere and anywhere. No one could see through and feel her agony. It was entrenched only within.

In her twenty-fifth year, her whole being was shrouded in hatred, distrust, bitterness, grief, and most of all, deprivation. She turned and gazed around at the happy attendants. They all appeared relaxed, assimilating every salient purpose of the topic. Since success itself depends on your backbone, not your wishbone, the class was an interesting one. The attendants laughed when necessary, and contributed to the lecture in one way or the other. They found it really motivating, unlike Do thi Ngoc, who had a lot etching on her mind. They should also have their own worries too. She concluded. No human exists without a worry. Having no worry at all is also a huge worry. But it occurred to her that hers was the worst of all: from the looks on their faces. She knew, without being told, that sadness had implanted needless seriousness in her life.

The lecture had ended when her mind travelled back to the hall. She realized she had not written anything within the two hours it lasted. Why was she even attending when it was difficult to learn? What was she doing there if she couldn't listen? She questioned her negligence, looking down at the exercise book and pen she prepared for the lesson. Only the date and course title were written on the page. No topic, no note.

She sighed, folded the book and put it back in her old hand bag. She felt a little relief at the end of it all- a relief from the same unswerving lecture, calling her to attention for the past three years. All her real course mates had graduated, had even forgotten receiving lectures on ENG. 205 but hers seemed never to end.

'You don't have to meet me here for project supervision. Please, visit my office at the right time. *Bangwe!*' the middle aged lecturer, Mr. Sakubu, shunned one of the students shoving his file in his hand. It fell on the ground and disclosed its emptiness.

'I'm sorry,' he ran after his five papers busily.

'You deserve that apology, not me. That is how far you've gone for two months. Two whole months. Please, get out of my way', he walked out of the hall surrounded by a number of students waiting to see him. They all followed like chicks to the hen either to beg for consideration or whatever- whatever Do thi Ngoc didn't care to know. She had long sealed her fate and wasn't prepared to beg for his acclamation.

She shot a vengeful look at him as he hurried to his office, yelling at, yet, another undergraduate. She cursed bitterly. He was the worst of all the instructors she encountered- the most inconsiderate of all. An ordinary pass would have been in her favor to, at least, graduate from the school and stop repeating the same onerous course every year. She knew his mind was always prepared to fail her. She wondered if he ever read anything she wrote. It is his headache anyway. She thought with a shrug and straightened up to leave. As far as she was concerned, she understood it would be the last course she would live to carry for the rest of her life.

At a glance, she checked the time on her leather watch. It was past three: the restricted time she must follow through on certain rules to avert another phase of trouble in her life. She swaddled herself with her ancient shawl and hurried to the main entrance of the campus to commute to her destination. It was still lecture hours so; lots of students were very much around: reading, writing, eating and just watching the liveliness of the environment. Not everyone had someone pressurizing him to return home for any reason. She wished she had such a chance.

'Hey, Do thi -hey!' Kapa, her ex-course mate ran after her, her artificial hair falling over her shoulders. She didn't hear. Her mind was on home- to arrive home obediently.

'Hello? Someone is calling you', a young man from the Faculty of Law motioned to her and pointed at Kappa.

'Oh, thanks. *Urakoze Cane*', Do thi Ngoc said, admiring his outfit.

The law students are marked out with their colors, eloquence and elegance.

'How are you now?' Kapa walked up to her.

'Fine. I'm rushing home', she proceeded to the gate, admiring her classy wears. She was one of the swankiest in their department, one of the best in the University of Burundi. Beyond a shadow of doubt, she was spending all her money on her good look.

'Are you sure you are fine?' she eyed the ancient shawl around her. She was the odd one out in the Faculty of Arts, for her mode of dressing.

'Do you see a symptom of sickness?' she looked around confused.

'Yes, this is not proper', Anna lifted the shawl with the tip of her finger irritatingly. Her antiquated lifestyle was her most despising trait.

'Don't worry about me', she rebuffed her correction with a wave of hand and asked instead, 'why did you stop me? It wasn't because of that, was it?'

'Em-ehn, it's because of painful English- ENG. 301. You're

carrying it over, remember? We have her class this afternoon and I learnt she's giving a test and taking attendance too. You don't want to repeat it again, do you? I've been looking everywhere for you', she swept a strand of curly hair away from her face.

Do thi Ngoc was dumbfounded, enervated. What was she going to do? She didn't recollect there was yet another course she had to clear before graduating. Painful English, Phonetics Phonology was, indeed, very painful - not only because of its theoretical aspect of phonetics but the phonological form which they had to learn. The lecturer of the course, Mrs. Niyonkuru, got her nick name from the way she squeezed and strained her face to produce the English sounds. And as humorous as her class was, only thirty students often passed out of forty, her own name included in the list of failure.

'Where are you off to? Can't you wait and write this test? Your exam is useless without a test, you know?' she tried to talk her into attending the lecture she wasn't positive about.

She anticipated failure like other attempts she had made earlier. It's excruciatingly hurtful.

'O-kay, but- I have to call home first'.

'Home? Why? Do they not know that you are in school? And did they not send you here to acquire knowledge? *Kuki*?' she inquired.

She darted a fixed stare and replied, 'thank you for reminding me but you don't understand anything. Let me just call home quickly. I'll be back'. She hurried towards a nearby Call Centre, tucking her arm under her shawl and wearing a static smile. A stupid smile. Kapa thought to herself, staring at her wonderingly. What a strange girl in this new age! A genuine puritan.

That was the only outward appearance they could all see and perhaps, use to misjudge her true prickly problem. Such imagination as being raised by one from the eighteenth century or not having enough to live up to the growing trend may be true. There might, possibly, not be a mismatch between her dress sense and her domestic problem as one situation leads to another. But the truth is that, they are unrelated.

'I'm so sorry, I can't attend the class. I have to go. I really have to run right now', she announced to Kapa who stood, for all practical purposes, gazing at her.

'Sorry? Did you say sorry?' she grinned at her unfounded apology. She had another topic they were going to discuss in the girls' hostel that night. It was all about her three days ago.

'I mean, I'm sorry to have disappointed you'.

'Me? Me KP? How have you disappointed me? What do I gain from getting you to re-write an exam you failed? It's your choice', she left her still standing and smiling, scourged by her damnable excuses.

'Thank you-', she appreciated her once again and pranced out of the gate.

As she began her journey home, she thought briefly about the number of courses she had to clear before graduating that year. They were five altogether. A wave of panic swept over her. She wished she attended the painful English class and write the test but that was precisely the time she had to return. At that point, adherence was the watchword.

She had to set about fulfilling her household tasks in as much as her authorized day- out- time was over. She wouldn't spend an hour more.

'You haven't paid your fare!' the driver of the bus she boarded home shouted after her as she alighted without paying. She was, at first, jolted, had forgotten completely that she hadn't paid. All her attention was on home –nowhere else but home.

'What are you thinking?' a woman said, watching her reaction. It was palpably clear that she forgot.

'I'm sorry'. She handed him a crumbled note and waited for her balance, looking amazingly flustered.

'*Urakomeye*? You better remove the shawl and look serious. You wish to be old as sweet as life is. Incredible'. He gave her some notes back and drove off.

She wasn't affected by whatever anyone said. She only nodded with equanimity. That wasn't the first time she would be ridiculed for her cherished lifestyle. Someone had once stolen the shawl from her and she got another one in less than two weeks. It's the way she desires to dress and live- it's her lifestyle. She shook her head at the driver's infuriating character and proceeded home. She wasn't brought up to be saucy, malicious or cruel to people. She was the respectful, old fashioned girl she liked to be.

On the street, her street, people stared, she noticed but didn't care. She moved at a steady pace, checking her watch intermittently to keep to time. She had only five minutes more to arrive home, however she knew that to run is not to arrive. The previous week was hellish for her when she spent thirty minutes more, buying the ingredients for preparing dinner. She didn't want to go through that anymore. Not anymore.

When she was a stone throw to her house, she walked past a broken car parked along the street. Her image appeared to her and disappeared. Is this me? Using a mirror had suddenly turned a sinful act in their home, so it was long she set her eyes on herself. She returned to the car wonderingly. Again, her round face appeared to her on the blurry side mirror. She noticed her round face first, then some slimy bogus pimples, mostly on her cheeks and lastly, her virgin hair. She knew she was unattractive, untidy. She wished she looked better than that, still a dedicated Christian, and not straying like the skeptics in her school. She accepted that, in their school fellowships, there were attractive members who were also as committed as she claimed to be. Her personal lifestyle had, unquestionably, turned her off youthful enthusiasm. When she made every effort to improve on her look, be that as it may, her blemishes wouldn't budge. It wasn't long before she withdrew from the spot and hurried home to make up for the time wasted.

In their own living room, the third floor of a six storey - building, the second of four apartments, she met no one around. She clapped her eyes on a fluttering bible in front of a laboring standing fan. She took three steps ahead and turned it off. Of all the three rooms in the apartment, she was obliged to enter the first one submissively whenever she just arrived from school. She dropped her handbag on their sofa and shuffled tiredly to the room – to a place where their unforgiving illicit act was recurrently committed - her den of incautious practices.

She heard the shower running when she got there. Her eyes travelled round the room then rested upon a well laid bed. She thought she liked the evocative smell of the perfume in the air. It smelt tasteful, should be another one he just got for her like he did three weeks ago. Why did he have to do all of that for her? Her face was suddenly smoldered with displeasure at the frequency of their act. And she wanted it to stop by all means.

The shower shut off. She pulled herself together, folded her arms behind her obediently. She was standing, smiling when Oricana appeared stark naked. She turned away sharply, looked in another direction.

'What are you turning away from?' he subdued the impulse to touch her and rather said 'you don't have the courtesy to greet? What rubbish is this?' He ranted, absolutely bereft of love and attention.

'I'm sorry sir- I- you were bathing when I came in sir, so-', she explained courtly, still looking away. She had to pander to his wishes.

'How many times have I warned you not to address me that way? Uhn? He moved a step away from her and sank into an old bed. He was all ready for her before, had spent a couple of minutes in the shower, lusting for her and she ruined it all. He regretted how she reminded him of who he is.

'Please, leave my room', he raked his fingers through his wet hair, angrily.

'Sir-you-s', she pleaded with a timorous voice.

'Are you mad? Leave, right now!' he stood up with a start, pushed her out of his room and shut the door. She was pleased he did. One of her topmost prayer points is to be pushed, not just out of his house where she was indisposed to fighting for her right, but out of his life. Then, precisely, is the time her unfeigned dream would come true. However, slowly, slowly, porridge goes into the gourd.

She stood meekly at the entrance for a while, waiting for him to change his mind and call her back. She had to be apologetic. Merely complying with his outrageous demand meant the same distress. She peeped through a keyhole in the door and saw him lounging on his bed, still naked, legs crossed. What kind of man is he? What precisely was his problem? She gaped at his senseless thuggery. Since he started suffering from depression, she had been supportive to him, consoling him, making his meals and of course, warming his bed to make him a happy man. Shouldn't he feel guilty, at least, for once, for what he was doing? Was she the right person for him? She moved away from the door slowly, her eyes glistened with tears.

Nothing changed in the apartment-the same lifestyle, inexcusable affair, and repeated courses into a new year. In all, what saddened Do thi Ngoc chiefly was the notification she recently received from the University. She had to clear her repeated courses on a final trial or withdraw from the school within the same year. What a life! In order to accomplish her goals, she had to break free from the problem as soon as possible, after her eight years of failure. It was all the effect of Oricana's culpability and her stoicism. For the first time, after her involvement, she went berserk, frowned at her furtive acceptance of their immoral act.

She brought out her bag and rummaged through it to glance over her time table. It wasn't there. She emptied the whole content on the floor then ran her finger through them but she couldn't find it. There were three of them living in the apartment. Her sister, Dagmar, wouldn't have taken it. It wasn't useful to her. If Oricana took it, then why? She remembered she gave him a copy at his request. What did he want to do with her copy?

She rose to her feet, leaving all the content there. She had to find it immediately if she wasn't prepared to lose all her eight years in the school. That was a way to turn a new leaf: to attend lectures regularly and pass the courses.

When she got half way to his room, she was gripped with fear. She walked to his door surreptitiously and peeped through the same key hole to see what he was doing. Nothing serious. He knelt in front of his bed, clasping his hands above the holy Bible, head lowered prayerfully.

'Forgive me oh Lord-forgive me', he whimpered for God's forgiveness.

For few minutes, she stood gazing at him, wondering why he chose to remain discreditable after asking for forgiveness. If God had presumably forgiven him now, why did he have to lust for her again? It was all so confusing. And she really despised him for taking advantage of her weakness.

She ran into the kitchen as he straightened up after the prayer. He put on his flip flop and padded to her room.

'Do thi! Do thi? *Bwakeye*' he pushed the door open to have a full view of her room. He didn't see her there, so he proceeded to the kitchen. Seeing him coming, she quickly came out and met him on the way.

'Sir-I'm sorry-h-honey', she tilted her head back and smiled. It wasn't real. Hidden within her was the detrimental thought of how to extricate herself from the crazy act. Maybe a poison would complete the work.

'Yes-yes! Come here my baby. Come here', he wrapped her waist with his arm, his eyes falling on her chest sheltered with the shawl. He removed it without her consent, saying 'always remove this when you're with me. I like to see everything and go cra-zy. Can you do that for me? It's what I need to be happy'.

'Yes-y-es-s-honey', she hesitated, watching him strip her inner wear. She reached for his hands and discontinued his drive.

'What? What is it?' he asked bluntly.

'I have a test tomorrow and I haven't read anything. I'm not prepared', she put on her wear, fastened it in a rush.

'Is this an excuse for not giving me attention? I need only twenty minutes from you. I need you right now', he unfastened it again.

'No, no, I have just this year to graduate and I've not been-been reading'. She saw the expression of shock on his face and stated, almost crying 'I'm sorry sir. I didn't mean to- but I have to prepare for my examinations'.

'You are very stupid and disrespectful. Do you remember who I am to you? How dare you yell at me that way?' he rasped. She was dumbfounded. She understood she had no right over herself anymore. He controlled the females living with him.

'Get inside my room now!' he ordered.

Like a string-puppet, she walked into his room obediently, her eyes filled with tears. He followed her and shut the door against every speculative eye or criticism. He liked it that way-living a life of ease in a heart-rending situation. He had managed to move on with his loveless life, in the face of tribulation- even when he knew that, not any right- thinking man would agree with his steadfast and untraditional approach to survival. However, it remained a secret buried in the confines of the apartment for as long as the victims remained servile to him whenever he was on the pull.

Do thi Ngoc returned to the institution the next day, looking pale and drawn. She had to find one of her ex-course mates to get the examination time table. There was no pre-conceived idea of a particular location to get in touch with them so, she already wasted an hour out of the three hours she was instructed to stay. She realized the time was too short for her, so fast and unfair. And she frowned at the surliness of time. Another thirty minutes went by and she hadn't seen anyone yet. She sneaked a look at her watch as she hurried to the auditorium. There was no one there! She held her head miserably, her heart hammering like a pestle in a mortar. She was suddenly filled with a pang of fear-fear of the precognition that everything would soon crumble away. All her eight years wasted. What would become of her? An old fashioned girl living a purposeless life in the arms of a mindless lover.

In a rush of uncertainty, she made her way back to her department to glance through their notice board again, in case she skipped something. Nothing new was there. This was the last straw that broke the camel's back. Maybe the examination was already written, she concluded, still in vagueness. She began to feel empty, nauseous and stultified. She didn't hesitate to find a seat in a shady garden when she almost slumped in the public.

She got more despondent about her misfortunes, watching the serious undergraduates around. No extra year, only their duration of studies in school. They went about their activities unperturbed, focused. What truly affected her was inattention to her studies and Oricana in her life. He caused much mental turmoil and failed her. She reflected on how she started out well in her first year, dropped her head and wept bitterly. So much more that she drew someone to her agonizing cries.

'Hey, what's the matter? Are you okay? You are crying in the public. Are you okay?' She covered the space between them on the seat, a look of alarm on her face.

'It's nothing- it's nothing, I just-', fresh tears streamed down her face when she remembered the examination.

The stranger sat still, taking a long hard look at her. What was her problem? What could have made her cry in the public? She could be heart broken by a boyfriend. Or she just lost a beloved one, someone so special to her. She didn't utter a word, merely stared at her, guessing right or wrong. Her bespectacled eyes ran through her pitifully. Her appearance was enough to tell a little tale about her sorely sorrowful life.

'Let me help you', she said, finally. 'I've been in a sad situation before- but I shared my problem with someone and solved it. A problem shared is half- solved. The longer you keep this burden in your heart the more harm you will do to yourself', she brought out a handkerchief and handed it to her.

'No, thanks. I have mine'. She sought for hers in her handbag, lunged for it and began to wipe her face. Her new friend kept gawking, particularly studying her disposition. She seemed too diffident and furtive but she was bent on drawing the truth from her.

'So, sister-please don't feel sad or cry anymore. I don't know what the problem is but -'.

'Thanks'. She pulled herself to her feet and left. She was not ready to tell anyone her sad story. Strangers aren't trustworthy. What if she was her enemy's informant?

'Take it easy and take care of yourself, okay?' she shouted after her solicitously but she gave no reply.

She hurried back to the auditorium to find a familiar student. It was probable that someone could linger for some time, spend extra time around. Her eyes journeyed around the scene tiredly. There was no familiar face. Examination over, maybe. She removed her bag from her shoulder and sat on a chair in the hall way. If the exam had been written, then it was over, she concluded. There wouldn't ever be the slightest chance to muddle through. All her eight years of chancing her luck was over. What next? The list of failures would be printed in a newspaper for all to see and use as a precautionary measure to correct all their unserious children studying in the school

Again, she sighed, holding her head desolately. In a world of her own, her eyes wandered on the ground as she diverted her attention from self-criticism to her uncaring ex-course mates. Someone should have informed her about the date, location, and what to read for the exam, considering her academic woes. But how? She asked herself inevitably. How was it possible when her number was concealed from everyone except her instructor: the ruler of her life? It was Oricana's fault, she agreed. Thirty minutes after she sat there, her phone began to ring. At first, she ignored it. Her mind was too occupied to receive any call- too occupied with how much damage Oricana had done to her life.

She felt a wave of dizziness when she stared down at her watch. The time limit he gave her was over. He must have waited for his meal to no avail and started fuming. Should she run away? She considered the possibility for a while and stood to leave, her face devoid of joy, her mind silenced by deprivation and her body desirous of freedom. She understood she was into mire but for how long? She shook her head and filtered through the bustling school gate with multitude of students.

'Do thi Ngo! Do thi!!' a rapturous voice followed her through the gate. Her long pleated skirt made a swish as she turned around. Oh God! It was Kapa. She smiled broadly and Kapa stood watching her approach nervously. To her, she still appeared strained.

'Where have you been? Uhn? Why have you not been coming to school?' she questioned her impatiently, her attention on her shabby clothing. That was one of the two sickening issues she detested about her- her primitiveness and dressing.

'Me? I've been around, looking for everyone- looking for you. I've been to the auditorium, lecture hall and- *amakuru?*'

'Why have you not been coming to school? That's what I'm asking you', she cut in sharply. Annoyance traversed her face when she recollected the way she liked being discreet.

'I've been busy. You can't understand, there's something I'm doing that's taking the whole of my time', a shiver of fear ran through her when her phone began to ring again. Its tasteless caller tone filled the air. Kappa grimaced, turned away abruptly. Oricana wouldn't give up until his call is received to explain the grounds for her delay. She never minded it, she ignored it again. Kapa gave her a knowing look then said, 'answer your call. Why are you ignoring the caller?'

'Don't worry about that. It's from home, they want me back and I won't go until I straighten out what I'm here for'. She tried as much as possible to hide her stinging feelings. Kapa mustn't know her secret and crying in front of her would unravel the mysteries of her failure she wasn't prepared to recount to anyone. Yet she read her thought and asked a related question.

'Are you working for someone at home? Or are you doing something more serious than your degree program?'

'No-no, not really. I can explain that after. Have you written your final examination?' she changed the topic deliberately to prevent letting the cat out of the bag. She wanted her to mind her business.

'Before we talk about the papers, your mummy was here. She came to find you about seven times last month and five times this month. She really wants to see you'. She announced, smiling.

'Wait! My mum? Did you just say my mum? Kapa, my mum?' she exclaimed in total disbelief. She wasn't expecting to see her soon after she left them for ten years. Dagmar was only ten years while she was fifteen at the time their father divorced her. They both longed to see her and get the feel of good mothering after a long time.

'Tell me-did she leave her phone number or home address? I really need to see her', she inquired in high spirit.

'Of course, she left her phone number with me. If you need to call her now, you can'. She brought out an expensive phone from her pocket. Do thi Ngoc swallowed hard, admiring the luxury of the cell phone. It's not built for an old-fashioned girl like her, she assumed.

'Alright, please- call her for me. I don't have credit on my phone. It's been a long time I saw her last. Ah-mummy?'

'She said so'. Kapa dialed the number and it began to ring immediately.

'Is it ringing?' she bursts with impatience. Kapa didn't answer, only smiled and waited for her to receive the call. Finally, a sharp voice came from the other end.

'Yes, hello?'

'Good evening ma. It's Kapa, Do thi's friend'.

'Yes, how are you my dear? *Urakomoye?*'

'Fine ma. I want to tell you that I've seen Do thi Ngo, your daughter and she's here with me'.

'Really?' she sounded exhilarated.

'*Ego*, she's right here in the school', she patted her confidently.

'It's okay; I'll be there with you in the next thirty minute. I'm on my way. *Kira*'. Her phone rang off and the two friends stood smiling at each other.

'Thank you-thank you so much I don't know how to express my gratitude to you. Hmmn? I can't believe I'm going to see my mummy today', she shook her head in sheer disbelief. Kapa paused, staring at her curiously. What kept her mother away from her for that long and why? When she met her the first and second time in their lecture hall, she never spoke a word about her motives. She only explained that she has been away for long- that she wanted to see her daughter. No further explanation. Seeing Do thi Ngoc, she quickly seized the opportunity to hear from the horse's mouth.

'Well, thank God mummy is back now. What made her leave before? I know you must have been badly affected by her disappearance'. She tried as much as possible to hide her nosiness, feigned compassion.

'Yes, have you written the exam? Please, tell me- I need to know', Do thi Ngo also avoided her question wisely.

'No, you're lucky. We are going to start next week'. She felt a little dissatisfied with her blurry secrecy.

'What?! I thought you had written it last month'

'Why were you not here at the right time? If you knew the date, why didn't you come to the school? You're too unserious with your studies. Anyway, it was postponed due to the strike action on increment of workers' salaries', she explained curtly, then returned to what really interested her, 'mama looked really worried. She must have missed you a lot. Let's sit somewhere and wait for her', she takes a few steps towards the closest garden.

'No- don't worry. Shouldn't you be going? I'll wait for her. We have a lot to discuss and am sure-you'll –also have something to do'. She smiled sardonically, already tired of her overmuch concern.

'Alright. I'll leave you- if you insist. I wish you luck. *Turabonaye*'. She sounded bitter as she began to leave.

'No, what about the exam time table?'

'You can copy it from Faculty of Arts; it's not in the department. Goodbye', she clarifies, striding away.

Do thi Ngo stood watching her, a look of surprise on her pale face. It always amazed her when someone wants to know her secret: a top-secret no one should know about, under any circumstance. In as much as she suffered a lot from her family's turbulence, she wasn't going to spit it out to anyone. Every family has a dark secret; they had theirs too.

She returned to the gate to wait for her mum. That was the easiest way she would find her after Kapa decidedly left with the phone number she needed to connect to her. On her way there, her phone started ringing again. Oricana! He gave her only three hours to stay, irrespective of any occurrence. He didn't care about anything despite all she told him about her list of failure in the school. All he wanted was the same indispensable attention he got from her.

She sighed and leaned on the wall when she got to the gate. She wasn't, an inch, swayed by his disturbances. She folded her arms obstinately, her lips tightened in deep antagonism and frustration. Each time she got obsessive of his absurdities, she wondered why an elder defecates on his palm. It's unheard of: a dirty talk. If not for his insanity, is she the right girl for him? She asked herself again, shaking her head at his incongruity.

'Is someone waiting for mama? *Amahoro*?'Mrs. Senagul arrived. Do thi Ngo rushed into her arms excitedly. Was she really the one? She ran her eyes over her transformed physique.

She appeared bigger than before and more beautiful. Obviously, she was more Godly, judging from her new look: head heavily shielded with a turban, skirt covering down to the ankle and body protected with a long sleeve shirt.

'Mum, you've really changed. You-have really-really changed. Look at you! And I've missed you a lot. We have missed you a lot', she hugged her again, crying. Her illusion about her interest in them was wrong. They were both badly affected by the shattering experience. She also missed them as much as they did.

'Oh my dearest, God knows how much I've missed you all, especially your younger sister who needed me more at the time I left. I tried to get in touch with you but, I just had to keep off to avoid fighting and imprecation. He told me to leave his children alone'.

She wiped the tears on her face, and then wiped hers too. She looked around for somewhere to sit and said 'we need to talk. Shall we enter your school and find somewhere to sit and talk? We have a lot to discuss'.

'No, mum. I'm going back with you today. I just don't want to discuss with you today. I have to leave with you right now. If not, I may commit suicide', she pleaded.

'Suicide? *Kuki?*'

'Yes ma. I must leave with you right now before we're caught together'. Mrs. Senagul was shocked. For the moment, she kept silent and her daughter noticed her indecision. She didn't welcome the idea but liked to, at least, listen to her reasons.

'Do thi Ngo- my darling, I've come to see you and keep in touch with you afterwards, not to run off with you. Please, you need to understand me'.

'No, mum-you've stayed away from me for too long. I want to

leave with you right now, *ubuyene*, even if I have a few months to stay', she looked at her squarely, her expression grim. She had always wished to elope to wherever she was hiding. And there – they met in the school- that evening.

'Listen to me Do thi, I won't deceive you. The truth is that, you can't live with me. Very soon, you will also be free; I understand what you're going through there without me. And remember, darling- no matter how long the night, the dawn will surely break. Pretty soon you will be free'.

'You have no idea what I am going through, do you?'

'Do thi-no matter what, you can't live with me'.

'Why? Why can't I live with my mother?' she stared at her quizzically.

'Why?' she broke into a smile and called her fondly. 'My dear Do thi, I'm living with my new husband. Your daddy divorced me ten years ago, remember? He divorced me for being saintly. I tried to reconcile with him, he refused. So, I met this God -fearing man and married him. He knows I've had kids before but I didn't tell him I will bring you today'.

'Hmm', Do thi Ngo sighed feebly, was about to start crying again. She couldn't help but ask another reasonable question.

'Mum-do you have another kid?'

'Yes, I do. His name is Dilon. You will meet him next time I visit. I love my husband and my son, same way I love you and your sister. Do thi, that divorce was a blessing in disguise. I have my peace with my new family all the time'.

'Mum, do you care for us at all?'

'How? I do care for you-every one of you. Your father drove me away from you'.

'I'm sorry to say, the truth is that you don't care. No- you don't. You care for only Dilon and your new- I'm sorry'. She fell silent and stared blindly into space.

'Why? Why did you say that?' she shook her arm for a response and there was a serious look on her face.

'Well, I don't understand why you don't want to help me after leaving us for ten whole years. This is the time I need you. You don't have an idea of what I'm facing presently-',

'Tell me what is going on. That I can't take you home doesn't mean I can't help you. I'm your mother, remember?'

Do thi Ngo sighed again. Should she let the cat out of the bag or keep her lips sealed? What would happen after the secret is blown open?

She contemplated for a moment.

'Do thi! Tell me what's going on. If you don't give me a good reason to help you, I won't', she said frankly, getting tired of her indecision.

'My daddy is having a love affair with me', she let it slip.

'What?! Incest! I'm doomed', she held her head drearily. She turned shockingly disgruntled at her ex-husband's heartlessness, marveled at the way he'd given full vent to his feelings.

'Mum?' she brought her hands down from her head as she noticed the number of people pausing and watching her. She had unknowingly attracted them with her outburst. She ignored them and asked her amidst tears, 'Do thi Ngo! For how long has he been doing this to you?'

'It's been seven years now but I don't know the relationship between him and Dagmar. I only caught her wearing a towel in his room once'.

'It shall not be well with Oricana. I will get him arrested!'

'For taking what is rightly mine? *Sindabizi*' Oricana himself answered from behind her. He had crept up on them after seeing them from afar. His primary mission was to detect Do thi's whereabouts when she refused to receive his calls. On his arrival, he realized he had a secondary mission too.

'You- what are you doing here with this devilish woman? Liar! Pretender!' he looked from mother to daughter fiercely, a perverse expression on his face, a fiendish thought running through his mind.

'Mad man! You are a mad man. Thank God you've come out here in the public to expose yourself. I'll make sure I punish you for what you've done ', Senagul yelled with a voice loud enough to move a mountain. A crowd began to gather around them. And Do thi Ngo feared exposure of her secret. Her eyes went around the spot for Kapa. She wasn't there yet.

'Will you shut your mouth now? Or I should shut it for you. You don't have any right to discuss anything with my daughter', he stuck his finger in front of her eyeball.

'If that filthy thing touches me, you will be sorry forever. Useless man, useless father! Did the court order you to sleep with your daughter after the divorce? Uhn? Answer me! Mad man', she asked repeatedly, glaring at the onlookers' reactions. They were horror-stricken. Was it true? They exchanged glances.

'Ehn? So what? What if she told you that? Did you remember to tell your mother that you promised to replace her and console me after she left like a stray bullet?' he fired at Do thi, who just hung her head in extreme shame. Tears moistened her burdened face.

At the scene, people had mixed feelings about the happening. Should the shameless father be blamed for committing a crime, which is not just gravely against the law but conversely against divination? Or should her mother be castigated for leaving her children to suffer in the arms of absurdities? Perhaps, if anyone is to blame, should it be the girl, for her utmost laxity? They all murmured as the wrangle persisted.

'And that is why you need her younger sister too. She is also consoling you, isn't she? The Almighty God I'm serving will spare you to see the end of this. You are a disgrace to paternity. I will deal with you for ruining their lives'. She hit her chest, removed her scarf from her head and tied it around her waist in readiness for a fight.

'Hun? You want to fight with me? You want to fight? You are a useless mother. Worthless woman! Shame on you! Shame!! You left your kids and ran away with another man. Shame!' he grabbed her hands and stopped her from hitting him the second time. She struggled to free herself.

'You want to beat me outside here? Go ahead, beat me in the public. Beat me for exposing your evil deed'.

'Mum-can't you just –leave him?' Do thi pleaded frailly.

She felt an overpowering weakness around her. A sudden blaze of darkness sprinted through her face before she slumped at the point. Mrs. Senagul crouched beside her unconscious body in despair and cried for succor.

'Oh no, please- help me. Do thi- Do thi Ngo!' She was first, at a loss, what to do. In the next few seconds, she realized she had to act fast and began to take measures she learnt from her secondary school teacher. She twisted her fingers together, and then flattened her palms on her chest to resuscitate her. She shook her body repeatedly, calling her name. Her tension heightened and in the midst of her great anxiety and uncertainty, Oricana left in silence. Nevertheless, it wasn't long before she sensed his disappearance and screamed.

'Where is he? He mustn't run away. He must come and wake my daughter, else-'.

Ten to eleven heads turned to look around for him while three bystanders gathered around Do thi concernedly.

'You too- you are a troublesome woman. What do you want from such a desperate man? Let him go away. The hands of justice will soon reach him. Don't you know his house? Or is he not your husband?' one of the campus marshals corrected her sternness, keeping the crowd under control.

'Never! He's my ex'.

'Whatever he is, you will still get him. We need to save the girl'.

Do thi Ngo's unconsciousness lasted for about six minutes after series of resuscitation methods were carried out on her. She was conveyed with a school's shuttle to the campus clinic for further medical examination as a student. Was she suffering from a kind of sickness or the psychological effect of the untimely disclosure? The crowd finally dispersed in an hour, everyone leaving with different opinions. On the whole, Oricana was mostly blamed for being immeasurably cruel to his family: committing incest, a punishable offence in the country. Was he really punished for this? How was he punished and who punished him? They actually wanted to witness the end but had to part their different ways.

The same day, in the clinic, after all tests were conducted by a school doctor, Do thi Ngo was confirmed pregnant. Senagul found the unanticipated consequences too shocking and overwhelming for her at the onset. But in the long run, when the police mediated, the matter was sooner resolved than expected.

Oricana was seized by the hands of law twelve months after Senagul's persuasion. She finally had a smile on her face when he was arraigned before a judge in a magistrate court in Buterere on the count of incest, child abuse and rape. He pleaded not guilty to all the counts, giving reasons for his incestuous affair with his daughters. Finally, he was sentenced to ten years imprisonment.

What became of Do thi Ngo and the unwelcomed pregnancy after justice was meted out to him? She had an abortion that almost claimed her dear life. She suffered the incurable trauma as years rolled by, especially when she decided not to get married for the rest of her life- for her barrenness. Although justice was rightly effected, nevertheless nothing changes. Nothing changes the reality that her biological father had a carnal knowledge of her. Nothing changes the infertility problem that subsequently led to her unending spinsterhood. And the society, of course, will never wipe the thought off their memories or erase the subject from their overly busy lips. It's insane and strange to everyone.

Each time she set her eyes on her hard earned first degree certificate, in a newly rented apartment, away from speculative eyes, she got more embittered. An ordinary pass wasn't what she envisioned on her admission in the school. She worked hard towards a first class degree in her first year, following her academic record. But, Oricana made it impossible- her broken family made it impossible.

In her present life, she was starved of all her ambitions: her blissful marriage to the man she loves, her own children she wished to have and nurture in a different way and her aspiration to become a television presenter. They all occurred in her dream and never prevailed in reality for her inescapable deprivation.

4

Dafina

…a family enjoys fortunes with one; flees from trouble

News is like wildfire. As fast as lightning, it surfaces, travels quicker than expected. Often appearing in different shades: the truth, added truth and false, it grows stronger. It depends on whoever is involved. For a non-entity, there's a magnitude it can travel and the number of days it would last. But for the rich and celebrated, it goes on and on. It seems endless, turns a vagrant and travels everywhere for prominence. Shortly after Dafina discovered the nature of her illness in a government hospital, in Kisumu, on a sunny Tuesday morning, she was panic-stricken. She read through the medical report she just received from a nurse, the second time, in a rush, to be sure there wasn't a mistake. No mistake. She just saw it and read it that she tested positive for Human Immuno Deficiency Virus (HIV): the famous deadly disease.

'Excuse me, please. *Habari* ', she hurried in the direction of a receptionist, still holding the report in a trembling hand.

'*Sijambo*. Y-es, can I help you?' she replied, not looking up at her. She was engrossed with the compilation of old files on their choking shelves. She had spent hours sorting out some disused records. Most of their patients don't visit the hospital another time after their recovery.

'Please, I want to see the doctor', she demanded with a shaky but familiar voice. This served as the driving force for looking up to match the voice with the face in the middle of her work.

'The doctor?'

'Y-es'.

'Was it not you that came for a test two months ago?' She pointed a pen at her. She almost denied but the truth was inevitable at the time.

'Yes-yes, but-'.

'Have you seen the result?' she pushed the files aside and raised her face. She didn't sound, at all, surprised or anxious to know something.

'Yes, but I still need to see the doctor', she looked down at the report: the saddest news she ever read in her whole life. Nothing like that ever happened to her. She drew a deep breath and looked up at the nurse again.

'He waited for you for two whole months and you didn't return. That's not fine. It's not okay to take your own health issue lightly', she picked another file, and cross checked the information busily, the pen roaming the page. She has done as much as she was assigned to do. She however left her to take a decision. After all, the life is hers.

Something in the nurse's voice rang true to Dafina. She also recognized that look in her eyes-that she had already read her report and the whole world must have seen it, probably. Its undeniable she saw the same look on everybody's face, including the cleaners. The news of her ailment had long travelled around before her arrival. That didn't really matter to her like its verification. Was it really true or it was a mere illusion, following her overmuch complaint in the doctor's office? The report could be for another patient. She believed there may possibly be a mix-up somewhere, somehow. She pulled herself together and concluded that she had to wait and see the doctor. Right there, she was determined not to be shaken by their nosiness. You care for what you need from a market, not the noises surrounding it.

'I still need to see the doctor immediately'.

'Well, you are not our patient. You need to register here before you are allowed to see the doctor'.

'And-how much is that?' she asked impatiently, still shivering.

'You pay five hundred and get a personal card, one thousand for a family card. After seeing him, you-'.

'The personal card is okay', she cut in abruptly. What would she need a family card for? Was she playing games with her? She flashed a wrathful expression while she searched for a new registration card.

'Well, after seeing him, you may need to pay for your medication if you have any', she drew out a crisp file and began to pen down her number.

Dafina sighed, slipping a hand in her armpit unconsciously, the other hand still holding the bad report and trembling. She felt their eyes stuck to her body even though she didn't see them. The unprofessional nurses allowed pessimism to creep into them and they gawped at her as if it never happened before. What is new under the sun? She wondered as she waited for the registration to be completed.

'Here'.

'Thanks, your names, please?'

'Dafina- Hamadi'.

'Address and age?' she cocked her head to pay attention.

'Helen Street, Kisumu'.

'You may have your seat and wait for your turn to see the doctor', she pointed at the reception hall, where other patients were waiting and handed the file to another nurse to submit it in the doctor's office. It took another thirty five minutes before she finally had a chance to see the doctor on duty that day. As the bell rang, the same nurse that presented her card came out to call her name.

'It's your turn to see the doctor, please'.

'Oh, thank you', she stood up from her seat, hastened into the office. This was her life issue, it had to be so. Never before, in her twenty five years, had she thought of becoming a victim of a deadly disease. The report was unbelievable until she set her eyes on the skilled practitioner.

'Good afternoon sir'. She walked in; meeting the steady gaze of a small man in a white doctor's uniform, waiting to attend to the line of patients in attendance.

'Miss Dafina Hamadi?' he read from the file.

'Sir?' she folded her arms behind her like one in a court of law.

'No- you may have your seat, please', he stared at her for a moment, a pitiful countenance on his face. He dropped the stethoscope hanging on his neck and sat up in his chair seriously after recognizing her face. He was the same doctor on duty on the day she fell critically ill and reported in for a test. And she disappeared before the result was ready.

'But, why didn't you wait for your result on that day? Why did you disappear?' She gazed at him for a moment, ran her tongue over her parched lips and said, 'sir, it's not like that. I- I-received a call from my brother in Eldoret- that my father was dying and I don't live with my parent. So, I had to quickly leave here and run to-'.

'Save him before saving yourself? That's not true. I don't believe you', he interrupted, shaking his head. He looked at her sternly and repeated 'I don't believe you'.

'I-'.

'I think you were scared of your test result. You already presumed what it would be and you disappeared. Come off it, we've had patients like you before. Actually, hundreds of them. Their reports still lie in our safe- for the time they will make up their minds to collect them'.

She gave no answer to his conjectural explanation of her absurd departure. She merely lowered her head, her eyes dropped on her laps. It was true. What kept her off was the result, nothing else.

'Well, you have been confirmed HIV positive, meaning you tested positive to HIV'. Not looking up at her face to observe her reaction, he picked his pen, opened her file and began to write on a fresh page.

'Doctor, what do I do? How do I live with it? Please help me', she fell on her knees from the chair and broke into tears. 'Please, help me'.

'Ahn?' he leaned forward from his table. 'Please, be seated. If it was this important to you, why did you leave? Why did you disappear for two months even when you suspected a deadly disease? Please, sit and listen to me if you need our help', he continued writing on the paper in her file.

'Eh- my God, I'm in trouble. What am I going to do? AIDS is deadly', she lamented in fear, trembling.

'No one said it's AIDS. AIDS is the last stage of the HIV infection. It's the most severe stage. If you can sit and listen to me, you will save your life. There's no magic we're going to perform here', he grimaced, seeing her restiveness. Being the only doctor on duty, he had to attend to other patients queuing up for consultation.

'O-kay sir. I'm listening to you sir', she cried silently, burned within. She rubbed off the tears on her face with the back of her hands, then looked up at him sniffing and still crying, her eyes bloodshot.

'Sit down', he pointed at a seat opposite him and watched her sit slowly, unwillingly.

'Yes, I have to attend to you now because there are other patients waiting to see me.'

'Hmmn'.

'Thank God the disease is no longer as it used to be in the past years when people died helplessly from either their unbroken silence or lack of proper medication and diet. *Hakuna matata*. You are at the HIV stage now, meaning Human Immunodeficiency Virus stage- your lucky stage to put it under your control. HIV can lead to AIDS- Acquired Immunodeficiency Syndrome if not treated. Unlike some other viruses, the human body can't get rid of HIV completely, even with treatment. So, it stays for life', he sighed, removed his glasses and rubbed his eyes. He wasn't crying but felt sorry for her. He also had a daughter of her age studying Law in the University. How she contacted the disease is not a mystery. He's a doctor.

'Sir- you said it's my lucky stage', she fidgeted. Her eyes were glistened with tears.

'Yes, because there are steps you can take to lengthen your life. There are lots of HIV Testing and Counseling Centers (HTC) all over the country to support the victims. Also, there is the Anti-Retroviral Therapy (ART) that can prevent you from progressing to AIDS and make you live longer and lower the risk of infecting others. That is if you take it every day'.

'How can I get that sir?'

'Don't worry, we are going to give you every direction on that and all the orientation you need. Remember; don't share any sharp object with anyone. And don't have unprotected sex. You mustn't spread it. Do let the people around you know your status and don't run away. You have to consider the uninfected people around you. You mustn't spread it', he drew a long breath and concluded 'I will refer you to the nurses now and you will be told the next thing to do'.

'Thank you sir', she wiped her tears with a clean handkerchief she was holding and stood up when the doctor pressed the bell for the next patient to enter. A nurse rushed in, collected her file and led her to another office.

On that day, only one statement from the doctor recurred to her: she was still in her lucky stage. She looked through the reception hall and saw the sky. It looked strange as well as everything around. She also felt like an outlandish phase of her life just emerged with the disease. She was empty and nauseous. The only good news is that people live longer with the infection nowadays, although it cannot be wiped off. However, in her affliction, she thanked God it wasn't a disease that would claim her life in a number of days like EBOLA or Corona Virus- contemporary diseases in Africa. And was she going to declare herself diseased? Never! She made up her mind to disclose it to her parents alone, to prevent being stigmatized like other infected people she knew.

Maybe Dafina was wrong when she got home that day and called her parents' attention to the root of the matter. They both exchanged glances then fixed her with a questionable stare. Her sixty-four- year-old father, Mr. Abdalla Hamadi, had heard news about the disease and also read information meant to edify the society. Most times, he would discuss it with his friends over their ludo games too. Besides, he had met an AIDS victim on their street before except Dafina's mother, Mrs. Budya Hamadi who had a little knowledge about its outbreak.

'*Hatari*! What?! That disease in this place?' he exclaimed, his Swahili native accent profoundly noticeable in his spoken English.

'That sickness? That one you told me about?' his wife fished for information.

'Yes! She's infected with the disease. We're all in trouble', he stood up, walked to the door then returned. He was confused.

'Eh! Jesus! My good lord, help me. Jee-suuu-s! Dafina! How did you get it! Dafina, how? How?!' Mrs. Hamadi burst out crying, giving her a distance.

'Keep your voice down. Did you hear that? Keep your horrible masculine voice down! If not, we may be asked to quit this one room we're managing here. I have no money to rent a new place', he shot her a frustrating look and turned to Dafina.

'You! You must find another place to live right now. I can't live with death itself. I cannot', he shook his head in utmost disapproval of the idea.

'That thing in your body can destroy a whole person. It can infect and kill!' he pointed at her aggressively, bitterly. Dafina began to cry again. All she dreaded before disclosing the news to them began to manifest. Stigmatization, deprivation, and segregation. Her biggest trouble was getting a new home to live. She fell on her knees and held her mother's legs for consideration.

'Please, beg daddy for me. Mum-please, I have nowhere to go'.

'What do I do? What am I going to do? Dafina, you have killed me-eh!' she continued crying.

'Keep standing there and let her infect you. Keep asking her what to do, she will soon show you how to live or die. Ears that do not listen to advice, accompany an unfortunate head when it is chopped off. Nonsense! I even heard that her tears mustn't touch you. Those hands are also infected', he removed Dafina's towel from his bed and flung it on their bare floor. She had left it there when she was rushing to the hospital in the morning.

'Ehn? Dafina, Uhn?' her mother stood up and stayed away from her. She used the tip of her wrapper to wipe her tears.

After seeing her parents' uncharitable reactions towards her,

Dafina decided to keep her lips sealed. They lived happily in that same room for thirteen years when all was well. When trouble came, there was no room to swing a cat. They detested the incurable disease and took it out on her- their daughter. It is always said that he who earns calamity eats it with his family but for her, it was different. For how long would she survive with the disease after her biological parents gave her only three hours to quit the apartment? Where was she going? To a friend or another relative for further discrimination?

By 5pm, when she had finished packing all her stuffs in two suitcases, she dragged them down from their old bed, set them both on the floor. She stopped crying and pulled out a handkerchief from her hand bag to wipe her misted face. Her strained eyes hurt but she didn't care. What befell her was worse than losing a sight. She needed a moment to sit down alone and plan thoroughly. The room already appeared like hell to her when they both fled for their dear lives in the wake of her bad news. She admitted she was responsible for their hassle, wanted to leave. Leave to escape deprivation in all forms. She shuddered as she thought of the humiliation she would face wherever she was relocating. If her own parents could elope from her, who would stay? She paced around the room, brooding over where to go. There were lot of choices but only one place occurred to her.

Mr. Darweshi. Yes, that was the only person she supposed would welcome her into his home anytime, any day and for as long as she wanted to stay. They were together three weeks ago, in his three-bedroom suite in Mumias. He was always a wonderful friend. She finally put two and two together then clutched her bags to leave Kisumu at exactly 6:45pm.

'Karibu. You didn't call me before coming. You didn't tell me you were coming to see me', Darweshi stared at her, full of surprise, his hand still on the door, an unserious smile caressing his lips. Dafina walked past him, struggling to enter with her suitcases. He didn't offer to help and she had no smile on her face.

'What happened to you? You almost missed me. I was about-about leaving for my night shift at work', he looked from her face to the suitcases, wondering why she came without a notice and of course, with bags.

'I'm sorry to bother you. I'm so sorry. *Pole sana*. Darweshi? I lost my dad. I just lost him yesterday.' She rushed into his arms and hugged him tightly. Her head ached as she began to cry again.

'Oh my God, what happened to him?' he asked disinterestedly. He held her head and looked straight into her eyes. Poor girl, he felt so sorry for her.

'He drank the tea I prepared for him and died. They suspected that I- I –killed him. They accused me of poisoning his tea'.

'Who?'

'My relatives, especially my mother. They almost arrested me this morning and I ran away luckily', she cried convulsively, dramatically. Darweshi sighed, was short of words.

'Trust me, I can't kill anyone. I didn't kill my father. Help me, I can't- I – can't kill anyone', she hugged him more tightly, almost crushing herself on him. He was dumbfounded, motionless. He was possibly considering her plight and what he would do to assist. Would he accommodate a culprit in his house? What if he was also involved?

'Dafina, it's okay- it's okay. Come, come- have a seat', he led her to his guest room. She slept there three weeks ago, wrapping herself in his arms. The bed still laid the same way she left it. It would be the best resting spot for her, she thought.

'It's a good idea you came here for help but you can't hide here. What if they come looking for you?'

'What?! *Nini*?' she was surprised he believed what she said. She never knew a flawless lie could block her chances. She shook her head, his hands and cried more.

'I didn't do it, I did not. Trust me Darweshi. I just want to hide here for like- em- three weeks, and then I'll return home. Help me, please', tears rolled down her face. What more would she do to convince him? He sighed, rose to his six feet and pondered on what to do. He had something else on his mind, not that.

He met her two years ago in a cosmopolitan city. She looked so young and attractive in her shorts and mile long heels, illuminating her luscious legs. A wave of seduction swept over him. They fell for each other on that same day and since then; they've been having a secret love affair. She had the freedom to access his home from time to time after she must have lied to her parents that she was either travelling to Nakuru where her elder sister lived or Gede, her only brother's home.

The affair was unperturbed all along, only that they didn't know much about each other. If Darweshi should disappear from the apartment today, she had no idea where to find him, just as he knew nowhere she came from. It was all in the dark. Dark life, dark relationship. He gave her one hard, long look and finally spoke out his mind in all sincerity. 'Look, young lady', he called her that for the first time in their affair. 'I must tell you this. I don't know how you're going to perceive it. Look, I can take the risk to let you sleep here for only one night, and leave tomorrow'.

'Darweshi! Ahn? Wh-', she retorted, her eyes burning with incredulity. He was the only confidant she had. If he could deny her for falsehood, then he would strangle her for the disease living in her.

'Listen! Keep quiet and listen to me!' he yelled at her. This was unbelievable too. He was always so sweet, friendly and calm. He rose from the bed aggressively and stood in front of her.

'I've never told you this before and I'm going to tell you now. I mean, I was preparing to explain to you on your next visit. And thank passionate God that you are here today.' he clasped his hands together, took two quick steps towards her and elucidated what she didn't know about him.

'Look around here properly; does it look like a place I can occupy alone? No- seriously, take a good look around', he watched the way she craned her eyes around confusedly and said, 'listen, and listen attentively. This is my matrimonial home. I have a family- a wife and children- four of them. The oldest of them is about your age', he watched her reaction but felt no compassion for her. After all, the affair was about give and take. He assumed he had given his oldest daughter the best training she needed to elude what she suffers now. She had his financial support, even though she stays in her mother's custody. What lured Dafina into their affair was evidently her penury and lack of home training. He knew this and took full advantage of her. Most parents do not care how their children get the money they spend even when they know they have no supported source of income. Her deprivation lured her into the immoral act.

She was in shock. What she heard from him was like pepper upon injury and he knew it. He knew that she needed consolation at the moment, not desolation. With the expression on her face and her pitiable frame of mind, he was close to hugging her and helping her solve her problem, nevertheless he was determined to dismiss her, and face his family affairs. He thought it was all lust.

Dafina decided to keep silent and contain all her agonies. First, it was the discovery of a disease, then it was heartbreak on the same day. She sighed, tried to restrain the pain but burst into tears unbearably. She felt the warmth of her tears on her face and its saltiness streaming into her mouth. Nothing mattered anymore. What slouched within was treacherous.

'God knows I'm not being wicked to you because of what you did to your dad. Am really sorry about your daddy's death – only- that it coincides with what I wanted to discuss with you. It happened when I wanted my family back. I've just reconciled with my wife', he leaned on the wall impassively and watched her cry her eyes out. He wished to walk up to her and calm her, even though he had no feeling for her. He could not. He didn't want her anymore.

'Darweshi!' she raised her clouded eyes to his face.

'Yes?'

'You didn't tell me that you have a family', she sobbed.

'Wait-wait-wait. Think about it, just think about it. Take a good look at me-how old do I look? Like 28, 32, 41?' he arched a brow, waiting for her answer. She kept crying and he added 'if at fifty two, I had no family, then, come on, I need someone to pray for me'.

Her mind boggled at the mention of his real age. She thought he was forty and still single. He had a deviously slim, athletic physique that one could hardly believe had lived for that long. She threw herself on the bed and cried more. He didn't budge. He kept a distance away from her, didn't care. For him, it was over, no matter what. He walked out of the room quietly.

By the time she stopped crying, her head ached and a familiar sound kept reverberating from her tummy. She remembered she hadn't taken anything aside from the tea and bread she took in the morning before she started having a disastrous day. Her eyes flicked open when she heard the noise again. And she peered around for Darweshi. Where was he? She wasn't astonished that he left her alone there. Nothing would change his mind about his family. In their short lived relationship, she discovered his strictness and ageless determination. He had said all he was going to do and that was it.

She rolled on her tummy and faced the bed, her hand by her side. The stale smell of the mattress penetrated her nostrils, travelled down her lungs. She pressed her face harder in an attempt to suicide but couldn't hold for too long. She released herself for a while, gasped for air. Fresh tears appeared in her eyes. She cried until she drifted into sleep.

When she awoke from an unmet slumber, it was past 3am. It looked like rain. She thought as she peered at the heavy sky through a lustrous window. She enjoyed the coolness of the humid air, raising herself up with an elbow. Pain radiated all over her body. And all of the symptoms that led her to the hospital set in again- the acute flu and feverish condition, sore throat, tiredness and joint muscle pain. They are all acute retroviral syndrome.

She shifted her attention to how she got the disease. Was it from Darweshi or Robin, another man-friend she had in their boulevard? She remembered she had an unprotected affair with Robin twice. What if he infected her? She set her feet on her slippers, wrapped her shoulders with a scarf she found in the room.

Darweshi was accustomed to being protective anytime he was with her either to avoid accepting an unwanted pregnancy or contacting a venereal infection. However, she could still recollect when he was carried away and he forgot to do so once or twice. Hence, she knew he was likely to have a fair share of the ordeal with his family. This disposition re kindled her hope and at least, alleviated the painful memory of losing a cherished one- a treasured one who didn't care about her feelings or problem. She burned with contempt.

She rose from the bed, stretched her body feebly and made for the rest room. She clapped her eyes on the shower and remembered their happy moments together. It wasn't, at all, regretful that she wasted her time with him or lied to her family for him. She was only pained by her negligence to ask about him, even though she had no intention to marry an old-fashioned man like him. She reached for the door and pulled it close angrily, her lips pursed. She wanted to shut him away from life like that if she had a way.

As she proceeded towards Darweshi's room, she saw her suitcases still standing in the living room, where she left them on arrival. Her mouth fell open in bewilderment. That, to her, is a way an unwanted guest is disallowed into a home. He obviously did not need her anywhere around him. Two weeks ago, when she visited, he took her bag inside his room. He also unloaded it and admired her slinky wears fondly. And now, she turned an unwanted guest. She took a long breath then blushed at the distressing scene. She took a few steps closer to her bags but suddenly changed her mind. He had to explain why he treated her like a piece of rag for no good reason.

'Yes? Who is there?' he asked without leaving his bed. He wasn't asleep. Her presence provoked his wakefulness and edginess. His utmost wish at the moment is her leave- she should leave and make him the happiest man on earth.

'We are two here, Darweshi. Do you have another visitor? Open and let me in'. She tapped the door again. Still in his bed, he gave her request a thought, his eyes glued to the door, brows furrowed. When he finally sat on the bed, anger crept over him. What did she want from him? Hadn't he made his point clear? He wondered, pushing his quilt aside. He stormed to the door and in two seconds, he stood facing her.

'*Samahane*. What do you want from me?' he raged.

'I –I –', she was overpowered by his thunderous reaction. Her face fell and she became speechless.

'Look, you're leaving tomorrow evening when I return from work.

I can't go to work today because you're here. Look, this is the truth-you can't spend a day more with me. You have to leave', he peeked at her suitcases. Good, they still stood there. He planned to see her out of his house the next day.

'What?! Darweshi!' her face twisted, a twitch of perplexity running through her.

'Yes, I've been on the phone to my wife all night and she said she can't wait to move in and live with me again. Meaning that you have to leave before she catches you here. You don't want to ruin my life, do you?' She kept gazing at him, amazed at the sudden turnabout of his feelings for her. Was it all fake? He confessed he would lay down his life for her.

'This is what I'm going to do. I'll give you some money now to get an apartment in the city. That's all I can do to support you'. He slammed the door beside him as she began to cry again. Again and again and again. It was an unfathomable life he never wished for in his entire life. What if she killed her father? Shouldn't she find somewhere else to conceal her demonic face? Why in his apartment? He fumed as he rushed to his wardrobe. He threw it open and brought out a wad of notes without hesitating. That would resolve her problem. He made to divide it but was smitten with sympathy. Poor girl. She was a poor and helpless girl motivated by the forces of evil to thwart every man's dream. First, it was her father, then it was him. He craned his eyes around the room wonderingly and finally decided to give everything to her.

'Dafina!' he looked around the apartment for her, holding the money in his hand. But she wasn't there. She was gone with her bags. She couldn't bear the pain anymore, he understood. He didn't attempt to find her after God had finally answered his prayer. He turned back into his apartment and shut the door.

At about 6:50am, on the same day, Dafina emerged in a different street, struggling with her bags. Stress and illness had taken a heavy toll on her. She was next to nervous collapse. Her mouth went dry, tasted bitter. The pain from her empty tummy couldn't supersede the heat of the sizzling emotional distress within her. When she looked ahead a lonely street, the world seemed empty. No parents, brother, sister or a beloved one. There was no one living for her in her tough times. She felt so deprived.

When she arrived at a junction, she stood for a moment, just staring. She sooner realized the seriousness of her situation, the need to seek refuge and the danger of loitering with suitcases. Darweshi once told her about how people fall victims of attacks on that same street. She pulled herself together and walked back to the bus station, where there were lots of commuters.

'Hey, are you lost?' a young man asked, following her. She neither replied nor turned around. She hurried along, even though she had nothing expensive in her suitcases except the little money she got from Darweshi two weeks ago. She needed it to survive the crisis of hunger.

'I – I – just want to help you. It's risky roaming around this neighborhood. You may get robbed and killed', he followed her.

'I'm fine. *Sijambo*. I know my destination. Please, leave me alone'. She walked faster, fearful of being attacked by him.

'Alright then, good luck. *Kwaheri*'.

She turned and looked at him for the first time. He looked young and responsible, different from a pretender she knows- a real lion in sheep form. However, whether good or bad, she didn't want anyone in Darweshi's locality to assist her.

It was 5pm when she arrived at Narok. It looked like rain again. She had spent the whole day, looking for where to stay. No one wants to help, on the ground that she's a stranger; except an old dirty man living in a poorly maintained house. Her eyes surveyed a busy road of four lanes. Workers just closed at that time and were hurrying home to beat the traffic congestion on the way and prepare for the work schedule the following day. Everybody seemed to have a destination except a maniac. What about her? Does she have anywhere in mind? She looked down at herself and felt a lot of pity for her life. She realized she was deprived of good health, home, education and happiness. Film of tears began to form in her eyes when she thought of where precisely she was heading to. Nowhere.

She walked to an angle, under a pedestrian bridge tiredly, leaned her bags on a broken chair she found there and sat down on the floor. All she needed was to eat and sleep in the filthy environment. She perceived a strong smell of old urine in the air, observed debris disposed everywhere but didn't care. She reached for her bigger suitcase, unzipped it and brought out the bread and butter she took from home. She ate slowly and watched it drizzle.

The rain began to pour shortly. Everyone ran into hiding, in different locations, away from a chilly lash. The bus stop, which was always uninhabited, became useful to fifty five passengers at once. It got too enormous that some were forced into the umbrellas of strangers while opened shops received unexpected visitors. This isn't new to them; it's an act predominant in rainy season.

No one, except a man headed towards where Dafina wrapped herself under the bridge. She was already drenched by the outflow from rainstorm. She was a pitiable spectacle. Only one with a heart of stone wouldn't feel sympathy for her. Her bags were wet, everything was wet.

'Hello? Are you looking for someone?' the man asked after looking at her with profound amazement. He hadn't seen a traveler caught in a rainstorm before. She turned around to meet his steady gaze instantly. He was a young and good looking man, officially dressed in a black suit and shoes – absolutely following the trend. He was apparently returning from work and locked there by nature with a dejected girl. Dafina's eyes dropped to the ground, a gust of shame running through her. She nodded then continued gazing at the busy road.

'So, haven't you seen the person? It's getting late and- my God, you're wet. And you're with bags', he looked around her and added, 'I'm sorry for being nosy- I just feel- sorry for you', he shook his head and brushed drops of rain from his sleeve.

'Thanks for your con-con-cern', she shivered with cold.

'God! For how much longer do you still want to wait for this person?' he asked deeply concerned, paying attention to her impassioned explanation.

'No, I have-no-nowhere –to go'. She rushed after her bags as the rain started afresh, heavier than before. She arranged them under the chair, where the downpour couldn't reach and looked up at the man again. He wasn't looking away. He watched every move she made and gave the impression of being more shaken by her plight. It was strange but real.

'So, you don't have anyone at all?'

'No, I have a lot of relatives, it's a long story', she explained diffidently.

They both fell silent for a while, sneaking a look at each other. Yet, he couldn't take his eyes off the wet suitcases, shrouded with mud. What on earth could such a girl in her youthfulness be finding around? Why didn't she stay in her home and why didn't she have a place to stay? He speculated, still gaping at her. Nevertheless, it was his haunting day, meeting a pretty stranger in heart-rending state. He was partly afraid of the unknown and he wished he hadn't met her in such a situation.

For Dafina, she felt shame, sorrow, and anger. That wasn't a day she liked to run into a likeable man. She knew he was drawn by her beauty as it happened with the other men that desired her love. But, something about this guy seemed different. He looked much like someone that would impact her life immeasurably on her health regulations. He seemed caring, responsible. He was all she needed to survive. She concluded.

'I – want to', he was speechless, possibly searching for the right decision to take. His gaze shifted from the bags to the subsiding rain and back to her hopeful face sadly. He wanted to help, needed to assist but was scared of the outcome. He finally gave a long sigh and said, 'right now, I want to help you but I don't know your intentions'.

'No-no bad int-', she cried in agony but he wasn't finished yet. He was quick to cut her short.

'Listen to me', he said with a wave of his hand. 'I don't know you- and many people have fallen victims of robbery and spiritual attacks. I really need to be careful helping a stranger. I just wanted to walk away but I can't. I can't leave you in this state. Now, this is the point'. He looked at two passersby staring at them and quickly drew a conclusion, 'I will take you to my house. Yes, I will help you'.

He tried his best to help her out of her ignominious situation, even when he knew he needed time to mull it over, thrash it out with a confidant or possibly pray about it to escape the consequence. Considering the unfathomable news of tramps giving hell to their saviors and sometimes robbing them of their belongings, he should shut his eyes to her plea and walk away. In all sincerity, he never, for once, rendered such a favour before but Dafina magnetized him. He had no choice other than praying for God's support.

Atieno stooped down to lift her heavier suitcase. He watched her carrying the other bag on her head.

'Be careful there. It's wet and slippery', he warned softly.

'Yes'. Dafina followed him, taking her steps gently. Her flip flop slippers slithered her wet feet, made a thwack sound consistently.

She met another man different from other men she had seen in her entire life- a unique personality. Although he was prudent in taking his decision, his neighborly gestures created a lot of good impression about him. He was humane and hospitable. The closer she got to him, the more she knew about him.

Atieno lost his parents in a plane crash fifteen years ago, when he was only nineteen years of age. He had his only sibling, Halina, in his care. The large, impressive house they were living in was their priceless patrimony since their paternal family didn't fight for their own share after seeing the deceased's last will and testament. Atieno's father was mostly hated by his own people for his selfish and freakish behavior. He cared only for his family and no one else. They scarcely visited his mansion when all their exigencies met no support. God knew, could enter their minds to know their true feelings when he travelled one day and died disastrously with his wife. Were they happy or sad? However, much of these were shown in their obnoxious avoidance of the home and most importantly, their children. Little did they know that Atieno wasn't his father. He was an odd one out. Dafina also observed the difference between him and his sibling on her first night in the house.

Halina did not, in anyway, hide her displeasure with her brother for bringing a stranger in their house, without cluing her in. What was he thinking? Did he want to risk their lives?

'What?! Atieno, are you crazy? What crept into you? The evil in her? Did you fall in love with a stranger? Are you sightless of all the happenings around? Oh God!' she sank into the sofa behind her, her head in her hand.

'No love for anyone. I don't love her; I merely helped her solve her problem. I wish you saw what she passed through today in that heavy rainfall. It was terrible that a person with a heart of stone would feel sorry for her', he shook his head in pity.

'Help? Did you say help? Help my foot! That is how you guys go about entrapping helpless strangers. You want to have an affair with her. You want to take advantage of her. Humph'. She pursed her lips and turned away from him, her face wrinkled in considerable disgust.

Atieno was dumbfounded even when he had his mindset to stand by Dafina, no matter what his sister said. That was not to say that he didn't know she would disagree with him. She was like their parents-mean, self-centered, snobbish and rude. She never pretended to be nice for once. She was always herself. Both of them were two sides of a coin.

'What do you mean I want to take advantage of her? What do you mean by th-?'

'Send her back to the street- to the cardboard city. Homeless like her are there', she cut in rudely, gnashing her teeth, clenching her fists. Atieno wanted to walk away, walk away like he always did but he stood his ground that night. He noticed she was beginning to glory in winning him in the house, possibly because of his gentlemanly behavior. And that had to stop. He wanted to have a mind of his own. He is a man.

He took two steps closer to her, looked at her sternly and said, 'no, she stays here on my own side of the house. Simple as that'.

With that, she took two big steps towards the door and yelled, 'fine! Don't come close to me. I don't know her. And when trouble begins, don't remember me'.

He shut his eyes against the bang on the door, and then heaved a sigh of relief. After that night, there was no mention of Dafina living in the house again, except for the times she reported her missing stuff to her brother. And that didn't change the cordiality between them. They were still fond of each other.

Dafina, on her own part, tried all she could not to cross her bound or upset her. She eaves dropped on all their argument that same night she arrived, heard it all. Halina did not want her, so she watched the time she came out of the room Atieno gave her. There were ten apartments in the mansion and he gave her one of his own. He hardly stayed in the house except on Sundays when he wanted to clean up. He arrived from work at 8:30pm.

Halina worked with the Ministry of health in the department of community services. She also had no time to lumber around like her. At precisely 6 o'clock every morning, she was prepared to commute a long distance within one hour, from home to work. Her arrival time was always 9:30pm after Atieno. She usually returned quietly to her apartment, avoiding an intruder.

One night, Dafina forgot her lingerie on the line and rushed out to get it, thinking Halina was asleep habitually. She was wrong. She barged into her in their commodious living room, sitting a silver tray on her laps and taking her supper in front of a television set. Her head dropped in shame; she got weak and managed to lift her legs from the tiled floor.

'Goodnight Halina', she greeted her but there was no response. When she greeted again, she turned and looked at her sullenly. She withdrew from the spot and took the flight of steps to her door without looking back. She knew she sat there calculatingly to upset her. She must have seen her when she sneaked out of her flat.

Consequently, Dafina tried not to show the shadow of herself whenever Halina was around. Fire and gunpowder do not sleep together. She enjoyed her freedom only when she went to work in the morning. From 9pm, no noise, no sound from television or radio set until Atieno arrived.

Atieno was awesome. He was the best friend she ever had. He

had given her all the support she needed unknowingly. At the time she got there, her look improved, no poor nutrition and much fear of the disease like before. Not much damage was done to her immune system: she had sneaked into a nearby hospital in Kakamega to begin her anti-retroviral therapy consistently. She noticed she had also regained her stunning beauty. Her average height cushioned a hauntingly beautiful contour. And her face, a round perfect frame with all hair of woman's great look. Atieno himself was beginning to extol her physical charm although he didn't confess his true feeling of seduction. He hardly left her room on Sundays and feared that Halina's prediction was true. She enjoyed their cheerful moments, but was focused on precluding herself from hurting anyone. Not Atieno, not anyone.

On a delightful night, there was a turnabout of their gaiety as Halina rushed into the living room looking for Atieno.

'Atieno!' she hollered his name from the living room, waiting eagerly for his response.

'What is the matter? *Mambo*? Halina?' he hurried to her. He loved her dearly, cared for Dafina. He noticed his sister was a bit withdrawn due to his acceptance of Dafina; nonetheless, he was never partial.

'Please, come. I want to see you', she beckoned to him, smiling. Atieno, not knowing why, looked down at her from the staircase and began to approach her slowly, unwillingly. He was actually enjoying his conversation with Dafina, was in the middle of some important information about her when she interrupted. It was a decisive jealousy, he supposed.

'Atieno- how many ears have you?' she held her ear warningly, her eyes on his rolled up sleeve, mind occupied with what he was doing in the room.

She added decidedly, looking straight in his eyes, 'Atieno, can you hear me?' He noticed her hazy eyes and sensed there was a hitch. Halina never cried except there was a problem. He began to panic.

'Two Halina, I have two ears. What's the matter? Why are you crying?' he wiped the tears on her lid and pulled her closer. She used to cry often, after the demise of their parents, when she was plagued by solitude. And that had long ended. They had moved on with their lives-they both graduated from the university with a degree and were rewardingly employed. It wasn't easy without their parents and relatives- even so, they succeeded. Whatever made her cry should be something different. He looked at her wonderingly and asked, 'Halina? What's the matter? Tell me- am here by your side', he held her two hands and gazed into her eyes.

'Atieno, you know you left me sleeping on this sofa', she reminded, him still crying.

'Yes, I can remember. I left when you fell asleep and went to-'.

'Atieno, there's trouble', she cut in looking up at the stairs. And without saying anything yet, she knew she had seen something. Halina was respected by all for her gift in dreaming and prophesying. She was dreaded by some. She herself didn't revere its effectiveness until she dreamt their parents died and it happened precisely the way she saw it, two weeks after. She also dreamt their grandfather disappeared and he was lost. What she saw next, he was eager to know.

'I'm listening to you Halina', he cocked his head aside and listened to her, holding her quivering hands.

'Atieno, listen to me. That girl you brought home is infected with a disease. I saw her – all covered with rashes'. She closed her eyes in reminiscence of the dream, a part of it already fleeing her memory.

'Yes, I saw her face', she depicted, remembering the first scene.

'She had a disease all over her and I saw her reaching for you and grab-bin-g you clo-ser and closer. Atieno!' She pointed in the direction of Dafina's apartment, blinking back the fresh tears in her eyes. Atieno was dumbfounded. He sighed and dropped her hands. He paced around the room, ruminating about the revelation.

'Atieno, believe me. I've seen a lot that materialized before. This is not about hating her. It's about what I saw in my dream. She's been with us for four months now and I've- forgotten about her', she spoke convincingly. She looked around for a seat, having relieved herself of the weight on her mind. A problem seen is on the way to solution.

'I believe in your dream, Halina. *Asante*. I believe in you but why were you crying to explain to me? We can fix it'.

'Fix what Atieno? Fix what? You are having an affair with her, aren't you?' she stood up again.

'No, she's my friend. Just a friend and nothing more'.

'Good. Go in there now and ask her about it. Go ahead or I'll report her to the police'.

'What?! With no evidence? Take it easy. Calm down- I want you to calm down', he held her shoulders gently, led her back to the sofa and sat her down.

'I don't want to lose you Atieno. At the end of the dream, you vanished with her. You are all I have', she spread her arms and cried her eyes out. Her shoulders heaved with sobs.

'Halina, this time, you win. I will do exactly what you asked of me. Don't worry, I won't vanish and you won't vanish too. We will live longer than our parents'.

Atieno rose to his great height and advanced towards the apartment. Before he took the first three steps, Dafina swiftly retreated from where she glued her ears to pick on all their discussions, scurried back into her room. She quivered with fear: fear of being thrown back in the street and deprivation. She heard every word of their conversation, felt chastened and started planning her next move. What next now? To run away or face the music? Yes, the hour of truth had finally caught up with her. She admitted her wrong and prepared to spit out the truth about her health.

'Dafina, are you still awake? I want to have a discussion with you', Atieno said from behind the door. Fear made a clutch at her heart.

'Yes? Come in'. She swallowed the lump in her throat, as she reconsidered taking him into her confidence. That wouldn't be easy.

'Atieno, please- sit down', she patted the bed she sat on, next to her, reading his cool face burning with rage.

'No', he refused, not smiling. She expected much more from him but he was calm and collected.

'Dafina. I'm here for something very important. I need you to tell me the truth about something.' he closed the door, took a few steps into the room and added before she answered him, 'if you lie to me, remember there are doctors here in Kakamega. I will simply take you to a hospital for a test. So, tell me the truth'. This got her adrenalin flowing. First, she moistened her lips, then began stamping- her own way of expressing anxiety. He ignored her stagey display and asked his question.

'Dafina? Are – are- you infected?'

She nodded unflinchingly in response. It was a moment she awaited: a moment of expiation she did not expect to manifest soon. It happened pretty soon. As he wanted to repeat the question, the door opened slowly. Halina entered the room, looking from Dafina to Atieno. It got more difficult for him to interrogate her with Halina standing beside him, a derogatory expression of distrust on her face. Was she really sincere or she was taking that out on her to dismiss her from the house? He wondered why she put herself in the position of the interrogator when he was already there. After all, he brought her into the house and her claim had not yet been substantiated- real or fake.

Dafina's face dropped, she couldn't say a word in her presence, knowing how much she detested her. Atieno saw this, grabbed her arm and took her out of the room. Outside the room she flinched at his stiff grasp, yelling.

'Leave me alone. Are you ashamed to ask her in front of me?' she gave him a flinty stare.

'What do you mean by that? Look, Halina, why not leave me alone. Leave us alone. You are getting on my nerves'.

'If you know you're not having a love affair with her, then feel free to ask her anything in front of me', she rumbled on.

'Halina, you are so heartless, so heartless. Put yourself in her shoes. You know what she's been through. I can't hurt her. Just leave me alone'.

'I can't ever be in her shoes. You just go ahead and ask her if it is true or not. Stop beating about the bush'. She stormed off, seeing the look on his face. Atieno was cool-headed; he knew how to keep his temper down. With his expression, he proved to her that everybody gets angry. Since he was left alone, he said nothing. He merely walked back into her room and shut the door behind him. He saw Dafina in the same foul mood she was on the day he met her. Again, the surge of protection he felt for her was rekindled. He never meant to hurt her, not for any reason.

He proceeded in the room and sat on the same spot she offered him earlier. There was a longish silence before Dafina finally spoke with a trembling voice.

'Atieno, I am HIV positive'.

'What? Dafina! Dafina!! Why didn't you tell me this before? Dafina! Why?' his eyes widened with disbelief. She turned away from him, crying.

'Dafina, tell me it's not true. Tell me it's a joke. Dafina – tell me it's not you', he ran his eyes over. Was he dreaming? He stood up, hit the wall and clasped his hands behind his head. Miserably, he looked down at her, almost shedding tears.

'Atieno, it is true. *Tafadhali*', she nodded, convulsing with sobs. She noticed shame in her voice as she spoke to him. She told him all he had to know. How unbearable it had been for her to live with the disease, but for the anti-retroviral therapy and her doctor's recommendation. She confessed to him for the first time that, with him by her side, she survived till that time and had high hope of survival. She declared how she managed to progress into the clinical latency stage with the support of Doctor Chitundu she met in the hospital of Kakamega. For the period of time she was in the situation, no one gave the white hope except the doctor. He had helped give some vital recommendations and advised on the healthy foods her body required, how to care for herself, and take her therapy in consistence. He was, indeed, her life safer.

'You should have told me. It doesn't change anything. I would have still helped you. Oh my God!' he fell silent for a while, sneaking a look at her until he asked the question on his mind.

'Dafina, how did you get infected?'

With this, she sighed, wiped her glistened eyes and thought of what to say. The truth and nothing else. She told him first about

Darweshi, then the other man and another man: all the men that existed in her life at the same time. Like a tradition, Atieno sneaked a look at her again and shook his head. He formed a different view about her at the moment. She was no longer the modest Dafina he thought he met.

'Wow', he heaved and dropped his head sadly. She kept quiet for a moment and started with her family story. She spoke about all the three of her siblings and her parents.

'If my parents could deny me, who will accept me? Who else would care for me? That's the reason I decided not to tell you a thing about it. That's why I didn't tell you- Atieno. I can't hurt you, my good friend'.

'It's okay', Atieno pulled her closer as tears streamed down her pretty face. She rested her head on his shoulder and he rubbed her arms fondly.

'Dafina, don't worry, it's okay. You should have explained this to me', he blurted finally, his face wrapped up in anger. She could have infected him without knowing. He couldn't deny that what he felt for her was true love and something serious would have happened between them if Halina hadn't seen it in her dream.

'I'm sorry-I'm sorry. I wanted to tell you but I was afraid. I needed a shelter badly'.

'Dafina, it's okay. I won't leave you. Stop crying, we will figure out what we're going to do, okay?' he doubted what he just heard. Did she really have the disease? It was hard to tell that she was in her asymptomatic stage. She looked okay, felt well. All the symptoms she felt earlier were drastically suppressed.

'Dafina, I promise to assist you. You don't need to worry. A friend in need is a friend indeed. I will do my best to save you. But we have to do something', he scratched his head for ideas. She removed her head from his shoulder, lifted her face at him then looked away in shame. Atieno didn't think so, but she felt dangerous to him. Her attention coasted to the problem again and she shifted away from him.

'Why are you doing that? I know what you're thinking. It's not like that. I am educated and I know what it's all about. You need me,

Atieno, to survive. You don't have to worry. I love you so much to keep you save and alive', he declared his true feelings finally, however, she didn't believe him. She said nothing. She merely nodded.

'She needs you to stay alive but not in this house! Not anywhere around me. Atieno, are you crazy?' Halina broke in on them. She heard all her confession at the door. She only pretended to leave and later returned there to overhear them. She had a premonition that the truth would be hidden from her to subdue her unconsidered approach. And that was precisely their intention.

'Atieno, if you don't tell her to leave now- right now, the whole street will soon gather here to hear the secret', she snapped her fingers and closed her eyes furiously. Atieno looked startled.

'She has to leave now. Right now', she rushed to carry one of her suitcases standing in the room, and took it to the door. She looked at Dafina implacably then shifted her gaze to her brother.

'Halina, stop acting like a maniac. Where did you get the information from? Where? I don't believe there was any dream with the way you over react. You must have stalked her or paid someone to do so. You hate her so much. That's it', he stood up, got even with her. He grabbed the bag from her and took it back to its position.

'I'm warning you. I'm running out of patience. Leave us alone. What if I wanted to marry her? Would you have stopped me?'

'Ehn?', she smiled bemusedly, a flush of anger spreading over her.

Dafina was confused. She looked from brother to sister and finally stood up. Was Halina really stalking her? She looked at her curiously.

'Leave her alone. Why are you so jealous? I'm your brother, remember? I'm not your husband'.

'Ehn- no problem. I'm done being over-protective of someone who doesn't deserve it. But I want her to leave here for my own safety'. She walked off, disappointed in him. When she was gone, Dafina stood motionless, speechless. About ten ideas occurred to her, however only one rang true. She had to leave immediately. Though the atmosphere was neither hostile nor peaceful for her, she decided to end the tussle due to Halina's confrontation. She had to leave and they both thought alike.

'You are going to leave today. I don't want her to involve our relatives in this. Halina may bring them here to send you away', Atieno concurred with her thought. Dafina said nothing. She sighed afterwards and started packing her stuff, first in the biggest bag clumsily.

'Dafina, you don't need to worry. Like I said, I'm with you. You will lodge with a hotel nearby and I will get another apartment for you in two days', he promised.

'Thank you', she said, not looking at him. She focused on the suitcases, nursing the displeasing thought of leaving the house, leaving Atieno. She forced more wears inside the bag. At that point, she realized she got more wears after she got there. Unlike when she arrived with only two bags, she needed two more bags to clear everything.

'Atieno, I need another bag. Could you give me one?' she pleaded, almost crying. Unable to hold the gaze for long, she returned to her packing quickly. Atieno saw her emotions, walked up to her and consoled her again. He pulled her closer again and embraced her.

'Don't worry, everything will be okay and I will never leave you Dafina, don't feel depressed. It's not good for your health. I'm with you, remember? I promise to be wherever you are. Like before, nothing changes. You are still my best friend'. He took the biggest bag from her and helped her to fold some clothes in the bag. With all Atieno's supports and assurance, she was relaxed. She felt better. If there was only one person living to support her and never discriminate against her, life continues. She had to move on.

In the entire situation, she was pained by just one thing. Her impatience to meet Atieno at the right time. He was all she wanted in a husband-to-be: a brother and father, everything a woman desires in a man. But as fate would have it, he came at the wrong time.

Dafina calculated that, she was wrong after the assistance she got from Atieno. He was never far away from her even when she was no more in their house. He opened a grocery store for her to make money and proceed with her therapy and maintain a healthy living.

In her fifteenth year after contacting the disease, she returned home. She got an affectionate reception from her parents, to her utmost surprise. They had been informed by an enlightened friend about how much support she needed from them. They both regretted their actions towards her, had looked everywhere for her until she finally returned by herself.

'How is my brother? Is he still in Gede?' Dafina asked a few minutes after her arrival. She had asked about other siblings except him. She really missed them within the period she was away.

'Your brother?' Mrs. hamadi rejoindered sadly, a noticeable pain in her tone.

'Dafina, we lost your brother ten years ago', Mr. Hamadi broke the news before his wife uttered a word. He didn't want her reminded of the saddening experience.

'What?! How?' Dafina exclaimed, rising from her seat. He was only thirty four when he died and was the strongest of them all. She didn't hesitate to ask the cause of the occurrence.

'He had an auto accident on his way back home after work. You know how strong and hardworking he was. May his soul rest in peace', Mr. Hamadi explained, still admiring his long lost daughter. Words were not enough to express how much pain he felt when his son suddenly died, and he concluded that he had only two children left.

'Dafina, I thought you were dead. Thank God you are still alive. How did you survive it?' he asked her to clear the air of doubt.

'No, daddy- in as much as I do the right thing on daily basis, I can survive for as long as I try', she explained, smiling.

'Hm. Hodari died a healthy man; you survive with a deadly disease. God is wonderful', he shook his head crying.

'No, a disease is not a determinant of death but a man's destiny. Hodari is forever loved. I wish he saw me today'.

5

Senami

No one kills an innocent soul, begging for wisdom.

In the earliest time of the day, Senami took a surreptitious leave from the church she was worshipping, still in the middle of service. She clutched a medium sized King James Version of the holy bible to her chest and groped through the darkness to find her way home. From the time she obstinately left for the vigil till 3am she was heading home, her heart never ceased to pound. She could picture the specter of violence she was about to face in her miserable matrimony. The sudden unbeatable pang of guilt she felt at the moment, was as overpowering as her sense of misgiving- another chapter of humiliation in her life.

Marriage is a fulfilling and enjoyable union, when two hearts are married together as one to succumb to the power of love. But Senami couldn't elude the bottomless pit of her disputable union with Gbenupo. It became so unjustified and unknowable as God turned their matter of concern. Each day passed by with the same uninspiring and disinterested view about who should hold sway over the other. Sena confusedly maintained her detestable state of dilemma while her marriage lurched from one religious issue to the other.

It was 4am when she arrived. Fear flickered in her eyes as she saw their low-price bungalow reaching out to her. She stood at the entrance, drew a long breath. How best is it to knock the door? Should it be just a loud or light tap, considering the gravity of her offence? Or should she wait till daybreak to avoid interrupting his peaceful repose; and causing more trouble. With all these on her mind, she stood worried and perplexed. She admitted to herself that, the whole situation was monstrously unfair. For the passion of Christ, she had turned a mutinous housewife, willfully embarking on a journey without her husband's consent. She merely left for the vigil, tucking a letter under his pillow to disclose her disappearance.

And with her complacent move to please God, she envisioned the disastrous consequence of her action. She shrugged off the thought and presumed that, the harm was done already. You don't dispose of a knife after the harm is done.

Twenty minutes after, she rose to her feet again, knocked the wooden door three times and stepped back. She nestled the bible closer to her chest and waited for his reaction. She finally hardened her heart to prepare the ground for acceptance of her religious faith. Under no circumstance was she ready to relinquish her love for Christ.

Gbenu stood in the middle of their room, staring at the door with growing anger and frustration. He folded his arms around his squat muscular body, his dark shaven head shinning under a bare bulb in the room like a mirror in the sun. He had gone to sleep the previous night in the same uneasy mood. He had his mind set for vengeance. If not for her impudence, he supposed, she wouldn't rebel against his rules after he had castigated her repeatedly over the same issue.

For few minutes, he shot his dark, vengeful eyes and opened them with a start when he heard the knock from the door again. He took two steps closer, questioning the veracity of her faithfulness to him in the marriage. Was she truly visiting the church or elsewhere? She had an impulse to open the door and she came face to face with her fearsome spouse. She dropped her clenched fists at a snail's pace. He didn't utter a word. He turned around sharply and proceeded in the room enraged.

'Good morning -dear', she breathed and closed the door gently, the holy bible still in her hand. Prayer should be her next line of action on her safe arrival but she bowed to the situation. Her gaze drifted to his round back turned to her on his bed. He bit his lower lip and shook his legs, profoundly embittered by her impetuous moves. She couldn't help but sigh in emotional turmoil and sense of guilt. It wasn't long when she dropped off on the couch, still in her sitting position. Her chin sloped steeply downward the palm she rested it upon and her head fell at a tilt.

Gbenu woke up first at 6am. He was still very indignant at her hurtful behavior. He looked at her evilly and rested his eyes on her thin veined hand, and the dribble snaking down her cheek. It was surprising to him how his beautiful Senami turned out. He met her, an unbeliever, seven years back, in a restaurant where she served as a waitress. What attracted him to her was her charming voluptuous body scantily clad in a skimpy dress, and carried with an aura of confidence. That, truly, had always been the woman of his dream-young, beautiful and fashionable-like no one else but Senami. He could recollect how much he frequented the spot, especially when he had works to do at the factory he was working until he finally proposed to her. At first, she was amazed. He barely knew anything about her-that she was once a prostitute. She noticed he didn't care much about it even after she disclosed the secret to him.

'That doesn't mean anything as long as you're not in it anymore. I will marry you and you will be mine forever', he confessed with deep admiration and indication that he was beguiled by only her beauty.

Three years after their marriage, Senami's inglorious past began to haunt her, especially when she tried to no avail to have another child after Viyan, their only child. Before the end of that same year, she met a devoted Christian who introduced her to their sisterhood and changed her completely. In all, he got more obsessive about her physical transformation.

'Good morning sir', Viyan's tired voice brought him back to the scene. She had cried continuously, for a couple of hours when she missed her mother at midnight.

'How are you? *Mi fon dagbe?*' he shuffled across the room absent mindedly, pulled back his window curtain to observe the morning weather. It was past seven and the sky was still grey. He had no car; the rain would be a great disturbance to him. He glared at it sullenly and withdrew from the spot.

Viyan had already woken her mother before he turned back. She sat up and stared blankly, struggling to get back to the physical world. While asleep, she dreamt she was in her hubby's arm and he whispered amorous words in her ears. It didn't last for long; it lasted only fifty five minutes before she woke up. She wished it continued or perhaps occurred in reality. For three months, their love had always existed only in dreams even though they shared the same bed together and lived in the same room. Gbenu thought the only way he could win her over is by neglecting her, other than hitting her and making himself impious to others. He heard all the rumors making the rounds that he was wicked and evil after he maltreated her six months ago. And he had since then vowed not to touch her again.

'Mummy, daddy gave me some cookies and tea last night I cried to see you. I cried more because I wanted you, not cookies.' She took her arms and used it to wrap herself affectionately. She merely smiled down at the child and wore back her woe- be-gone face.

Gbenu peeked at her gaudy dress as long as a pole, with a neck long enough to consume the head of a new born and its blinding green color. He felt mostly downhearted seeing her accustomed hair-do. She often indomitably refused to unveil it on account of his overmuch objection. That didn't affect him as much as her recurrent fasting which sometimes took two or three weeks and seemed never to end again. It all made him sick.

'Good morning honey', she greeted, self-consciously aware of his stare. Her voice quavered emotionally.

'Hmm-', he slipped a shirt over his singlet and stormed off the room, banging the door behind him. She was filled with sobriety but understood it was her day of reckoning. However, she chose not to look where she fell but where she slipped.

The situation remained the same after she stopped attending

her church's vigil, abiding by her husband's vehement disapproval of her commitment to the church. His desire was to transform and transfigure her into the woman he wanted. The woman he loved and gave his heart.

Gbenu saw this difference within the next few weeks and also made moves to fall things back in shape. Two months after, he arrived from work and announced they had an outing. Emotional confusion churned within her. She sprang to her feet and feigned indifference.

'*E yan gaji!* That's won-der-ful, but where. Where are we going?' She sank into the couch beside him spuriously, an unserious smile playing around her lips. She had to be foolish to get him fooled.

'We are rocking in a club tonight and I want you to look exactly as I met you in that restaurant. I want to fall in love again, okay?' he read her expressive face.

'But-'

'No but-listen to me', he cut in angrily, gazing at her squarely.

'The time has come to put an end to this and enjoy our marriage. It's either you choose the church or your marriage. That's it. Get prepared for tonight's party'. He sprawled in the seat next to her, wearing a face smoldered with anger. To him, she's just too annoying. She will never be a good fit for him anymore, in as much as he tried. He wished she was the same woman he met; he wished she was still the same. Just that and only that would have restored peace in his crashing heart and also proffer all the peace she wants in life.

'Honey – I'.

'Get prepared for the party'.

She sighed and looked away confusedly. What was she going to do? Visit a club with him or lose her marriage? She regretted she married such a man who was not only set to ruin her relationship with God but also selfishly rob her of integrity. She should have known this long ago, before she turned born-again Christian, that her husband would turn hostile to her transformation. That he would be devoid of the compassion, reinforcement and espousal she needed to submit to God. That he would be a stumbling block to her. When she was in a world of her own, they both had similar ideas, interests, tastes and desires. Who would have known or predicted by then, that, by the twist of fate, they would become obviously incompatible in the nearest future.

'I hope you've not disposed of all those skimpy wears I love seeing on you. If you need money to get new ones, let me know', he smirked. She glared at him for a moment and picked up the Holy Bible to save the day. According to their father in the lord, you cannot lie down where your enemies have thrown you. You have to make effort to rise up and triumph over. Then was the time she deemed it fit to chance it, probably win his heart to Christ bit by bit. Christ loves him too.

'Well, there's something we have to discuss now', she began to leaf through the pages of the bible, looking very serious.

'Ehn- will you stop this nonsense?' he seized the bible from her, slapped it back on the table.

'How many times have I warned you against preaching in this house? Do you see me as a devil or something? Tell me! Do I look satanic?' he yelled at her. Her heart flipped when he turned to her and added, 'look, you can't turn God's back on me. I'm not God's enemy. If that's your intention, you've failed. *Mawu!* You have failed.' In inexplicable confusion, she turned to him and clarified, 'no, how could I do such a thing to my dearest. I just-'.

He stood from his seat and drew a conclusion. 'Shut up! And get prepared for tonight's party or leave my house tomorrow', he swung the door open and left the room. Again, she was left devastated. She hated to think that the one she loved the most in the world was strongly against her submission to a new life. His overreaction had simply justified an objection to her interest. She wished she could reach out to him too and touch his heart, so they could move ahead together in the journey to eternity.

On that same day, before Gbenu arrived home, Senami needed a benevolent and dependable confidant for proper counseling. She waited for Viyan to close from school then proceeded to the church with her to see their parish pastor. It wasn't difficult to find him as he lived in the church premises with his family. After listening to her, the elderly man of God in his late fifties, Mr. Ahumenu, hung his head in deep thought. He had handled matrimonial issues of that nature almost all the time in his district, but not a strange invitation to a club. He shook his head with disbelief then fixed her with a pitiable stare. Without living with them, he could imagine all she had been through to embrace the Christian faith. However, he considered the significance of her marriage.

'Humph'. He sighed and requested, 'is your husband around now? I need to see him right away', he folded his arms, shook his legs in profound concern.

'No sir, not yet. He returns at 6pm and it's just 4:02pm'. She dropped her gaze on her watch and returned it to the pastor in anguish.

'Alright, you know what?'

'Sir?'

'I don't want him not to meet you in the house. That will make him angrier than before. Go back home now and- *Mi wa yi wegbe*'.

'Sir?'

'Listen to me. I'm coming to your house tonight, okay? I'll be there before you leave for the er-', he tried not to mention it. He deemed it unjustifiable inviting a devoted Christian to an unholy venue with lewd dressing. What was he up to?

'Sir, please don't come. He will take it out on me and conclude that I'm reporting him to everyone. And that may lead to another issue', she explained, terribly hurt by the subject

'Then, what do we do? I can't go to him, he can't come to me. How do I see him and resolve the repression? You can't hide a smoke when a house is burning,' his brows rose thoughtfully.

At that point in time, she was enthralled by the outcome of what she was about to do. She didn't know the right answer to give to the minister's question. From her unfitting presumption, she had suffered chapters of remarkable issues she decided to handle alone, without involving the church or her family. Eight months ago, when she suggested inviting him to the church for counseling and orientation, a huge problem broke out between them and he gave her a black eye. Again, at the time he was absent from the church determinedly for almost two years, and the pastor offered to visit him, she didn't consent to his plan. She decided to handle every situation alone. As the issue of visiting the club emerged, why wouldn't she handle it alone?

'My sister in the lord, listen to me clearly. For your victory in this battle, you need God. You need to submit to God and at the same time; you need to save your marriage. That's why I want to see him right now. Without effort, no harvest will be abundant', he stood up to follow her home. 'In proverb chapter 28:1, the bible says that the wicked flee when no man pursueth but the righteous are as bold as a lion. Also, in Philippians chapter 1:14, the bible says that- and many of the brethren in the lord, waxing confidence by my bonds, are bold to proclaim the gospel without fear. So, sister Sena cast away the fear in you and let's do this. You have tormented yourself long enough and it has to end somewhere, one day'. He walked to the altar to collect his bible and returned to her. 'Your husband is spiritually blinded and a blind man doesn't lead another blind man else both of them will end up in a ditch. You have to fight his battle for him and win his soul like you won his heart. Let's go', he led the way to the exit.

Senami wasn't content with his suggestion. She chose to talk to him herself for serious, indisputable reasons. She hurried after him, staring at him unflinchingly.

'No-no, don't worry sir. I'll go home and talk to him'.

'What? To visit the club with him? Sister Sena! Listen to me. In the book of Timothy, chapter4:4-5, the bible says that: they shall turn away their ears from the truth and shall be turned unto fables but watch thou in all things, endure afflictions, do the work of an evangelist, make full proof of thy ministry. Sister Sena, don't dare backslide. Win him for God, don't join him. Happy is the one who conducts herself honorably. *Mi se?*' he held his ear warningly.

'No-no sir. We'll talk this over. I don't want you involved in this. I – I – only need your advice', she explained, almost crying. She looked around for Viyan. She was busy playing with the pews in the church, using them to count numbers as she learnt from school. She was just on fifteen when she was discontinued. She fixed her eyes on her, beckoned her over.

'Well, sister Sena, I won't impose my wish on you but I'll advice you to be discreet about whatever decision you take. You can't go back there anymore but you should win him over for God. Shall we pray?' They both prayed for few minutes and at the end of the prayer, she scooted out of the church without waiting for the evening programme held on Tuesdays. It was already 5:30pm. She had only thirty minutes to return home before he arrived. He mustn't arrive before her, according to his previous warnings.

Viyan found it difficult to keep pace with her as she rushed off, dragging her along like a piece of kite. There wasn't a room for complaint, she knew. She was excellent at reading her mother's mood and her sudden transfer of aggression. She heard and understood nearly all their conversation in the premises and knew quite alright that her mother was in low spirits.

At 5:45, their house came into view. Two of her neighbors stood in front of the house lazing away the day with engrossing topics. They both turned their attention to her when she was a few steps closer to them. And they continued looking till she was at the entrance of her house.

'Ahn? You went out with your daughter?' the skinny one reached out her scrawny hand and pulled Viyan's cheek, playfully.

'Good evening ma. *Mi ku dowe.* How are your children?' she greeted them grinning from ear to ear.

'Welcome back', the dark skinned and plump accomplice looked away jealously. She never pretended to like her lifestyle. She had spent the whole day discussing her with her friend right in the same place she met them. In their idle gossip, they had talked about her shabby dressing and lurid colour combination, how she related with her hubby and the way her mouth stinks while she talked to them. The skinny lady looked at her till she entered their apartment.

'Look at your friend, Mrs. Pemede'.

'She's not ashamed of herself. Is she the first to accept the Christian faith? Was she not a mere prostitute before? She turned

Mariah overnight. Holy-holy-holy', she mimicked the way she walked and fell about with laughter.

'Sussy! Watch your mouth. Remember you're talking about a woman of God. Woman of God', she cautioned, also laughing.

'Hun! Save that threat for yourself and your own day of judgment. I have something to do inside. See you tomorrow'. She strode back into her own apartment still laughing.

Gbenu felt very depressed after overhearing their derisive discussion about his wife. His eyes dropped on his laps as he gave the situation a thought. Shouldn't she cogitate about his own likes and wishes before turning him into an object of ridicule? Was it not because of the same matter they quarreled every time? Why must she allow someone to mislead her in the ministry?

He got up to his feet and paced around the room. He had arrived from work since 4pm with the mindset to spend some time with her, take Viyan to her grandmother, and embark on their amorous adventure. On the contrary, he was disillusioned by all he overheard from their loquacious neighbors, who seemed to awake him to the verity that Senami wasn't right for him.

'Hello dear'. Senami threw the door open, smiling. Her daughter followed closely. Gbenu didn't answer her. He just walked to the door, slammed it shut angrily.

'Now, drop that bible in your hand and answer all the questions I'm going to ask you now'. He shoved her away from his daughter with growing explosive temper. Senami lost balance and fell down on the floor. She struggled to get back on her feet, her eyes fixed on her spouse. She grabbed the bible and went down on her knees curiously.

'Please, honey-please- I beg you in the name of our lord Jesus Christ. Please, let's resolve this peacefully'. She held up the Bible, pleading amidst sobs but he stood his ground.

'Keep quiet and answer my question. Pleading with God is never the solution'.

'Honey please'.

'Where are you coming from? I want an answer to that question, not your stupid apology', he loosened his belt, drew it out from his trousers. She knew what he was up to. She dropped the bible and prepared for the rage of the slave in his hand. It had to dance to his tune.

'From the church. From the church. Ah, *mawu-* am in trouble today. Please, forgive me'.

'Yes, you are in soup. You stubborn and wretched wife', he lashed out at her furiously, his second hand busily pushing her backward. She tried to seize the belt from him but he was too strong and controlling.

'Did you take permission from me? Did I marry you from the church?' he paused to catch his breath and persisted. It got tougher than the onset, more penetrating than expected. She felt it burning deep into her skin and cried like a baby. Finally, she succeeded in gripping the metallic end of the belt. She struggled with him-struggled to protect herself. He didn't give up. He surrendered the belt to her, then turned more resolute with the use of his fist.

No one had the gumption to save the suffering woman from violence. It was a hellish night for her. Viyan stood watching her mother groaning, writhing in pain. Her heart thudded as she snatched at her father's arm firmly. She thought she was about to die.

'Leave my mummy alone! My mummy- mummy', she rubbed her palm over the inflammation on her forehead then burst into tears. A swell of panic was implanted on her little face. Gbenu retreated from his outrageous act feelingly. 'I have just started with you. I won't stop until you leave the church', he blustered, catching his breath.

Senami crept on the floor sorely brutalized. When she ruminated about why she suffered that much, she got more pained. All the feelings, hopes and everything she aspired for in the union began to crumble into nothing. And she wanted to be estranged from the family and stick to her consolatory God. It wasn't long when Gbenu actualized her dream. He sprang up like a wild fire then got down to moving her belongings out of the apartment. The upheaval finally breathed asymptomatic dividing line between them. Everything got out of control.

As Senami wrestled with the wind snatching away her stuff, friends and neighbors hid and glimpsed at her. She had nobody with her, including her daughter who Gbenu restricted from getting to her. Her unsettled cry filled the atmosphere before she finally left the spot shamefully.

'Oh Jesus, oh God almighty, why me?' she wept on.

Like a withered leave disclaimed by its tree, Senami ended up rejected and forgotten in the church. Her condition soon turned nightmarish when all her regretful pleas to return to Gbenu fell on deaf ears. He remained vengeful, unconcerned.

'I don't need her anymore. Jesus needs her more and she's available in the church. *E* yan. The church is the right place for her'. He retorted bluntly when three of Sena's family, including her mother visited for settlement.

'But- what precisely is the problem. I don't quite understand. Are you pushing your wife out for relating with the same God, your creator or what? Please, make it clear to us', the eldest of them; pa Danianou, in his late seventies, questioned his blurry decision. He looked from face to face, read the same countenance. They were all confused.

'Well, you all may not understand what I've been through in this house. I mean- it wasn't easy coping with her. She obstinately goes to the church without taking permission from me and treats me like Satan in my own house! Listen, most time, Senami wouldn't allow me to touch her because of fasting or her supposed relationship with God. Why did I marry her then?' he explained breathlessly.

'Fine. We apologize on her behalf. We promise you that she won't do that again. We've really warned her and you will see the changes, *mijale*', Sena's aunt chipped in, almost going on her knees. Sena's mother interrupted bitterly, saying, 'I want you to consider that she's not in a good condition right now. She moved into that same church and I'm sure she's not serving God with joy. Please, forgive her.'

'Well, that's her problem, not mine. That's between her and God, since she wants it that way. Her home- sorry- her matrimony is less important than the church. She needs more time with God and she's there now', he stood up from his seat, tired of their war of words.

He wanted them to just leave him alone. Sena's issue was settled as far as he was concerned. You cannot exchange peace for war. Yet, they did all their best, trying to resolve the issues but Gbenu remained same as ever. He wouldn't accept. She had to be punished for always disobeying him.

'Come – come back here. If you don't respect the grey hair on my head, respect God almighty that crafted you. You didn't come to this earth by accident, he made it possible. Respect God, *Mawu tin* or are you satanic? 'Pa danianou exploded, when he got tired of his obstinacy. His intention was to storm the place with officers and arrest him, but he was restrained by their tradition to resolve it customarily. After all, he was still her husband. What if they reconciled after? How would they delete the police case from history? However, he could not contain his arrogance any longer. It seemed to him like they were begging to find a space for their daughter. He also stood up with a little effort and called a spade a spade.

'Why are you stone-hearted? Uhn? God owns your soul. He can claim it at any time or right now and you will drop dead. That's all, that's the end of your pride'. Gbenu let off a confrontational stare and flung his door open.

'Get the hell out of my house now. I don't like disrespecting elderly people, so please leave my home now. The marriage is over, there's nothing to discuss here. And kindly help God react if he cannot. Leave'.

Sena's mother stood up first, followed by her aunt. The elderly man sat still, fixing his anguish stare on Gbenu. He wished he had the power to act like God and give the right judgment promptly.

'It's alright, we will leave. You don't have to be rude to anyone here. None of us is your mate. Think twice; think twice about what you're doing. This is unfair', she stormed off the room.

'*Ato gblaja*, we should leave. Thank you. Remember you begged me to marry her', Pa Danianou picked on him again.

'Leave here, all of you'.

'What a wonderful son- in- law you are'. Pa Danianou left the room last.

A few days after Gbenu drove his wife, he handed Viyan to his mother for the maternal care she needed. He hadn't any time to look after her or give the attention she wanted. She accepted the child from him, though she wasn't in support of his decision. In the face of the tribulations, she also devoted herself to reconciling him with his wife even when he was undeterred, unconcerned and reclusive.

Time rolled by into two full months and the couple was yet to reconcile. This was outrageous for Sena. Within the period, she was kicked out; it took her two weeks to acclimatize to the church premises. Her lonely time was exhausted on reading the scriptures, and cleaning the premises. She admitted within herself, by and by, that she had made an unforgiving mistake, choosing from going after God or her husband. What happened to the women that marry the two together? They earn themselves eternity, possibly; even so Gbenu was too complicated for her.

In point of fact, her anxiety did not only border on the unpleasantness of her predicament. Over and above that is her deteriorating health. She had taken ill for the past two weeks she relocated in her new abode. She feared chronic malaria and typhoid, bearing in mind the indicators living with her desolation: frequent headache, fever, and nausea. The pastor's wife subsidized her need to see a doctor from the church's nest egg, since they had been responsible for her upkeep after the incidence. Notwithstanding, the unanticipated cropped up after her medical check-up.

'Oh, you're here. I've been looking around for you', the pastor's wife, Mrs. Ahumenu, grabbed one of the plastic chairs dis arrayed in the outdoor, stomped to where she positioned herself in a melancholic mood. She rubbed her palm against her blurred vision, blinked repeatedly then managed to wear a smile.

'How do you feel today?' she concealed the tears in her eyes.

'Hm? Why are you crying? Stop crying. Look at your eyes; they've turned reddish from overmuch weeping. You don't need all this brooding'. She filled her massive size in the chair, the back support tilting rearward tiredly. She ran her fingers through her traditionally plaited hair and continued.

'Have you lost your faith in God? What does it profit a man to gain all that is in the world and lose his soul? Sister Sena, the Bible says in the second Chronicles 20:20 that-believe in the lord, your God, so shall ye be established. Sister Sena, if you don't believe in the wonders of God in your life, then, you're not helping us in this matter. I know it's not easy for you, despite that, you have to be strong. Please, be strong', she threw a plump, comforting arm around her.

'Is he rejecting me with pregnancy? Is he? Why? Why does he have to do that?' she wept bitterly. 'This is what I've ever wanted from God. A comforting life of eternity'.

'We haven't told him yet, have we? Since the pastor followed you to him and he chased both of you out of his room, this is your next visit, right? Daddy will go back there with you in the evening. Don't worry *e na yan*. You will be together again by His grace.

That they would visit the second time restored her lost hope to reunite with her family. She couldn't wait to welcome a new born they had been longing for in the past years. That, precisely, was her reason for building a new life. Her dream finally came true, however in a saddening mood. She set her heart on breaking the good news to him on a gleeful day- possibly on a Sunday they would all worship in the church in gratitude to God. As fate would have it, there she sat viewing herself alone in the same premises she believed she received her blessing from, thinking of how she would be accepted with an unborn child. She shook her head in utmost self-pity, sighed tiredly. All the same, she fell on her knees and began to pray fervently for heavenly mediation.

The time was 7:30pm when pastor Ahumenu got set to embark on the mission with her. He had spent two hours in the church ministering to his congregation on that Wednesday but bearing in mind the schedule. His initial plan was to wait for Gbenu ultimately, after he gave them the cold shoulder on their first visit. What more would they do when he drove them like sewage. As the pregnancy issue was involved, he had to return with her as instructed by the general overseer.

In less than two hours, they found themselves standing in front of Gbenu's door, the pastor in front, his bible in his hand. She wrapped her arm behind her like an offender, awaiting retribution. He tapped the door continuously and waited for him to surface.

'Yes? Who are you?' a young and pretty lady came out of the room. She cocked an eyebrow at them inquisitively.

'Oh, you haven't introduced yourself because you are not a resident here'. Mr. Ahumenu stood on the threshold smiling. Sena stood behind him in profound disbelief. Impossible. Could Gbenu have filled her vacuum within that short period she left? Was it planned before the dispute? Mysterious. She remained silent, didn't say a word to the lady, even so she shook her head in a climate of distrust.

'Okay. I'm-'.

'Who is it?' Gbenu's deep and heavy voice interrupted their interrogation. Hearing him from inside, the pastor clutched his bible with his second hand preparedly. It was a serious war between them the previous time they were there. He was, indeed, a complicated creature.

'What do they want?' He strode from the living room to the door, wearing a hot face.

'Peace be unto you, brother Gbenu. It's good to see you today', the pastor bowed reverently, Sena did the same.

'Sweetie, let them in', he went back inside, not looking at Sena.

'What? With the woman?' the lady gave Sena a revolting stare then allowed only the pastor in. She stood in her way, blocking her outside. She had seen her photograph in Gbenu's photo album, could still recognize her, even her shadow.

'Medese let her in, come and sit here'.

Pastor Ahumenu shook his head heartbreakingly. He looked over his shoulder to catch a glimpse of Senami's mood, before proceeding into the unwelcoming living room. She didn't budge, didn't argue with her. The smell of cigarette around the apartment made him ill at ease. He sniffed from time to time as he stood adjacent Gbenu. It was so overwhelming that he couldn't breathe suitably. By all indication, they must have frittered the whole day smoking, having lot of immodest fun around the place. He shifted his gaze to Gbenu who clad only his waist down to his knee with a short towel, his laps showing as he sat beside the unknown lady. He shrugged and concentrated on the rationale behind their visit.

'Peace be unto you, brother Gbenupo. It's quite a while', he peered around for somewhere to sit when he didn't offer them a seat. He read his moves, knew what he wanted but didn't care. They were seen as intruders, especially Sena he was determined not to love again for the rest of his life. He turned his gaze towards her and sized her up from head to toe. On that day, she was wearing a long pleated skirt, almost touching her toes and extremely oversized, and a turtle-necked blouse matching a heavy turban. He fizzled then turned away irritably. Mr. Ahumenu watched his countenance, sighed and asked, 'sorry, may we be seated?'

'What for? Haven't we finalized this issue? Why getting on my nerves every time?'

'Mr. Gbenu, you let us in because you respected the grey hair on my head and you want to listen to me, if- not- her-', he pointed at Sena feebly, tiredly. He didn't like that kind of mission from the church. The man was too complicated for him. He had always been his best to his wife, never treated her like debris, for once, after he married her. What possessed the man was a mystery to him.

'Listen to me. Your general overseer sent for me and I sent a message to him, asking why he wouldn't come to me. Is he claiming to be better than everyone?' he hit his chest, raised his voice. Sena began to freak out.

'No, it's not what you think. He travelled with some ministers to the north for ministration the following week and that's the reason he assigned me to see to the matter'.

'Humph', Sena sighed and lowered her head with anxiety, nervousness, uncertainty, hatred, and disbelief. Her heart thudded like it was about to go off like a booby trap. In her own home that used to give love and fulfillment, she felt like a disheartened stranger. So different. It's akin to a new life – the same way she felt when she accepted Christ in her life. As she raised her face to look at her husband, she met a different gaze from a different man. The Gbenupo she met eight years ago was pleading at her feet for her hands in marriage, promising her the whole world. He'd suddenly changed into a plump, bug-eyed, and ugly devil with a bulbous nose, sitting upon her glory and seeking for her destruction. If not, he wouldn't reject Christ and eternity or find an accomplice in defiance to persist in his sinful life.

'Honey- good evening', she greeted him tremulously.

'Hmmn? What do you want? What is this greeting for? Have I not told you that it's over between us? I can't accept you back', he sprang to his feet, advanced towards her with a tightened fist.

'Hey, brother Gbenu, calm down-sit down- and listen to why we are here. Don't touch that woman again. It's okay', pastor Ahumenu also stood in defense of Senami. Why would he hit her for greeting him, despite being met by open hostility in her home?

'Tell me why you're here and just leave. Leave my apartment for God's sake. I have a date with my dearest'. He folded his arms across his belly, leaned on the wall and shook his legs furiously, in readiness for another brawl. The situation was completely beyond Senami's control. Was it real? She was sure, what brought about his retribution and revolting behavior was a mere turnabout from her to a new love. Maybe the new lady. She should be the indispensable barrier between them. She thought to herself bitterly. She turned and looked at the lady where she sat with much confidence. She still wore the same menacing look, possibly praying for their separation to make a way for herself. What a life! It seemed the pastor was reading her mind when he gave the stranger the fairest share of the matter; just at the right time.

'Er- madam, I'm sorry to say but- it's crystal clear that you're brother Gbenu's girlfriend. Why not just excuse us for a moment?'

'Why? Why do you want her to leave? Is she disturbing you?' he sat back in the sofa, laughing gleefully. 'Go ahead I'm listening'.

'Alright, to save our precious time', the pastor cleared his throat, began with a scriptural reference.

'Pastor, pastor- we need no aggravation. Go straight to the point. We have a special outing now; you are delaying us', Gbenu interrupted.

'Your wife is pregnant, Mr. Gbenu', he announced, plagued by his overmuch tension and stiffness. He was shocked, although he tried to hide his feelings. He sized her up the second time.

'She's expecting your second child. That's why I've accompanied her here to tell you', he concluded coldly. Gbenu broke into a sardonic smile and rejoined, 'congratulations'.

'Yes, congratulations to you. God has finally answered your prayer', the pastor said smiling'.

'Answered your prayer indeed. I knew it; I knew it would come to this- when she was spending nights with you in the church. I knew you would impregnate her, it has finally happened', Gbenu accused Ahumenu. He was short of words. He watched him with a full expression of shock on his aged face. For the past twenty nine years in his ministry, he has not, at any time, encountered such an open confrontation and embarrassment. If it occurred, he wouldn't have ventured it anymore. Sooner than he imagined, he realized it was time to back off from their family affair to uphold his deference in the society. Ugly rumors spread quickly.

'Sister Senami, God almighty is your witness that I've not, at any time, had an affair with you and the Lord almighty is your witness that you innocently came to the church to worship. There's nothing else attached to it. And also, your husband is responsible for your pregnancy', he stood up from his seat and made to leave. 'Sister Sena, it's time to leave'.

'Pastor!' Sena cut in impatiently when she saw her only chance slipping off her hands.

'Listen to me. We have to leave right now. We need divine intercession', he waited for her to follow him but she did not. She crept to Gbenu's feet and held him tightly amidst tears.

'Gbenu, my dear husband- please, don't. Don't do this to me. *Asu che*, I promise to give you attention when I get back. Please, forgive me, I promise to-'

'Get out of my apartment now! You want to get back to where? Leave me alone and follow him now. That's the result of your vigil and fasting. Follow him and get out of here!' he pushed her out of the apartment.

'Na wa oh. This is wonderful', Medese laughed her head off.

'Well, whatever goes around comes around. Sister Sena, follow me, let's go back to the church'. Pastor Ahumenu forced her on her feet, and dragged her out to avoid further disaster.

'Leave my house right now before I lose my temper'.

'Let's go – let's leave now. It is well with you in Jesus name. The lord is your strength, let's go, I can't leave you like this', he continued taking her away insistently. Gbenu followed them.

'It's a lie! You impregnated her. Do you think I am foolish to accept that thing from you? Go! You're compatible, I wish you the best'. He followed them outside.

The man of God was beginning to regret his mission. Nothing made him as discreditable as that in his entire life. Neighbors and passersby, amongst who were members of the church, gathered and watched as Gbenu disgraced them. He set off after them barefooted, at a steady pace, until they were out of sight. It was obvious he was under the influence of alcohol he took before their arrival. At the end of the day, he was pleased he expressed himself extraordinarily. He had no regret whatsoever.

The next three days were terrible for Sena. Each time she remembered chapters of the incidence, she blamed herself for being an extremist- the one who devoted all her time to only the church and paid less attention to her marriage. The one who saw her husband as an unbending sinner she should avoid to have her way. She had forgiven him, despite his ill treatment. She wanted to carry on, nevertheless it was impossible.

Mr. Ahumenu did not mind Gbenu's rudeness. He was obviously still supportive to Senami for the next five months she was living with them in the church. Her tummy had protruded and people were passing speculative comment about her matrimonial problem. She was less concerned about whatever they said; after all, people talk about people. She had been through a lot in her life. What could be more disheartening than the deprivation she suffered from their union? Maybe the denial of her birthright. She pulled herself together then concluded that it was their headache. Whoever hangs her burden on her shoulder and put her own bulk on her head would suffer considerable headache. It was her life and fate.

As she got into her third trimester, she partly pushed the thought out of her mind as advised by her doctor. The role her relatives also played in her life couldn't be forgotten. They visited the church most time to console her as her delivery approached.

'Hmm? It's just that, my husband, who is not your father, disagreed with bringing you to live with us. I've done all I should to make it possible, he still refused. He vowed to drive me like you if I ventured it, and I have nowhere to go', her mother explained, out of sheer discomfort, on a day she visited and saw her looking unhealthy.

'Iya che, I understand. I will be fine. I am fine. I just lost appetite two days ago. Mr. and Mrs. Ahumenu and the entire church are taking proper care of me.' She smiled then turned her attention to her aunty, Mrs. Valerie Hunjo, who accompanied her mother there to see her.

'You are welcome ma. What do I offer you to eat or drink?' she flashed a forceful smile at her.

'No, nothing-I'm fine. I feel so sorry for you. I wish I could help you out of here too but- my husband won't consent to the idea. We are managing only a room apartment with three kids. You know? The lord will strengthen you and I pray Gbenu regains his senses soon'. She shook her head pitifully.

'Humph- thank you ma. I'm doing fine here. Don't worry about me. If I'm doing this for God, He won't forget me, I believe. I believe He will settle my home soonest', she forced another smile and persisted, 'what bothers me now is not where I'm living- it's my Viyan. He stopped me from seeing her. He took her to his mother in the village and I can't go there to see her. He barred me from seeing my daughter or his mother'. A film of tears formed in her eyes.

'What about his mother? What kind of woman is that? Like mother like son? ', her mother inquired angrily.

'Hm? She visited here only once and never returned again. Not anymore. How I've offended her too, I don't know. But I know that the lord that I serve will fight this battle for me'.

'It's okay. Remember you've been praying for this baby. Who knows if this is the condition God has given you to have it? What do you think?' mama sought Valerie's opinion and she refuted her idea instantly.

'No, *soeurs* don't talk like an unbeliever. Does He give any condition to provide for our needs? God is good all the time. Her problem is a result of Gbenu's devilish behavior, its devil's handwork. He is only ruining the work of God'. They all agreed vehemently.

'Uhn- you are right and God will fight the battle for you. Satan is a liar'. She assured her.

For all the occurrences in life, it is thoughtful to admit that, man proposes; God disposes. No one could penetrate our minds to see what we plan and it's aftereffects of failure and happiness, except God, the originator. Senami wasn't enjoying herself in the premises. She believed God bestowed her utmost wish, however life wasn't fair to her. She knew she was suffering while her hubby basked around with a new love. That you know only your mind and situation but blinded from seeing people's true feelings and encounters is also factual.

Senami's assumption about her husband was wrong. Not any of them enjoyed their union six months after.

Gbenu failed in his comprehension of the new woman in his life, that not all women are completely satisfactory. Granted that he felt a weight off his mind when Senami finally left and there was a quick replacement for her in his heart, it wasn't long when Medese began to show the real stuff she was made of. Unlike his deprived wife, Medese's unacceptable problem centered on her unpermitted and unusual outing to night clubs and parties. Most times, without his permission, she would spend the night wherever she went: a life she was accustomed to before they began their love affair. Why should he raise a dust for what he knew her for? For a life they had always enjoyed together- a life that brought them together-for one thing they had in common.

As a leopard will not change its spot, Gbenu couldn't come to term with her extreme prejudice. Except for the times she sneaked to the church, Sena lived with him in the same house and never raised her voice against him, no matter what he did. She would apologize to him even though he was wrong. Medese was her indisputable opposite in all ways. She would exchange words with him, throw back his insult and blows. They lived like cat and rat in the same house for months. He tried all he could to be his best so he wouldn't be misjudged that he was a terrible beast but Medese was also a dare devil. She pushed him to the wall and he faced her on a day she returned home after spending two unapproved days away.

'Are you out of your mind? How dare you talk to me in that manner? Shouldn't you apologize?'

'For what? Why did you call me a prostitute? What makes me a prostitute now? Am I not better than that mess you called a wife?'

'Better indeed! She's not like you- she doesn't have the nerve to date another man but you-,'

'Cut it there! You just can't intimidate me like her. I'm better than her'.

'Keep quiet now. Medese. Keep shut now or you'll regret it', he advanced towards her but she didn't take him seriously. She didn't imagine being maltreated by him like Senami. In her mind, she was better and more special than the one he treated as his slave.

'What will you do? You want to hit me. Try it and see what happens, bastard!'

Bastard? He paused for a moment, and took a proper look at himself. Was he daydreaming? In his forty years, no woman ever had the nerve to call him names. He dropped the cup in his hand, took three sharp steps towards her, his hands ready to strike, his eyes blood shot. Anger crept into him, vengeance arrested his mind.

'What will you do? I am not that wretched slave you called a wife. If you hit me, I will hit you back'. She countered, not taking any step away. She stood gripping her dancing waist, her chest pitching in frenzy as she gave a malevolent look. Only one side of her face turned to him, but her two eyes busily washed his value off as a man. She feels he is a low- life compared with her last husband. She had been in two marriages before and none of her exes ever treated her like that. She rather left them before they had the thought. But everything she did upset him. Already, he had lost his temper. He took one last step closer and slapped her across her face. She had to learn a lesson and respect him for once.

'You are very stupid! Get up and call me a bastard again. I will beat the hell out of you. No woman, I repeat- no woman will stand in front of me and call me a bastard. What do you mean?' he stood over her body still ranting. He had to get even with her, must teach her a lesson to be nice next time. He didn't realize the gravity of the incidence until five minutes later.

'Medese', he stooped beside her and shook her body. She knew she was a prankster. Most times, she would play pranks with him in the room and that was what he thought she was doing.

Another five minutes flew by and she was still lying on the floor. This scared him. He instantly began to conduct a mouth to mouth resuscitation on her. He pressed her chest to revive her. All effort was in vain. Medese was dead.

With deep regret, he ran across his flat to his nearest neighbor who had been attentive to their argument. Before the next six seconds, he stormed out standing in front of him violently.

'Very good. You have killed her – you are going to pay for this- you are going to pay for this', he shut his door behind him eagerly.

'No-no, she's not dead. She can't be dead, she's only unconscious. I need you to help me', he turned apologetic for the first time in the vicinity.

'Go and revive her then. Am I a doctor?' he drew out his phone, dialed 911 for his arrest.

Before the end of that same day, the rumor filtered to the church shortly after Sena left for her ante natal care in a hospital. Intrusive neighbors took it upon themselves to visit the scene on her behalf. And by the time they arrived under a tense atmosphere, it was too late. The culprit and the corpse had been moved away in a police van. A lot of people converged in front of the house, weeping, lamenting and cursing. There were also different versions of the incidence, not forgetting to mention the way Sena was treated as his wife. No one spoke for him: everyone was against him. After two hours, pastor

Ahumenu left bitterly with his wife, having heard all they wanted to know. They felt sorry for Sena, yet were determined not to feed her with any information.

That Gbenu had been a terrible man in the past didn't discourage Ahumenu from seeing him. He left the church earlier the following day and visited the police division handling his grave case. He was short of words, bowed down by the situation when the criminal was called out of his jail cell handcuffed.

'Pastor- pastor-look at me. See what I've led myself into. Pray for me, pray for me. When I'm out of here I'll accept Christ as my lord and savior ever and ever and I'll sin no more', he cried convulsively.

'Mr. Gbenu, brother Gbenu-why? Why? Why can't you control yourself when you're angry? An angry man is different from a mad man, isn't he? And the fear of God is the beginning of wisdom. It surpasses all things in life'.

'Look at yourself now. Just take a look at yourself', he pointed at the bruises he got from the police and his angry neighbors.

'Pray for me. I will sin no more. I want to be out of here',

'Well, God is in control. Let's hope so because, all your neighbors testified against you and the deceased's family vowed to go any length with you. Only Jehovah jireh, the God we worship will set you free', he said prayerfully. He knew it would be difficult for him as every murder case meets a stringent judgement. Patience would have prevented the problem for him but he never gave it a chance.

As hard as it is to conceal news, Senami gathered the information from one of her friends in the neighborhood. She promptly walked to the police station with her younger brother, still in the early hour of the day. Her back ached while she waited for him to be called out of his cell, away from other inmates. She couldn't yet believe that Gbenu would end up in such a place. With all the atrocities he committed, she didn't wish him that. She still loved him, wanted to reunite with him. He remained the father of her kids, no matter what she suffered from him.

'Sena- Sena, my wife. I'm sorry – I'm so sorry. I'm sorry for treating you badly. Forgive me, am so sorry'. He remembered the way he had beaten her severally and regretted his action.

'Oh God, it is true. It is true- why? Why my beloved?' Senami wept.

'Even if I don't escape this judgement, I want you to forgive me', he knelt in front of her, placed his cuffed hands on her laps apologetically. He still couldn't believe the occurrence was real. Was it an unending dream? If not, when would it end? When would the bad dream end?

'Oh my God, why did you push her? You should have left her alone. Why is this happening?' she felt a sharp pain from her lower back and ignored it. What needed attention was how her hubby would be miraculously released from the station. Few minutes after, he was walked back into the cell, by an officer. Senami didn't leave immediately. She loitered around the station for close to three hours, crying before she finally left.

Following the unpredictable system of justice, Gbenu's case remained pending, unresolved. He had been in the court five different times with no judgement or bail. He remained in the prison for the next six years but as a different person. He was, however thankful to God for granting him the grace to repent and get close to Him. He always grabbed the Bible to pray fervently for his breakthrough.

Andre, his second son, now six and Viyan, ten always accompany their mother to the prison to visit their father. They maintained a united family, despite his situation. He spends each time with them to preach and pray. As for him, nothing is more important than a happy family and transformed soul. No one kills an ignorant ant that begs for wisdom.

6

Kenosi

...the art of negotiating is acquired from childhood.

As a child, growing up was like a scuffle between a net and fish: a challenging struggle to be functional to myself, my contiguous society and of course, my defenseless folks. This burden was crushingly distressing to me, being a child who had a whole lot of needs not in place. Someone, as it is appropriate, had to fend for me, and reduce my encumbrance as a youngster, for everything had its time- a time to hook on and a time to be hooked upon. At my own dependent time, I was depended upon. At the time I should think of only today, I was obsessed with my tomorrow, often uncertain about the pleasantness of hereafter. I could see, in my mind's eye, what more would befall me, without being told. I was afraid of my surrounding; I mistrusted my ambiance, got weary of subsistence. I tripped over an invariable livelihood revolving around me, year in -year out. Nothing new, nothing impressive but the same me- me –me, lurching in penury as designed by divine providence.

    The moment I watched my father slump in our house, in Francistown, when I was precisely six, I pictured my entire life crumbling with him into the bottomless ground he was entombed the following day. Since then, my life was not the same again. Although still young then, I could recollect his family's deliberation on his heritage and how we would survive afterwards. From their mindless certitudes, my mother was robbed of all her savings with my father, traditionally. We were left with nothing, except the house he built for us before his demise. All pertinent possessions, therein, making our home attractive was either shared or sold to generate cash for them.

'You are just sitting and weeping for nothing. You better get up and start finding what to do to raise all these kids you have. No one has money to raise them for you', my uncle, Mr. Boipelol, who hated her with passion warned, flinging his hands above our heads while we sat surrounding her hopelessly. According to my mum, he was the first to make an offer of marriage to her and was embittered when she finally agreed to marry my father. For that alone, he would revel in his sudden departure or roll in the aisles.

'Who could have predicted that he would end up like this? Now, it's too late for you and these kids', he taunted her but she gave no reply. She only dropped her head and cried her eyes out. Deep within her, she prayed for a prompt mystical judgement: maybe a thunder strike or his mouth shifting to his hindmost. Anything. Men like him deserve no mercy. Nonetheless, our almighty God is not always quick to react or judge a sinner.

We were eventually shared by the same people that doled out our belongings. Two of us, my sister and I, were left to live with my aged grandma who had only my mother while the other six children travelled to different destinations, away from my mother's restrictive eyes. Before my father's death, she was known for mollycoddling us, not allowing anyone to scold us, no matter what we did. We were about to begin a new life- an unforeseen living we didn't bargain for. Our journey into the world of poverty and deprivation.

Four years after I moved to the city with my little sister, we had grown older than when we departed from the rest of our siblings, who had also relocated to their new homes. Whether they were enjoying themselves or not wasn't our priority. The matter had turned to saving your own head before saving others. You barely think about others' condition when you are not living fine. My mother was the only one visiting to supply our needs. She would buy lot of foodstuffs that could sustain us and her parents for about a month and afterwards, it would take up to forty days before we would see her again. I couldn't blame her much for that because she was laboring to raise all the nine of us after my father's demise. She would, sometimes, hawk some food items or jewelry around, trekking a long distance and finding customers to patronize her merchandise. It wasn't easy for her, at first, for she was dependent on my father when he was living. He would tell her to stay in the house and enjoy all his struggles, after all it was all for her and the children. Contrariwise, she had to live and fend for us within her capability.

'Aw- *mma* is here. *Ngiya kwemukela*', Tchieu, my lovely sister of eight years threw the sand she was playing with away. She hurried to hug my mum as she saw her approaching our house on a sunny day, a big bag in her hand. She crouched down to lift her to her chest and she smeared her face with relic of the sand in her messy hand.

'Get down, you have stained her', I said dragging her down with one of her legs, jealously. She pushed my face away from her and I got so angry.

'Oh, it's okay. I'll carry you too but- not now', she measured my weight, then my height with her eyes. I had grown older and stronger than before. Lifting me may fall both of us. Just then, she changed her mind.

'You know what? Let's go in and I will carry you there?' she cajoled me and walked in slowly, still carrying my sister. I followed closely, holding her second hand.

'Is grandma around?' she inquired, almost at our threshold.

'Yes ma. Grandpa has gone to the mosque for Zuhr prayer'.

'Why didn't you follow him?' she asked us both and we shrugged distastefully. I got sick of following him due to his prolonged stay after worship. In the mosque, you mustn't make any meaningless noise; or you will be driven out instantly or shushed for the rest of the time. The last time we followed him, we were driven for wasting the water for ablution and grand pa was crossed with us.

'He sleeps in the mosque after prayer', Tchieu gave her reason that fled my mind. Old people like him loved to enjoy the quietness and freshness of the mosque after the noon prayer, like we adored playing with our peers in the field. Different times and dissimilar tastes.

'Nayna- you are here', my grandma welcomed her joyfully. She sat up on her bed the moment she set her eyes on her only child. She had spent the early hour of the day, complaining about how much food we took in the morning and the little she had left to feed all of us. On the date she gave for her return, we didn't see her until ten days after. It was considered too much for the old, jobless couple. They had to think of themselves and the little children in their care.

'My mother –sweet mother. I'm sorry you didn't see me on the scheduled date. I travelled to Kanye to see three of my children living there. You know only two of my children are with me', she explained, sitting next to her on her bed, blanket and bed sheet all scattered around, the smell of menthol in the air.

'Why didn't you cut your hair', she rubbed her feathery grey hair to the back. It got flimsier than before. Her eyes dropped on her wrinkled skin on the spur of the moment. She noticed her mother aged almost every time she saw her and said 'I hope you're taking all your medications'.

'What did you see? Am I looking too old? First my hair, then my medicine. It's all about money, you know? Money ends any form of deprivation'.

'Mother, I'm doing my best not to deprive you of anything in life, including all my children', she drew the bag she brought closer and began to unwrap the groceries therein. Grandma followed all things with her eyes anxiously. She had retired from her trading job that used to fetch her all her needs. Nothing seemed enough for a caged lion that used to roam the jungle and get all needs.

'Ah- that's my oat. I loved the one you brought last month but it wasn't enough', she reached out for it, looked at the label vaguely. In their generation, females were denied education, so she couldn't read or write. She only admired the colour and the picture saying, 'wonderful, wonderful'.

'This is for Ntatemogholo. Your children said that he's in the mosque', she handed a bottle of nuts to her. He loved nuts battling with his displaced and aged teeth.

'No, I won't give him this- he has diarrhea', she took it from her, hid it under her pillow.

'Nkuku- it won't affect him'.

My mother observed that I was watching anxiously and she gave us what she brought for us too. For each kid, there was a big pack of plantain chips and chicken she got from Kentuchy Fried Chicken. It was a jolly day for me; however I made a mistake. Only my sister thanked her the same way we were taught by Nkuku, as we fondly called her. I took mine and opened it without any word of appreciation.

She gave a bad eye and yelled, 'hand that back now! Is that what I taught you to do when you get a gift?'

I immediately handed it to her, looking sad. Nkuku is too stern, unbending and too disciplined as much as I knew her. I felt there wasn't any need to thank my mum for buying a snack I deserved for me- it was my right. I glowered at her glumly and she forced me out of her room. My mother shifted uneasily, feeling there wasn't a need to do that maybe but she dared not call me back when I was being scolded. Except she would take me with her.

'He's too troublesome. He just troubled me before I sent them out to play', she gave my snacks back to my mum. Mma took it back reluctantly, despondently. She really wanted to spend some time with us before travelling back, considering the space between us. She drew a long breath and diverted to another topic that she wanted to discuss with her mother.

'Tchieu, come down and enjoy your snacks. I want to talk to Nkuku', she dropped her on the ground concentrating on her hair. It was too rough and untidy. For lot of considerable reasons, it's been left untouched for six weeks, she understood. My observant Nkuku caught her demanding eyes then corrected her unknown impression, 'I will cut that hair because I can't afford to maintain it'.

'Don't cut my hair, cut your own', Tchieu pouted and she was also driven out of the room like me so she could enjoy her conversation with her daughter.

'Leave them- let them go and play or they will cry after you when you're leaving. They are birds of same feather'.

'Alright ma', she broke into a dull smile. Nkuku shifted closer, angling her head to pay attention. She was her only confidant.

'I visited Selebi, where my three children are. Remember I told you three of them travelled to Selebi with my brother- in- law'.

'Which of them? The one that hated you?'

'Yes, he insisted they were going to live in his house and I had no right to drag with them, you know? So, I accepted'.

'Hun- how are they doing', she twisted her eyes in eagerness for sad news. My mother's enemy is equally my enemy.

'He is enslaving my children to raise his own children and they are not even in any school. Can you believe that?'

'Did they not all promise to enroll these children in school when they took them from you? Are theirs not in school? They are so wicked!'

'I was appalled to see them wearing rags around the street. In short I couldn't believe they are my kids when I saw them', she explained with a teary voice.

'So, what are you going to do now?'

'I've removed my children from there. Without informing him or his wife, I took my children away from them and they are living with me now'.

'Why? You should have informed them. Won't you trouble them with your decision?'

'That's the only way I could get them from the rascal. And afterwards, his wife came finding and saw them playing in our compound'. She unzipped her purse and brought out some money.

'Dirty thing! What did she tell you?'

'She didn't utter a word. She merely told the cab driver to take her back. Right now, I'm expecting another family meeting to rebuke my actions'. She handed eighty of similar notes to her. She collected the money and dropped it aside. Her well-being was considered more important than the money at the moment. Only that moment.

'So, what about the other three in Kanye? Are they okay?'

'They are not in any school too but they are clean enough to make me happy'

'Cleanliness and no education. Won't you bring those three you brought back here? God will provide our needs'.

'Oh- sweet mother, what will I do without you?' she picked the money, counted note by note in Setswana language. She touched her tongue to moisten her fingertip each time they stuck together. Mma stood up to look around for us and she stopped her instantly.

'Leave those kids and let's talk. Are you going back today', she asked, tucking the money under her pillow

'Ummm- I think so, because of the children at home. I have five of them now, remember?' she returned to her position, beside her. Nkuku sized her up, remembering all her vainly persuasion to dissuade her from overmuch delivery of babies after she married my father. All advice fell on deaf ears, and then the unforeseen occurred. Suddenly, Nkuku fell silent and she didn't say a word to her again. She noticed her mother was a bit troubled as usual and started a fresh topic.

'Is there anything you need me to do for you before I leave?'

'No- you have to see my husband before you leave', she shunned calling him her father. She was too plain, unpretentious. Both of them knew she divorced her father on the ground of infidelity many years back, then married her quiet stepfather.

'Yes- so, mother when should I bring your other grand children?'

'Not all of them- you are bringing only two of them for now. A boy and a girl that can look after the younger ones'.

'Okay- thank you ma', my mother noticed me coiling my legs and peeping through a light curtain into the room, with a face laden with feelings. I wanted my snacks badly. She still didn't call me back until Ntatemogholo returned from the mosque. He hanged his *Tesbiy* on his neck, his great height keeping up with his apparent double pace.

His traditional attire made a clutch at his flat belly as he ran into the cool embrace of a light wind. I watched him approaching then turned away from him sadly. Not he or anyone had the capability to convince Nkuku to return my snack, except she had her mind made up to do it.

'What happened to you?' He asked as I crept away from the road he would pass inside the house. I didn't respond. I just shook my head and he asked no further question. He ignored and joined them inside when Mma was preparing to leave, bearing in mind the traffic on the way. She exchanged pleasantries with him, spent one more hour and rose to leave.

'Are you leaving right now?'

'I have been here. I don't want my children to fight before I return. I now have five of them living with me'.

'Oh- you may leave then. I will see you off'. He dropped his rosary on the bed, beside Nkuku and prepared to follow her. She squeezed some notes in his hand.

'Don't worry sir. Stay- stay with my beautiful mum. You've stayed away for too long. She needs your attention now'.

'Oh- thank you', he laughed from ear to ear, his ninety years written all over him. He tucked the money in his pocket and sat on his bed opposite Nkuku. He grabbed a wrapper lying on his pillow and dusted sand away from it. I had hopped on it earlier, messed up the whole sheet. He sat up still smiling and glaring at the greatness and the man inside my mother. She was too quick to recover from her loss, acting stronger than a man- an undisputable amazon. Like mother like daughter. It was what attracted him to my Nkuku.

'Hold on, I will follow you to the door', Nkuku searched the room for her head- tie while Mma smartly left the room to find me. I was hiding near the wall with a doleful face, like the one who just mislaid a hunted animal. She raced after me as I made to run, slipped her fingers through my hidden armpit and tickled till I burst out laughing. At the time I was down laughing my head off, she tucked two crisp notes that could feed me twice in a week into my left hand. I opened it curiously then gave her a big hug. She rubbed my head fondly before Tchieu came out to join us.

'Mma- don't leave today. I want to see you till next year', she clung to her sleeve seriously.

'Don't worry. One day- I'm going to bring all your siblings here and we will stay for a year'.

'Just a year? Can't we go to our house and leave this Nkuku alone?' I inquired unequivocally. I detested her ascetic way of life.

'Don't worry, be good kids to her. She saved your heads from lot of troubles'. I pushed her hand away, refuting her glorification. Someone else deserves that assertion; not my grandma. What would ever make me agree with her?

Just as we persuaded her to stay, Nkuku burst out of the room, holding her scarf.

She looked unbelievably stronger than her eighty six years. She carried her great height and robust body suitably and always bustled around with the energy of six strong young girls combined in a body. Her appearance alone ingrained enough fear in me unlike Ntatemogholo who was wiry and calm. They were two faces of a coin.

'Before I open these eyes now, get inside. Go and stay with your grandpa. Why do you want to follow her? Are you not satisfied here? You may take your leave now. Your children will be expecting you. Please don't be long before you get back to us. Do you understand? *hamba kahle.*' We immediately retracted our hands from her and waved desolately, a film of tears in Tchieu's eyes. I gave Nkuku a bad eye and walked in displeased.

'*Sala Kahle*'. My mother waved.

Not minding any of us, she cleared her throat then waved back at Mma as she took her leave. We kept waving, looking at her through a little window near grandpa's bed. Each time she visited; we felt detached from the parental guardianship we deserved. We wanted much more than living with our aged grandparents, although it wasn't anyone's fault.

'Come and pull my toes for me', Ntatemogholo hauled our attention back to the room. He had outstretched his two dry and scaly legs on his table. From recurrent farming and trekking, they had aged more than his look, needed enough moisture to revitalize them nonetheless he didn't care as long as they carried him to his destination every day.

'What is it?' I gave him the same bad eye the moment he grimaced. I pulled another toe harshly, intentionally. I didn't care if it hurt, he should let me be. Tchieu took his second leg, rubbing his bunion.

'I got that from wearing shoes when I was in my thirties and forties and was a civil servant in-'

'But you don't have any shoe', Tchieu cut in.

'Not again, that was then', he cleared her qualm, shifting another toe I grabbed. My eyes travelled round the room in search of the snacks Nkuku seized from me. It wasn't anywhere within my reach. I knew she wanted to chastise me till the next day as she used to.

'Kenosi- you are hurting me. Be careful with that one. I bumped into a stump on the farm yesterday. Do you see the bruise?' he showed me his injury but my attention wasn't there. I was enthralled by the frayed sachet of consumed chips on the floor. Had my snack been eaten by him or his wife? I dropped his foot, took steps away from him reproachfully.

'My fingers hurt, I'm tired. If your toes burn, why do we have to draw them?' I eyed him, wondering why he had to put me through that after enjoying my snacks. It's pepper upon injury.

'Grandma said no questioning an adult. You are rude-', Tchieu corrected and I yelled at her, 'shut up!'

Ntatemogholo didn't care if I got back or not. As far as he was concerned, he saw me as an unwise kid who needed appropriate training under stringent nurturing. To him, kids will always be kids, no matter what you do to metamorphose them into adults overnight. He presumed he was tired of me or didn't have the strength to handle me maybe, so he let go almost every time.

'What are you doing over there? Why didn't you answer all my calls?' Nkuku came in with a handful of some dried clothes we washed together in the morning. She dropped them on the carpet then picked the empty sachet on the floor.

'Why did you eat the snack without my consent?' she asked, looking from me to my sister. I rose my two hands up defensibly.

'Not me- I don't know who ate it'.

'I didn't eat it too'. My sister released the toes and fixed her eyes on grandpa. She caught him dropping the sachet when she entered the room first.

'Is it for him? I ate it', he declared, setting his feet on the ground. Nkuku went berserk. She had spent a lot on him the previous week, to heal diarrhea and pile. Their traditional doctor had also forewarned him to abstain from spicy and sugary foods. Why he consumed the snack that wasn't his was what only the two of them should discuss and understand.

'Leave here both of you', Nkuku drove us out of the room to correct Ntatemogholo, I knew. She never corrected her husband before us, irrespective of his offence. I strode out of the room, dissatisfied with them and my livelihood.

An idea struck me as I leaned my back on the wall, relishing the fresh atmosphere in the compound. If I could fortunately get money as much as I got from my mother, then I would get all I needed, I thought to myself. With that, I wouldn't be denied the opportunity to eat all I wanted, visit amusing places and be completely satisfied. I mulled childishly, rubbing the notes Mma gave me. How I would fulfill that wasn't yet clear to me but I had it at the back of my mind to fulfill my wishes, come rain or shine.

Two days after I kept the money in a pouch behind Nkuku's water pot, in her local kitchen made with mud and thatched roof, it disappeared. I rummaged the whole house for it, desperately needed to take it to school for nice snacks. It was gone! Nonetheless, I had no nerve to walk up to her and ask for my money, although I knew she took it from there. No one visited there like she did- she cooked our meals there every time or processed cereals for the future. Ntatemogholo barely visited the kitchen. His place was always on the farm. And my sister? She was taught that thieves wouldn't make heaven, would be roasted in hell like barbeque. She wouldn't venture hell. My lips curled in deep surprise. Nkuku. Was she stalking me?

Hiding myself behind the same kitchen, I cried my eyes out for minutes. I mustn't be caught in the mood; else I would be accused of stealing the money. I was absent from school on that day. I dropped my backpack somewhere, and meandered for the whole school hour. First, I visited a tennis court where truants like me took cover and frittered the whole school time, then proceeded to my friend's house. There, I spent the rest of the period. I enjoyed the sensation that was different from school and on that day, I conceded that school was a lot of trouble for me. I didn't leave until the closing time.

I waited for Tchieu to pass through the same route we treaded on every school day, to arrive and depart. She mustn't arrive home before me to disclose my secret movement like she did one day she didn't see me at closing time.

'Ah- what are you doing here?' she asked approaching me with one of her numerous classmates. 'I've been to your class twice during break. I wanted to share my candy with you'.

'I – was there. I went out to play with my friends', I joined them and we walked home together. She suddenly noticed I wasn't with my backpack. It was odd because every returning kid was with a bag either old or new except me.

'Where is your backpack?'

'I gave it to someone to help me drop it at home'. As I said this, her friend sneaked a quick look at me- a look unearthing all my lies. It wasn't her business anyway. At this, I changed the topic to what wouldn't favour their friendship.

'Mmaabo, why does your mouth stink?' I shot her a disenchanting stare and she didn't care. She continued moving with us, ignored me. However, I was prepared to annoy her and send her away from us.

'How did her mouth stink when she didn't say a word to you?' her friend defended her, covering the space between us. I crossed to her side and repeated the statement.

'What is this? Please stay away from me', she flared up.

'You- go away from us. We are siblings. Where do you fit in?' I held Tchieu's shoulder amiably and watched her walk away from us. Mission accomplished.

'You drove my friend away. Why?' she fell my arm from her shoulder.

'Let her go. Tchieu, do you know I have an idea'. I put my hand back on her shoulder and she removed it again and again- up to six times before she finally yelled, 'leave me alone!'

'You don't want to visit the theatre?' I caught up with her, faced her on the road, and then walked in reverse.

'Which theater?' she eyed me

'You know my friend Seth? He invited me to a movie theatre to watch a film for free because his mum is selling soda there'.

'Does that give us the ticket to enter?'

'Don't worry yourself. Through her, we will enter and enjoy a cool movie right now'.

'Hmm? That doesn't make sense. Nkuku is waiting for us at home', she deterred me from the plan but I didn't give up. I convinced her successfully and she followed me.

On that day, I succeeded in dragging her into trouble. We spent three hours watching the first interesting movie after we were luckily admitted as one of the theater traders, with the help of Seth. And we weren't out of the dark scene or able to check the time to know it was night. We waited to watch the next two films that ended at precisely 9pm. I already dropped asleep on my seat, mindless of home and my guardians. The seat was restful; the setting was out of my impoverished world and the movie, the best of the year for kids in our generation. No screaming face of Nkuku, no sad and silent Ntatemogholo. Just my sister and I, in a life of comfort I always dreamt of. I slept and dreamt on.

When the last set of spectators for 6-9pm movie streamed out, it was time for 10pm-12am audience to enter the overly busy spot. Fortunately for us, Tchieu looked through the exit door and saw the pitch dark surrounding of the venue. There was a bright light only within the cinema due to electric outage- a huge power plant was operated to show the films.

She hurried back to me, gave me two hot slaps on my face shouting, 'we are in trouble!'. Without looking back at me, she grabbed her backpack and rushed out of the big movie house. Still struggling to get conscious of my surrounding, I stretched and staggered after her.

'Wait!' I stopped her as she hurried home to find the right direction in the dark. Pictures of the castigation we would face on our arrival assailed her, arrested her mind. Nkuku would tie us like dogs this time around or flog us awake from our sleep. We were flogged and given marks the day we deflected and followed a dancing masquerade. She would definitely give the right punishment we deserved for staying out till night since we left for school in the morning. It was definitely too much to think of- a punishable offence only wayward children commit.

'Leave me alone. Shut up and just- show me the way home', she stopped halfway, fidgeting. She craned her eyes around in the dark and without asking again, she headed towards a route.

'Wait! It's not that way. Why not wait and listen to me first. I have an idea'.

'What idea? What else do you want to do?' she broke into tears.

'We are not lost. You don't need to cry. Come; let me hold your hands for safety reasons. We will soon be home'. I took her hand and off we went home. In all sincerity, I didn't desire to be home. I wished to sleep out there, in a free world of my own but for her. She needed their support to grow up, not me anymore.

'I saw the time when we came out. It was 9 o'clock. What time do you think it is now? I'm in soup!' she grabbed her head with her second hand, still crying

'Tchieu, you are crying because we are going home. Can't we use this opportunity to find Mma and remain with her? Nkuku will flog us like goats tonight. I can't bear the pain'. I slowed my pace as we approached our house. From afar, I caught the view of a little crowd gathering in our compound and heard the penetrating cry of Nkuku in their midst.

'Do you see what I mean? She has already gathered a crowd there for us. She is never peaceful'.

'You caused it. You took me with you and I don't have the gut to go home now. What do we do? Her spanking is terrible. She won't listen to Ntatemogholo's pleas this time around', she stamped her feet miserably, made to turn around.

'Except for you, I would run away from them'.

'Did you help me find them? Eh- my children. Are they kidnapped?' we both heard Nkuku's distressed cry in the distance.

'I saw them inside the theatre this afternoon', one of the onlookers spoke out.

'Take me there, please help me', we heard Nkuku still planning to find us that night. I was struck by pang of guilt and I made my mind up to take my sister home, then leave my resolution till another time. I would definitely leave and not return to that hut one day, I knew it. However, I didn't know when. I contemplated as I proceeded towards them, still holding my beloved sister- the one I loved the most of all my siblings. Maybe when that trouble was over, I thought, I would leave them for good.

'There they are. They have arrived. Nkuku, do you see them?' a man approached, grabbed our arms and dragged us into the compound. Thousands of questions surrounded us; though I answered only the one from Ntatemogholo.

'We were at the theatre', I dodged the slap from Nkuku. Tchieu took cover behind Ntatemogholo. Punishment was certain that night and we didn't escape it. Nkuku ordered one of our neighbors to tie us down like goats. We were flogged and brutalized that night by one of the retired soldiers in our neighborhood. Poor Tchieu cried all night. It didn't end there- we were driven to bed without dinner. As for me, I didn't feel anything next to remorse, didn't feel much pain or sense of correction since I was accustomed to flogging. Tchieu regretted following me and swore never to accompany me to break rules again.

That gave me no worry, since I had lot of accomplices outside, waiting eagerly to give me a free life. Little did they understand that I was different from the little and innocent grandson they carried home some time ago. I had metamorphosed into a young man, prepared to explore the mysteries of earning a better living, joining the fittest to survive at an early age. In as much as I eagerly anticipated the reality of my wondrous dream, I had to take my time with them and scheme that huge and bold step for the first time in my life, except I wasn't deprived.

Mma didn't bring my two other siblings as soon as she promised. They both joined us five months after, even though she had visited repeatedly before then. Was I really relieved seeing them? Yes, I was partly exhilarated being joined by my brother, not my sister of sixteen. My immediate brother, Azuel, was a direct opposite of me. Where he stayed before he returned to us, he wasn't given the slightest opportunity to misbehave like I did. Their guardians were much younger people with five of their children also living with them. It was out of their cruelty; they were denied education and made to look after the house and their children. They were their slaves, irrespective of the family ties between them.

I studied the two of them in only two days after they came. The first test was on Azuel when I invited him to join me to play snooker with certain friends in the neighborhood.

'*Umuqala*, have you washed all the plates we used to eat lunch?' he rather questioned as I pulled out my slippers. I peered around confusedly and he added, 'don't you wash after eating?'

'We don't wash immediately- until tomorrow morning, after gathering the plates together', I wore my slippers. He took two angry steps closer to me and removed my flip flop, one after the other.

'Go and wash now. It won't wait till tomorrow. Do you want flies to gather there or lizards to feed from the plate?' a flash of anger crept over me however; I had insufficient power to confront him. He was fourteen, four years more than my age. Instead, I pleaded.

'Please give back my slippers'.

'Not until you wash'.

'Why?' I demanded infuriated. We both had to define our position in the little hut. He just came and he was being the master.

'Why? You are asking why you should clean your own mess?'

'Our mess, not mine alone. Your plate is also there. Look, you are not here for me, so face your business', I added, pointing my warning finger at him. With that same finger, he pulled me closer, grabbed my hand, then dragged me to the stinking kitchen. I fought to break free and he pushed me on the plates. They all scattered, the leftovers of the traditional *Bogobe* my sister made stuck to the shirt I wore to impress my friends. I straightened up with a start and rushed towards him to get even. He pushed me and I landed on the ground.

'Come back here. *Ukubuya!* You think you are stubborn? Try me again. I will break your bone. Wash those plates or I will teach you some morals'. He insisted.

'What's going on here?' Lesedi, my sister, inquired, looking over his shoulders into the kitchen. She squeezed her nose, pinched it with her fingers irritably. He had blocked me there with his entire lanky structure.

'It's this naughty boy. He refuses to wash the plates and he was inviting me to join his stupid run-away friends'.

'Hmmn? Why worry yourself. It's the way they do here. *Angazi.* They hardly wash. I couldn't breathe in that room last night. I don't know why mother had to bring us here. I wish we could return home'.

'Everything has changed now. Get up and wash or I will kick you on those plates again'.

'You too, get up and wash the plates. Are you like this?'

'Like how? Are you guys here for me? Please mind your monkey business and leave me alone', I fired back at Lesedi.

'Our business?' they both burst out laughing, knocked heads together as I stood to clean up my shirt.

'Please tell us what business is ours here. Wash the plates! Where is Tchieu?' Lesedi walked away, leaving him to teach me a lesson. From that day, I understood his position and never saw him as a friend again.

He was a bully, a disciplined home rat, afraid to break rules. Hence, I avoided involving him in my ways. How did our grandparents see us or relate with us? It wasn't the same. He was more liked and appreciated. They sang the song of his praises around the house, liked to work with hardworking Lesedi. Within the four months they just arrived, everything changed, I also changed a little. All the chores they used to do for us were taken over by them and done to their insatiable tastes. Lesedi trekked a long distance to find water and filled it in all our buckets and Azuel followed Ntatemogholo to the farm. I think we lived better at the time because they both knew petty trading. They were industrious and we lived better. I felt useless.

While our family expanded, Mma continued visiting until when we didn't see her. Nkuku sent Lesedi to find her in her house to clear the dust of doubt. And the unexpected happened.

'Mma- what happened to you?' Lesedi inquired the moment she entered my father's house and saw her in a critically bad condition-her leg heavily bandaged around a decaying wound. Her mouth hanged open for a while before she finally joined my eldest sister, Mpho, on the mat, near the wound. Mma broke into a dreary smile, looking at her vaguely. She was the only person she was not expecting to see on that hot Sunday, after she returned from the hospital, where her leg was being treated.

'How are you doing? I knew you would come looking for me. I discussed you with your sister last night. Mpho, didn't I?' In response, she merely nodded, didn't utter a word. She fixed her wondrous eyes on Lesedi as she fondled the leg surprisingly. And again, she repeated the question, 'Mma, what happened to your leg?' She looked from Mpho to her and gave a long vague smile.

'It's a long story that I don't even know where to begin from but to cut it short, I was pushed on a nail in a broken furniture'.

'Oh my God! By who?' Lesedi clasped her hands above her head in utmost surprise, her mouth still opened.

'By your two big sisters while they were fighting three months ago. And I was about visiting Nkuku when it happened', she broke into tears and Lesedi joined her in deep sympathy. Mpho didn't cry, knowing she was responsible for it. She rose from her seat and entered her room rudely. Before Lesedi's arrival, she had begged her not to expose her to anyone anymore. She wanted the secret concealed forever but Mma wouldn't hide such a big secret from Lesedi, one of them.

'Mma, sorry ma', she drew closer to her. She wished she had the aptitude to heal her instantly, even so there was none. She was all she had –her father, mother and confidant. Her all –in- one. Maybe she meant nothing to them. She wondered as she followed Mpho into her room with a bad eye. The loud bang on the door returned her attention to her suffering mother. She gripped the leg and squinted in pain. And Lesedi switched to the other side of the mat she sat on to look closely at the wound.

'It's not bleeding anymore', she searched for any trace of blood but there was none.

'No, it's not. I had a fractured bone inside, that's why it's swollen. What have I not done to remedy this problem? I've sold all my stock to raise money to pay the hospital and it's still not enough'. She drew out a handkerchief and blew her nose inside it.

'Oh my God, we have no one. What are we going to do now? This is so serious', she examined the wound again. And as she was about to ask about Nkuku, there came a knock on the door.

'Are you expecting someone?' Lesedi rose to peep through a little window next to the door.

'People visit to sympathize with me or assist in one way or another. Open up- we are safe'.

Lesedi followed her instruction. She walked briskly and flung the door open. A plump woman stood in front of her, carrying a small polythene bag in her hand. The moment Mma recognized her; she motioned to the position adjacent her on the mat.

'How do you feel today?' the woman squatted then sat stretching her legs casually, smiling from ear to ear.

'Itumeleng- it's still the same feeling. I'm not enjoying the leg'.

'I'm coming from Tumelo's villa', she stole a glance at Lesedi then back to Mma. She immediately understood her countenance. She smiled softly then signaled to her to carry on.

'You don't know her? She's my daughter- one of my children. Go on, I'm listening to you'. Lesedi didn't bother to join them on the mat after seeing her guest. She wasn't taught to be nosy where she lived before returning home. She remained in the room on a different wooden chair positioned near the back door, pretending her attention wasn't there. But in all sincerity, she was all ears. What precisely did she have to say? She feared negativity as she listened. Everyone knew Tumelo was a soothsayer.

'Please, pay attention to all I have to tell you. Tumelo, in his consultation with the oracle, discovered that your problem is from your brother-in-law who you refused to marry after your husband's death. Do you understand?' Itumeleng held her ears seriously, depicting the gravity of her predicament. She watched her reaction for a moment and continued her explanation when she hadn't defeated her shock.

'According to him, he was responsible for the demise of your husband so he could have you as his second wife but you refused when he proposed to you again, recently'.

'Oh God! Humans are wicked. Is that why he doesn't want me to walk and fend for my children again?' she threw her mouth open again.

'Exactly what he said', she crossed her legs and looked at her earnestly. Mma pulled herself together. She remembered what she learnt in her childhood that, when there's a will there's always a way. A problem discovered is on its route to extermination. She also used the opportunity to discuss the solution with her friend.

'Did he actually propose to you again after your husband's burial?' Itumeleng cut into her wandering thought.

'Yes- he did and I told him it wasn't possible. Their family called a meeting and asked if I wanted to marry again and I refused. Not him- not anybody else. I already vowed even before I met my husband that I would marry or be with only the first man in my life'.

'Humans are wicked like you said. Is it by force to marry his brother's wife?'

'Well, the tree cutter suffers the pain of bringing down a tree. The tree will surely grow back again, shrouded by fresh leaves', she concluded boldly and drove at solution. Itumelang nodded in agreement.

'What did he say I should do now? The wicked mustn't overcome'.

'How is that possible? He said you should visit him and he will return the wound to the sender. That's the solution'.

'Itumeleng! Thank you and God will be with you too. The wicked shall have his reward right here on earth'.

'Surely'.

Lesedi drew a long exasperated breath after listening to all their discussion. She had learnt, yet another lesson from life that, a sibling can be more dangerous than strangers. That humans don't care if you grieve from a problem, when they pursue an interest inconsiderately. What a wicked world! She sighed again and drew Mma's attention this time. She remembered she had been there – that she had to return before Nkuku began to worry about her.

'Lesedi, you have to leave now. I will give you the little money I have here to give to my mother. Tell her everything you saw here and – explain everything you heard to her', she brought out a purse from under her pillow and gave some money, only enough to feed us in two days. She wasn't happy when she took it, after all the complaint she heard from Nkuku when she sent her on the journey. But what mattered was her well-being. She wouldn't fend for anyone when she was spiritually tied down like a chicken by a mindless uncle.

'Yes- mother. Take good care of yourself', she began to cry as she looked for her second shoe. And she did so for two irrefutable reasons: one, Nkuku had no means to raise all the four of us with her and two, for her mother's critical state. However, she had to return home that same day to divulge the sad news to Nkuku, regardless of its effect on her or any of us.

'Take good care of yourself. I would have added some money to that for her but I spent a lot on this charm Tumelo asked me to prepare for you', Itumelang pointed at the polythene bag she brought.

'Don't worry- she will be fine'. Mma wished to see her off but couldn't move or stand on the legs. She bade her farewell, still in the same position, her eyes loaded with depressing feelings.

By the time Lesedi arrived home, it was late. We all gathered around our palm oil lamp, digesting the saddening news she returned with. Every one of us was affected. To us, it seemed the only tree that bore the fruit we consumed had fallen. Without those legs she nursed, no more food or survival, except it healed prayerfully or spiritually as Itumelang assured her. Although we had a petty trade we were profiting from, once in a while, but it was never enough to feed all the six of us. Sometimes, we would hawk round the whole community and return with nothing. The little gain we realized from our merchandise was not sufficient to feed us for two days. So, the business was totally out of it.

'Humph- I'm in trouble. A very big trouble. How will I survive with four children?' Nkuku stamped her feet bitterly. She had given each one of us corn meal with the unripe baby chicken she killed the previous day. It was yet not enough when she gave up her share to please us. She gave all her remaining money to Lesedi to commute and find Mma when she was leaving in the morning. She had nothing left to feed anyone. She dropped her head in a melancholic mood.

'Don't worry; I will move some corn to the market to find buyers tomorrow. We will manage all we have to survive and God will heal her too', Ntatemogholo chipped in, feeling deeply concerned for his wife. She was a brave and hardworking woman. So brave that when he had no job, she stood by him for almost six years. They both came to a decision that, he should return to the farm when there was no job for him.

'Don't worry-my dear. You are too old to drag corn into a market with no ready buyer. I will visit my brother tomorrow morning. He's rich- he should be able to assist'. Nkuku lifted her old and wrinkled arms to the sky then began to pray. Prayer was what we needed for support. Yes- she knew what she was doing; she knew how tough her rich brother could be. He was a mean and stingy sibling, caring only for his family. Whether someone is hungry or not was never his concern as long as he satisfied his family. I've witnessed her plead with him on several occasion she needed his support. He always had a concocted excuse to give for his rigidity. But in that situation, she had no one to turn to except him.

That night, we all went to sleep without food. I began to imagine all I could do to safe myself from the twinge of hunger. It was a saddening encounter as I rolled from edge to edge on my mat, holding my tummy against the attack of starvation. Sleep eluded me in favour of my body needs, my mouth ran dry and I was left with no stamina to have a sound sleep. It was indeed an empty night-time for me. I laid supine, focused on our thatched ceiling. A spec of the sky glistened in my sight, peeked at me and saw me stirring. It turned my only witness to the ferocious feeling but it didn't last out. The climate took charge, wiped off all the sparkles in the sky and lightning appeared. Rain! It was about to rain. I sat up absently, feebly. What was I to do? Wake them all up and announced the coming of the disquieting rain or just ignore it and oblige myself to sleep? The later would be worse, reflecting what we suffered three weeks ago. The palm fronds in our roof was vandalized and taken away by a wicked wind. We lost; mostly part of the ones it snatched away but we sped after it to recover, at least, a tattered trampoline- the topmost part. And it was too late. Azuel and I went hunting for fresh fronds in the forest nearby and that was how we fixed it almost imperfectly, without the trampoline that served as a roof. Since then, rain became a burglar in our little home. It sneaked through the open parts and poured in hysterically.

Again, I heard a terribly loud noise from the thunder; saw the sudden flash of lightning. I shut my eyes and blocked my ears miserably. I had calculated the arrival of the rain afterwards. I drew closer to Tchieu. Only fifteen minutes after, I felt the unfriendly drops of rain on my knickers and my buttocks. It was our troubled moment again. I didn't hesitate to spring to my feet and wake my big sister from her deep sleep. I kept wondering how she managed to sleep that deep without any food in her tummy.

'What is it?' she asked, looking around the dark room, a little frown on her face. I recognized that gesture at once. I had woken her to kill a creeping cockroach near my mat the previous night. This time, she needed a good reason to be disturbed from a troubled sleep. And before I uttered a word, a drop of rain fell on her temple, snaked down her bare shoulder.

'Did you see that? The room is leaking; we will soon be swept to our feet'. I explained our fate to her and as if confused, she peered up at the partly opened ceiling then tapped my brother awake. He wasn't, at all, asleep. He had stayed awake all through the night, also feeling hungry and watching my reactions at the onset of the dilemma.

'There's nothing we can do about it until the rain stops. The whole house may collapse if we climb up there now', he whispered to us but Nkuku was awake. Only they had beds inside the room, although our august visitor wasn't biased in sharing its fountain of blessing. She was woken with some drops on her forehead that night. In the midst of our shocking unrest, no one wanted to be disturbed- no one was prepared to fix the problem.

'There should be something you can do about it. You can't leave it leaking and messing up our stuff like this'. She rose to her feet and watched Ntatemogholo climb a stool within the house. He reached for some opened fronds within with his spidery arms, then attempted to put them together. A lot of water poured on his face, a thatch fragmented and water splattered on Tchieu's belly. She woke up confused. I smiled secretly. Rain drummed inside the hut.

'Come down from there. You are too old to do this. Let these boys go up there and do something', Nkuku persuaded impatiently. I had the worst sad face of them all. Why did she send us to do that? No food in the tummy to strengthen me for such a task. How possible? I looked away sadly.

'What are you still standing and doing there? Go and get the ladder from the backyard and go up there!' Nkuku instructed harshly. My brother neither argued nor said a word. He merely walked to the backyard to find the ladder inside the rain. I calculated, within myself, as I followed him unwillingly, that there had to be a way. My life shouldn't be continuously spent in penury. The wards of the rich and average people around us had only one head like me; I should enjoy a good life like them. Why do I have to be subjected to suffering while they enjoyed all the time of their lives? If all questions are answered or resolved, only one remained a mystery to me. When would it all be over? When would I sing a new song?

Mma's leg had yet not healed despite all her efforts. Both Nkuku and Ntatemogholo had visited her when she didn't show up after two months. They returned with more saddening news that it had swollen and puss were emitting from the spot. What a wicked life! My uncle was, indeed, responsible for the problem as confirmed when he was visited in his home, only four streets away from her. According to him, the solution would be to marry him and be his third wife. Nonetheless, Mma's unchanging refusal maddened him more.

'How am I going to raise children without money now? Tell me. Why did he do that to a mother of nine? Does he have a human heart?' Nkuku lamented to her friend that visited on a dry Sunday morning. I was the only person at home with her. Others have followed Ntatemogholo to the mosque for a festival. At least, that would give them a chance to get some food to eat. What I had on my mind was far more fruitful than an ordinary *Sara* as it was tagged. I wanted more than feeding intermittently, wanted survival. I didn't want someone to offer me fish but to catch the fish myself. Young as I was, I believed I could fend for myself and my siblings- possibly everybody. My friends were also in the street, making ends meet. Some engaged in pushing trucks for traders in the market or carrying their stocks to different locations for them while others call passengers into commercial vehicles. However they made the street their homes and never had to return home again for the fear of being caught and controlled by their parents or guardians. A responsible parent wouldn't allow his child to turn a street urchin. But should they watch the child starve slowly to death? Yes, some kids died of starvation at the time I was growing up and they were eventually shielded in the ground with all their glories. Whatever purpose they had in life was already fulfilled- to join a wretched family and be killed with hunger. Such was never my ambition. I wanted much more from life, albeit I was deprived by the circumstances. Even though I wasn't really prepared for my adventure, Mma had shown me the path to follow. She had shown, by all indication, that she couldn't fend for me anymore, that I should become an adult. What more? No father to run around and mother's leg was on break. And without the fingers, the head will be a spoon.

'Kenosi! Kenosi!!' I heard Nkuku's voice as I sneaked through the back door with my little back pack, containing just my essential needs: a chewing stick to clean my teeth, my mother's wrapper to protect me from cold and mosquitoes, two shirts and a pair of knickers. I hastened up, cutting through a huge tree and looking over my shoulder in surveillance. They mustn't discover my hideout if I was out there to make it. I felt the breeze of freedom rubbing my face, although I wasn't conscious of my fate in the street. But I believed in miracle and God's protection over me. I was prepared to combat poverty and kick it out of my life forever.

On my first night, I had nowhere to sleep. My peer that introduced me to the job followed a bus till 10pm. I did a similar job on the same day, calling passengers heading to different destinations, even though it wasn't as easy as I thought. There wasn't a space for me to sit- I had to hang on the moving vehicle to collect fares from commuters. Some people looked down on me, some insulted me. A woman asked why I was in the street at that age. But I didn't mind any of them. What mattered was what chased me out of my guardians' embrace. I needed survival; not their opinion. I made some money enough to feed my family for two days and smiled. As long as I benefitted from my pain, nothing else counted.

My mouth dropped open in utmost surprise when I saw hundreds of children of my age, waiting to sleep under a concrete beam bridge, where I also hoped to rest my head. They swarmed around noisily, gabbing about the events of the day. Being my first time out, I clutched my bag to my chest then sat silently beside a boy that appeared quiet in the group. He possibly, should be engrossed with the thought of his lifestyle or he was tired. I looked from face to face before tapping him for some vital enquiries.

'Hello, I am Kenosi', I stretched out a hand for a friendly shake but he didn't take it. He sized me up and sighed. With that, I concluded there was no room for introduction. I went ahead with my questions.

'When are we allowed to go to sleep here and how do we get a position to lay our heads?'

'Hmm', he sighed again then cleared his throat before he responded. 'Not until all the vehicles are parked- possibly by midnight. No position, first come, first served', he paid attention to a boy discussing his encounter with an old woman that refused to pay her fare. My mind drifted to Nkuku. She hadn't seen me all through the day and I knew she must have searched high and low for me worriedly, from the time she called me, and I didn't answer.

'I think that same woman came finding a little boy called Kenosi this afternoon. She had no money and she boarded a bus. Old witch!' the boy said rudely and my eyes darkened with rage. He was obviously discussing my grandma.

'You should have helped her. I always help old people while I'm working. Not all of them are fortunate'.

'If I was fortunate, would I be in the street. Forget about her'.

I drew a long breath, then looked back at the almost empty road. Should I go back? I contemplated in indisputable confusion, fixing my shimmering eyes on the road. Vehicle lights beamed on my little and troubled face, my shadow one of the very many that glued to a hidden wall, waiting to enjoy the night. If sincerely Nkuku was there to find me, then she wouldn't return there again, since I wasn't there the first time. Good. I heaved a sigh of relief as I struggled to belong there once and for all.

Finally, at midnight, we all took positions under a very quiet and lonely bridge, draping our whole bodies with our wrappers. We laid straight like canned fish, encaged with different thoughts. I didn't know who my neighbours were, had never seen them before but I knew we had one thing in common- fleeing for survival. It wasn't long when I drifted into a deep sleep, tiredly. My preoccupied mind led me into a seemingly real dream. I saw Nkuku weeping for help, holding up a lantern and peering into our faces one by one, under the bridge. I struggled out of the dream and blinked awake forcefully. Sleep evaded me and my conscience surfaced. Why was I there? Why didn't I return home and get punished for spending a whole day away from home then the whole matter would be forgotten? What would my mother feel when she got the bad news? My good conscience set in strongly, rebelliously but my hardened conscience superseded it irrefutably. I listened to the stronger one, giving me more convincing reasons I should be there and forget my family.

In the morning, I had no water to wash but I was shortly introduced to a public bathroom where everyone washes in the morning before embarking on a daily job. By the time I arrived there, there was a rather too long queue, each person with his bucket of water and towel.

I was the twenty fifth in turn to use the bathroom. For a moment, I looked down at myself, contemplating staying without a bath. I was undeniably dirty and smelly, even had a blotch of oil from the vehicle we fixed the previous day on my shirt. Nevertheless, we used to make more money in the early hour when workers were hastening to work; I didn't want to miss that for a bath I could take another time in the day. Without a second thought, I dropped the bucket aside and hassled towards the bus station to resume my daily duty.

I took the next bus, busily running around, calling and finding passengers to occupy it in the shortest time possible. I almost lost my voice on my first trial but that didn't mar my efforts to perform wonderfully. Much of my techniques helped me fill the vehicle quickly. I begged for consideration, if possible, at some point. I was ready to work, full of life. And like that, we plied the same route twenty five times before I closed at 5pm, looking dirtier than before. I made double of the money I realized the first time. My hands trembled as I settled to count everything- note after note, very delighted that my dream was finally coming true. I wrapped them together then secured an account with a thrift collector operating in the axis. Unlike before when I would have to manage a plate of food with Tchieu, I could buy as much meal as I wanted or wear the type of cloth I liked. I also had my freedom to stay out for as long as I wanted or visit anywhere. I had all the freedom I wanted in my childhood. I became a fugitive street kid as we were popularly called and looked down upon. Good kids stay at home under the watchful eyes of their parents or guardians. Kids like us do not.

Two weeks after I did the job, I was introduced to truck pushing inside the market. Did I enjoy it like transportation? Not really, because it was tougher for me and there were lot of hoodlums involved in the occupation. Hoodlums in their forties, the type I couldn't drag a job with or confront for cheating me. Considering that the stress was worthwhile; I had no choice than to do it whenever I had no bus to follow. And I had to survive out there.

This kind of work was different from my previous job where I merely called the commuters' attention to a bus. In this, I usually carried loads for marketers from inside the market to their destination or vice versa. Whenever there was a job, we all gathered and dragged the load amongst ourselves-about twelve of us sometimes on top of a basket of tomatoes. I had not enough strength to compete with my rivals. I merely stepped aside for my luck to find me, wait for my customers to approach me.

From time to time, I was always approached by women that took pity on me, perhaps considering that I shouldn't be in such a pitiable condition in my young age. The same reason I was stopped and questioned by one of the marketers on a busy market day.

'Why are you doing this kind of work? And where are your parents?', she dropped her basket of fish I was to lift to the garage for her, then looked seriously at me for a good reason I subjected myself to that lifestyle.

'No one sent me to do this. I just want to help myself to live better', I answered smiling.

'All alone? Unbelievable. Where are your parents?'

'I lost my dad and my mum had a wound that prevented her from working'.

'That's serious. Sorry about that. But this is not good for a child like you. Someone should be out here fending for you', she corrected my wrong insinuation, dipping her hand in her purse. She brought out some money and gave it to me. 'Take this. It can feed you for two days but I advise you to return home and discuss this with someone close to you. I know you are out here on your own like the other kids I've been seeing around. Listen to me. This doesn't give you any respect'.

I collected the money slowly, sadly. She had said all I should know about my mindless act, nonetheless I didn't care. I felt better outside than inside a hut without food.

'You must return home', she added as she looked around for someone else to carry her stock for her. I nodded feebly then returned to my work, less concerned about her advice.

She had to mind her business even though I appreciated her support and counsel.

After that day, I received much of such counsel from the people I worked for and subsequently got tired of the job. I gave up on that and returned to my previous work. It was my third week away from home, with my new unknown family. We all knew our names, shared thoughts and problems leading us there but felt less concerned about our roots. Wherever I came from was no one's affair as I didn't care about them too. I lived my life the way I wanted and never told anyone about my family, especially Nkuku.

When it was precisely a month I began to live there, Nkuku returned to the spot to find me again. She was holding up our old lantern and accompanied by four strong men, also holding a bright torch each to peer at the faces of all young dwellers. They were strong enough to lift me home if peradventure I was found there. Nkuku's voice drew my attention from the sixth row away. I sneaked a look at them from under my cover and immediately crept back inside like a snail in its shell. My heart raced and thudded in my chest, my body trembled all over with fear. Was I about to be caught? Were those men going to carry me back home? I thought of all that might befall me if they successfully laid their insistent hands on me. It would be a fate worse than death. My neighbor felt my reaction and whispered to me.

'Are they here for you? Kenosi, are they your people?' At that point, I realized I had to say the truth to save myself from trouble. I would use him to cover up if he knew the truth.

'Yes- that is my grandma. I used to live with her. She is very wicked and-'

'Don't worry; they won't take you away from here. You are safe with us', he assured me quietly. How he was going to do it, with all those strong men involved was unclear to me, however I hid where I was, waiting for them to get to me. If I stood up to run, I would be caught.

'I have been here before and they told me they don't know him. Recently, my neighbor told me she saw him lifting stocks in a market- that this is where he lives. What kind of boy is this? Does he want to kill me?' Nkuku explained to the leader of the men that followed her and he drew a long breath after giving attention

'Nkuku- don't worry. We will look from face to face tonight. Tabansi-', he called one of the men with him to strategize how to fish me out from the numerous kids. Little did they understand that rules apply everywhere, anywhere regardless of who made them.

That night, they barged in on us without permission from our manager, who we submitted to and took orders from every day. He caught a glimpse of them from afar but waited to see which way the wind blew. Knowing that they were there for his boys, Nyang sprang to his feet and confronted them for infringing on his illegal rights.

'Old woman, what is it? What do you want from my boys?' he approached Nkuku who he noticed was responsible for the search.

'Good evening sir- I'm finding my grandson, Kenosi. He's been away for one month now and –I was told he is here', she explicated persuasively, eyes wandering from face to face, on the ground for me. But mine was covered securely away from her prying eyes. Only the nosy one raised their faces to listen to her, looked at her mockingly. We were all in the same situation. Different families visit there to find their kids day in- day out. We were incorrigible fugitives.

'I won't allow you to find any kid this night. Come in the day so we can see your faces', he ordered. But they didn't agree with him.

'I don't understand what you mean. What law restricted us from finding our boy that left home and we suspect that he is here?' Tabansi asked, flashing the torch on his face. He turned away from the strong stream of light irritably. Five more men living in our park also joined them in support of Nyang. We had the adult and children sections under the bridge. There were about fifty five male adults living in their section. And we had no female anywhere.

'You can't touch any of these kids because we've lost most of them to the ritualists, lying and touching their heads with demonic powers. They are under our care until they are big enough to look after themselves', Nyang concluded insistently. He just took some cannabis with his boys before their arrival and he was high-so high he could kill someone. Right under the cover, I prayed that my grandma walk away with the men. He was the wrong person they should quarrel with. He was insane.

'Well- it's okay, Tabansi. He can help us bring out the boy by himself. He must return home with me tonight. His mother is worried about him', Nkuku pleaded, still looking at the opened faces with her lantern.

'Don't look at anyone here again. Don't bewitch anyone. Come back tomorrow morning', Nyang asserted, under the influence of his addiction.

'Nkuku- let's return home and get back here tomorrow', one of her men held her arm mildly to take her away from the crazy scene. No old person goes out or visits such a place except for my sake. I began to pity her, considered following them. But taking into account my castigation, I could not.

'Are you sure he won't run again? Hah!' she lamented then decided to leave a message for me, knowing quite alright that I was there.

'Kenosi- Kenosi-return home. If you're there and you're listening to me, return home. I won't beat you for running; I will do everything you want- to make you stay. We love you-I love you. I can hand you over to your mother if that's what you want'. She broke into tears and continued. 'You are really punishing me. I can't sleep – I can't eat – I think of how you survive out here all the time. You are too young to live for yourself. Please stop running away from your future, don't break the foundation we are laying for you. I am old now. I am not training you to look after me tomorrow because I am very old now. It is for your own tomorrow. Return home- return home', she walked away quietly, followed by her aides. She said all she should and did all she could, although she wasn't pleased that she had to leave. She desired to sleep there and wait to see me arise in the morning and pay my usual homage to her principles.

After her departure, Nyang took a few steps and pulled me out of the group, my bed cover dragging along with me. Although half drunk, he understood all that transpired. He knew Nkuku was finding me and understood what led me to them. He himself absconded from his family when he was just twelve. According to him, he was taken home almost six times and he kept absconding until he was left alone and forgotten. Now, at thirty two, he still lived that way and was determined never to return to his folks or be controlled by anyone. He had a lot of encounters but he survived. He was, indeed, a survivor of a harsh weather, severe cold in the open we called home, hunger, threat to life, insecurity, and death itself. What had he not encountered outside his home? Maybe the return of his late grandma. By then, all that meant nothing to him or his type in the group.

'Look at me very well. I am a man of justice. I always listen to both sides of a story before drawing a conclusion and taking a decision', he peered into my eyes sternly, belched loudly. The gas of his alcoholic breath infiltrated my head, blurred my vision. I had a lungful of his drunkenness. He used one ruffled but strong arm to pull me closer as I nodded, then persisted.

'You have heard my story several times and you know for how long I've been out here. I regretted everything I did. I am saying the truth now but it's too late to return home. I can't go home because they won't accept me again. I have transformed myself into the kind of child nobody will welcome in my family. Don't become me', he hit his chest vigorously. He paused for a while, gathered a whole pack of phlegm from his throat and spat it aside, not too far from where I stood timidly. I swallowed irritably, feeling the same movement in my throat and the urge to do so, but I controlled it. My face fell in shame when I turned to meet the steady gaze of five of his mates. One of them jumped down from the rim he sat on and bolstered his opinions.

'The old woman needs you back. She won't stop coming until you return. She might be here with an officer next time and we don't like that. Return to her tomorrow morning'.

Of all the men there, only Ochen wanted to listen to me. He supposed I was pushed into their midst for one cogent reason he wanted to know. In his case, his step- mother pushed him away from his father after the demise of his biological mother, when he was fifteen. He had lived there for twelve years and nobody cared to find him as he didn't care to return home.

'What brought you here?' he asked tiredly. He had spent the whole day driving a hired bus around to find commuters.

'I had no food to eat. *Ngilanibile*. I was always hungry', I explained, almost crying. I forced the tears back, wrapped the cover around my body. I wanted to drive the unseen but diligent mosquitoes nesting on my legs but could not. I had to comport myself in front of our foster fathers under the bridge. I had watched them flogging my mates for committing any form of crime or being rude to them. We all had to obey them or leave the scene.

'Did you leave home just because of food?' Nyang inquired full of surprise. Lot of the kids he brought there by himself fled for safety from frequent maltreatment or molestation; not usually for food case.

'Well, a kid called Okal joined us here six weeks ago because of hunger so –it is a common reason to leave home. I left because of food. My step mum didn't care if I ate anything. The witch flogged me upon my empty tummy. This is my opinion'. They all fell silent. All heads turned towards Ochen for a laudable suggestion. He was the most thoughtful and they respected him for that.

'Leave the boy alone. Let him decide to return by himself or he will turn fugitive in another place. You know there are thousands of places like this in the country. Let him be, let him eat'.

'That's his cup of tea. I made a little profit today. Are people not travelling to Mokolodi again? I drove emptily all through the day and – I'm really tired now', the least concerned of them all yawned, interrupted their discussion. I was left standing alone, encaged in my own thoughts about my life while they switched from topic to topic noisily. I stared back at our side of the venue and saw some of my mates still awake and discussing my issue. It was all about me that night but I didn't care. It will last for only one night and it would be another child's turn the next night. There wasn't a space to sit there and talk in the day when the occupants returned. That space was a vehicle park in the day and our bedroom at night. Without notifying any of them, I sneaked back to my position quietly, slipped under my cover and shut my eyes, awaiting a deep sleep. My eyes were loaded, had since been battling with sleep and tiredness. Whatever would be would be, no matter what Nkuku did. Ochen had spoken my mind- I would rather elope to another garage than follow her home to begin a new phase of starvation. Little did she understand about the plan I had for my mother. The thrift collector had saved some money for me. Already, I had money enough to feed my family for two months but I intended to give all to her. I would send someone home to her with all the money, then stayed back to find more money.

The weather was too cold, my head hurt badly from wakefulness and fatigue. It wasn't long when I fell asleep on my frayed carton. I travelled back home with big suitcases, encasing gifts for everyone, as rich people do. The whole street was empty, our hut had fallen. I met only Tchieu sitting in front of two fresh graves and weeping bitterly. I rushed to her and began to console her then I woke with the advent of a heavy rain.

'Hah- let's move to that edge', suggested Oba, one of my very close friends in the group. Rain had never met me there before, so I looked around vaguely. I fled to the same direction with them, though we all had to stand till daybreak. Under the bridge is not a home, it was a wide opening, allowing the influx of all sort of weather. As we stood drenched like a wet chicken, our teeth clattered and we shivered in the cold.

Was there a need to regret? I supposed no, owing to my aim- my crucial aim. I grabbed the tip of my knickers and squeezed the water out then wiped my face with my wet shirt. After adjusting myself, trying to adapt to my new condition of living, I drew a long breath and began to reflect on my recent dream. It was the second time I had that dream after I began to live there. What was it all about? Were they okay? I wondered concernedly. But be that as it may, I had to fulfill my mission before returning to them or finding a way to speak to Tchieu. I knew how I could sneak into her school and speak to her.

I didn't work on the next day because I noticed I wasn't feeling well. I had to rest somewhere before setting out to find my sister. Out of the money I made the previous day, I kept some in my pocket. I joined my Muslim brothers to say the Zubhi prayer at 7:00am, in a different mosque my folks wouldn't dream of attending. I had to hide till I returned to my hideout. I knew Nkuku wouldn't catch me, even if she returned there in the day as directed by our leaders.

'*Salam alaykum*', a fellow worshipper greeted and my heart flipped. I lowered my cap then responded '*wa alaykum salam*'.

The prayer ended in thirty minutes and the congregation dispersed. I seized the opportunity to have a sound sleep I was deprived of the previous night. It wasn't for long. It lasted for another three hours when I felt the compulsion to use the restroom. When I was done, I embarked on my journey to Tchieu's school, my school.

It was a long trek to my destination. As I cut through an avenue into a wide junction, noises of children reading the English alphabets aloud in a nursery school pervaded the environment. The structure of the school wasn't that protective, so I could see their little heads through their wooden classroom windows. The break just ended and their teachers were busy rounding up with them before the closing time.

God knows how much I hated school: that early morning preparation, flogging for lateness coupled with yelling from our teachers, obligation to read and write even though it was complicated, all made me sick. I always looked forward to the break and closing time and felt better on week-ends and holidays. I was often a victim of castigation: at home and in school.

I can't forget the day Nkuku reported me to my teacher and I was stripped and flogged before my classmates.

I was downgraded to two classes backward for knowing nothing. A time came when I totally disagreed with my teachers' conviction that I was dull. What they meant by that, I didn't understand. Would a dull person do all the things I was doing to survive? Or be as calculative as I am? They just had to accept their fate as failed teachers. Yes, failed teachers propagating failed students. As they had competent and efficient workers in their midst, so we also have children of different capabilities and personalities.

I stopped beside a tree, the same spot I waited for Tchieu on the day I took her to the cinema. I wasn't prepared to answer questions from my teachers or get caught by someone. Who knows if Nkuku had set me up? I decided to wait for the next twenty five minutes the school would close. I stood, staring down at the stagnant water from the heavy downpour. My reflection looked imperfect in it; it's what I had wanted to see. I hadn't seen my image in the past days I left home. I noticed I had changed: my face looked unkempt, my hair bushy and unappealing and my physique the rugged posture of a street boy. The Insects and harsh weather I was frequently exposed to had transformed my skin. I had really changed.

'Kenosi! Kenosi!! Where have you been? Kenosi, we have been finding you. Where have you been?' Tchieu approached me speedily, laughing energetically. She grabbed my shoulders and shook me playfully. Her classmates stopped by to ask questions.

'Hah- Kenosi, where have you been?' I ignored all their questions, grabbed my sister's arm and drew her to a spot for enquiries. She followed quietly, observing my changed look in mystery.

'Where have you been?' she asked again, removing the leaf that dropped on my cap while I stood under a tree. She looked from my unpleasant look to my filthy wears. What would I say? That I travelled to somewhere or relocated? I stood, contemplating what to say.

'Kenosi', she demanded.

'I am working somewhere to get some money to bring back home'.

'Work? Money? I don't understand you', she rolled her eyes confusedly. How would she understand what I meant? That I was struggling at my age to earn a good living? I cleared my throat and tried to explicate it better.

'Tchieu- you know how tough it had been for us to, at least, feed twice in a day. I left home to work and make money to help my family'. She burst out laughing at my stupidity. Was I for real? What made me think I was grown enough to feed my family? But I asked her only one question that convinced her that I had to leave.

'I beg your pardon? What do you mean? Of course I'm satisfied with whatever I'm given by my grandparents. I'm still a child living under the watchful eyes of my guardians. Take a look at yourself, you have really changed. Can't you see? You've not been in school for a while now. Two of our teachers told Nkuku that they saw you in the midst of hoodlums in a market while our neighbor said she saw you calling commuters into a vehicle. Kobena, this is quite unfair. Let's go home. Come along with me', she grabbed my hand and began to drag me along, towards the way home. However, I wasn't prepared to leave, not when I was already ingrained in the system, not when I had a say and I've suffered to build a position for myself. Not until I had enough money to heal my mother. I took my hands back from her, stood firmly where I was and rather asked her, 'how is my mother doing?'

'Hmmn- she's feeling better. She finally met an herbalist that's closing up the wound with voodoo. You know it's an evil wound. Kenosi, let's go home. I know you're scared of Nkuku but she promised everyone she won't beat you when you return', she pleaded relentlessly.

'I know. I'm just not ready to return home. How is Ntatemogholo? Is he doing fine too?' I gathered myself together and focused on my purpose of visit. I wasn't there to be led home.

'He has been very sick. Some attributed that to your absence too', she stopped smiling at the moment, wore a serious look.

'What happened to him?'

'Nkuku said its old age sickness; he has no money to call a doctor to examine him. His eyes are always close like that- he doesn't talk anymore', she looked away sadly. I instantly understood the severity of his ailment. Tchieu doesn't exaggerate, she expresses occurrences as they are-no blue is painted black. Grandpa was really sick.

'Kenosi', she drew my lost attention back to the scene.

'Yes? I was thinking of what can be done to get him back on his feet'.

'I don't know oh. Azuel and Lesedi have left. They complained of hunger every day and Nkuku decided that they should return home. She had no money to feed them. I am the only one with her now, and we treat Ntatemogholo every day. We are so sad', she wiped the tears in her eyes. And I felt sorry, envisioning what she was going through alone. I wished I could be her companion in the depressing situation but I had a lot on my mind.

'Don't worry- I will soon return to- no- I'm returning to Mma soon. I will join the rest of my siblings there', I opened up my mind. I didn't intend to return to them, no matter what.

'Why? I told you she won't beat you. She has forgiven you. I can't be the only one there. Let's go', she persuaded me once more. I gathered all I wanted to know and I was set to go. I dipped my hands in my pocket and brought out the money I kept away for her. She looked at me weirdly then broke into a teasing smile.

'You are really with money. Where did you get this much from?'

'I told you I'm working. This is from the money I made yesterday; I didn't work today because I had to see you'.

'I don't believe you. I don't want your money'.

'You have to take it and use it for what you need mostly', I coaxed her, tucking the note in her hands. She refused. Nkuku had disciplined her beyond disruption. She left me with the money then walked away slowly, pausing intermittently and turning back to observe my mood. I remained at the same spot obstinately.

'Kenosi, let's go home. *Woza nami!*' she waited a distance away from me and I still did not budge. I clutched the note in my hand and I waved back at her. Her motionless body was visited by a busy air, brushing and engulfing her whole being. She swirled around, then walked home briskly. At that point, I went another direction- a strange path- as the black sheep of the family. My ways were diverse, my judgments were strange, and my drives were zealous and challenging. I was evidently absurd.

It is true that every enjoyable aspect of life has its bad side no one can escape, irrespective of who you are. As laudable as luxury is, it has its shortcomings.

I once saw a luxurious and new model car and admired it wholeheartedly, wishing it was mine. Was I covetous at my young age? No, every child likes a stunning stuff, wants a good life. We like to identify with rich parents that give us all life necessities - all we need to attain success and happiness in life. That was the reason I admired the car all the time I saw its owner and his children in it. As beautiful as the vehicle was, it took the wrong turn one day and rendered the owner paralyzed in a fatal accident. He had to utilize a wheel chair for the rest of his life. That was the bad side of his lovely, exclusive car. Another instance I witnessed in the street was about a man who married a beautiful lady he loved so much. Her beauty was breath- taking. She had an aura you would behold and send your whole being juddering through your entire day. She was extremely gorgeous and he married her luckily. His luck turned against him when she used his gun to kill him one day, for staring at another beauty. Such is life: for good and bad. And who owns too much remains unhappy.

My own newly- found money making zone turned bad when I got back from work one evening, after a year. I met one of the familiar faces I saw in my vehicle that morning, in the midst of my mates. He was obviously pained by something I didn't yet know about. He swung his arms in the air, gnashed his teeth and stamped his feet in desperation. It appeared he was reporting someone to them. I crossed the busy road to their side under the bridge and joined them to listen to him. And suddenly, he stuck his finger at me

'That is the boy. He is the one I just told you about. Yes- that is the boy'. He took two extensive steps towards me and dragged me out of the crowd. Without asking any question, he began to search my pocket. I was dumbfounded.

'Yes, this is the watch he stole from me this morning', he slapped me across the face and grabbed my shirt to pull me closer and assault me. My mates looked surprise that I was accused of stealing. I never stole since I got there. I attempted to defend myself, prove my innocence.

'No- I didn't steal your watch. You forgot it in the bus this morning. I took it and kept it for you. I was expecting to see you again and hand it back to you', I explained to the middle-aged man defensively. I sincerely found it lying in the vehicle after all commuters alighted that morning. I didn't give it to the driver because he would claim it.

I kept it safe in my pocket till the time I saw him again. Then, it resulted in what I never envisaged.

'I didn't steal your watch', I looked from face to face, hoping someone would support me or saved me from the trouble but they appeared unconcerned. Each man lived for himself when it comes to issues of stealing or other criminal acts. What if they interrupted and we were all arrested? They often choose to steer clear from trouble.

'Liar!' He sneered, curling up his lips. Nothing would make him believe me when he found the watch in my pocket.

'You are going to the police station right now! A bad fugitive like you should be locked up', he hauled me with him, ready to get me arrested. Two adults from our garage stopped him straightaway. We had our rules in the territory- rules that must be followed.

'You can't take him anywhere since we are accountable for them- for all the kids here. Take your watch away and we will reprimand him for you. Police is not our friend so, don't knock our heads together', Ochen took me back from him and yanked me in the big circle drawn by the crowd. I fell heavily on the ground and in few seconds I was back on my feet, my heart thumping hysterically, my eyes on the adults roaming the scene. Over time, I had watched them flog my mates worse than a street thief: in the same vein of jungle justice and in the name of reforming us before we return to our homes. I began to cry. I regretted absconding from home and fending for myself for the first time, since I settled there.

The man gave up on me. No one knew if he was about to remove me from the group with his initial plan to give me up to the police. He stood there for a while to observe how I was going to be admonished. Was he feeling sorry as a father already? Yes, I noticed that pity in his mood and moves when Nyang landed a callous slap on my temple. I staggered and fell on the ground. The crowd shifted backward, giving me a space to suffer my pain.

'Don't worry. You don't have to do all of these. And that's why we have the police. Let me take him to them and from there, his family will be informed about his movement. He's only a child that should be under someone's custody', the man rushed to my rescue. He finally unfolded his intention for pulling me out of the crowd. I could recollect he focused on me when I was doing my work in the morning. When I demanded for his fare, he rejoined with perceptible irritation.

'Mr.? *Umunz*? What is your name please?' Ochen blocked him from me, his face wrapping up in intense anger for two reasons. First, for leading me into that mess and second, for not trusting any fugitive. What next was he up to?

'Mr. Khama- I work-', he paused, succumbed to his interruption. He had no interest in him except his name.

'Back off. Mr. Khama, please leave him alone- and- leave us alone. You have done enough, we will correct our boy. In this park, stealing is not allowed. Good-bye'. He watched him leave before he got back to me and pulled me out of the crowd.

'I didn't steal the watch; ask the driver of that bus, I am not a thief. I don't steal', I explained pleadingly but all my pleas fell on deaf ears. It appeared they were starving for flogging and I became their victim. He took me to his mates without hesitating and like enemies on rampage; they took turn to beat me that night with belt and sticks. I was sincerely beaten to a pulp for an offence I didn't commit.

That night, I couldn't sleep. I writhed around in pain and cried my eyes out. My mind fled from spot to spot: it travelled everywhere. I thought of my father who never beat me till he died, then my emotional mother who pampered me each time we met. What about Ntatemogholo- the old man of the house? He was always so kind and friendly. Even Nkuku only twisted my ears or sent men to flog my buttocks. I was never treated that way. These were the people that raised me- the ones that know me so well; not the hoodlums that took advantage of my insecurity and insensibility. I regretted not being with my folks.

I was the first to get on my feet the next morning. Immediately I heard the call to prayer from a neighboring mosque, I forced my aching body up on my feet. A stormy ache snatched at my heavy head, and I couldn't straighten my hurting spine. My left black and ballooned eye struggled to unearth from a gummy lid sticking it down for a break. I tried to give my support to no avail. It had to remain close for days. It was like a million elephant sat on my body. I felt floppy.

I glanced around for some useful stuff I bought when I got there:

a mat and kettle. Were they still useful? I decided to leave them there. The money I saved was the most needful and the thrift collector often arrived in the evening. Putting two and two together quickly, I decided to return for my money at another time, and in a different location I always saw him. And I started walking away slowly, determinedly.

'Where are you going?' A stalking masculine voice called me. I strained my throbbing neck to catch a glimpse of him but I didn't see him clearly. I ignored him and proceeded. As if that wasn't enough, he turned around to face me and I could see him squarely with my right eye opened and functional. Mr. Khama again! What precisely did he want from me? Did he want to get me killed?

'Please-go away from me', I pushed words out of my inflamed mouth.

'Kenosi-it's time to return home', he stated without smiling. He beckoned to two policemen, accompanying him to take me away.

'You are coming with us little boy', a detective took my arm and led me into a police vehicle, waiting a few steps away from our sanctuary. It appeared they had come for only me as the other fugitives fled unperturbed. They were regular and known faces at the police station whenever they were arrested and released several times for invading the government property and absconding from home. At those times, some of their parents had denied their parenthood and refused to turn up at the station. Mine was a case of concern - since Mr Khama felt pity for me - after he accused me of stealing his watch. He was obviously visited by a great deal of guilt when he was dismissed from the scene the previous day. He also regretted putting me on the spot and was ready to make amends for all my serious suffering. But how could I understand his intention when I was swept that way into the custody of the police again?

He wasn't, at all, in a hurry to go anywhere on that day. He waited in front of the police station with me until my invited folks appeared for me. My face fell in deep shame when Nkuku walked into the station first, followed by my mother.

'Ah- Kenosi! What is this you're doing to us? What have we done to deserve this from you?' Nkuku sat on a bench opposite us staring squarely at me, still indignant at my unruly behavior. I couldn't raise my face to look straight at her or answer her insoluble question.

I chose to keep mute and fondle the bruise on my fingers.

'My God! Who did you like this?' Mma forced my face up persistently. I couldn't help but look straight at her, a heap of pain loaded on my pale face. She took a second look at my disfigured face then burst into tears.

'Where have you been? Who did this to you?' she demanded. 'Who?!'

I turned gently and pointed at the man beside me. He was appalled that I had to still accuse him, despite all his efforts to exonerate me from the den I confined myself in for months.

'Why did you do this to him? Don't you have your own children? Why did you treat my child like this?' Nkuku showered him with unending questions while Mma stood astonished at his mindless behavior. Mr. Khama rose from his seat without responding. He walked back into the station to inform the police about their arrival. They had released me to him on his demand to interrogate me and feed me before making every arrangement. One of his brothers was also an officer in the station.

'Come inside here- all of you', a police emerged and ushered us back in their office.

'You are the black sheep of our family. I am highly disappointed in you', Mma lamented, her eyes rooted on me.

'Did you fight with that man?' Nkuku interrogated but I didn't say anything. My eyes remained downcast.

'Shame on you. You won't talk because you are at fault. Useless kid', Nkuku added in front of the officers.

'Welcome ma', an officer attended to them and they exchanged pleasantries. Mr Khama gave us a respectable space like the leg to the face.

'Your son, here, Kenosi, was reported here at our station by Mr Khama', he pointed at him and persisted. 'For fleeing from his home and turning fugitive with youngsters like him. And-',

'Uhn! Didn't I tell you that he was with them? I went there and they hid him', Nkuku interrupted but was given attention for her old age.

'He stole Mr Khama's watch and he was refused this same arrest by their hoodlums- their street fathers, so they did this to him', he concluded.

'Oh my God! Why did you run away from home? Why? I couldn't meet up because of this wound and here I am now. I am standing again for you. Kenosi, you can't stand for yourself. You can't', Mma began to cry again and I followed suit.

'Why is he crying? Shut up your mouth! Donkey mouth- you are too greedy. Greed is the reason you left home. You wanted large chickens- not the *Bogodi* we were eating at home, foolish boy. You wanted executive meals and luxurious homes, not our humble hut. Do you see yourself? It has dawned on you now. May be you have learnt to be pleased with what you have and you will be yourself!' Nkuku hit the nail on the head, twisting my burning ear as she made each correction. I strained with pain but she didn't give up till Mr Khama chipped in.

'Maybe he had a different reason for this. You should, at least, hear him out when you get home. Then you correct him. I really feel sorry for him though'.

'Foolish talk. Senseless idea! Do you plant cereals just for birds to feast on them? Reason before you talk; don't just allow words to escape from the hole in your face,' Nkuku retorted, sizing him up. From the whole scenario, she deciphered he was behind my torture by the group. Had he not reported me, I wouldn't be that battered. Even though he had something reasonable to say, she would block her ears against him.

'You treated him like a thief before helping him. Is that the way it should go? You suffered him', she pestered on. Mma looked from the man to the officer and back to me. She was speechless. My eyes travelled to her leg. The wound had closed and there is a little black circle on the spot. She had recovered, finally.

'Nkuku, I didn't mean any harm when I went to find him', Khama tried to free himself from her conspicuous grudge.

'It's alright. He has really helped the boy to reconcile with his family so, let's appreciate him for that. If not for him, you may not see your son for the next five years. A lot of them have been reported missing here a couple of times and they grow up out there. In the next ten years, they may not return home again. We will release the boy to you now but we want you to appreciate Mr Khama's effort'. He clarified what seemed unambiguous to only my mother. It entered Nkuku's right ear and fled through the left. She deemed it unfit to thank him for dehumanizing me. And I love her for that. Without wasting much of our time, Mma rose from her seat, stretched her arm to show gratitude to him.

'Thank you sir. God will reward you for what you did to this child and your children will be rewarded too *insha Allah*', she said absurdly and he didn't reply or accept her outstretched hand. He was already tired of my folk's advances: an unruly reaction from mother and a spiteful prayer from child. To him, their attitudes were the reason for my escapade. He prepared to leave, putting his initial plan to help with my upkeep on hold.

'Thank you very much, officer Mazhindu. I will get back to you next week Friday'.

'Are you leaving? What about –?'

'No – I will see you next week Friday. Just collect their contact and – bye little boy. I will see you later. Be good and don't run again. Remember all my advice and promises'. He hugged me and slipped some money in my hand.

'Goodbye', I whispered to him. He shook hands with each of the officers with a big smile on his face and left the station without saying a word to my family. They also avoided him, avoided my glory.

The fugitive ultimately returned home shamefaced. Like a hunter on a fruitless mission, I got back with nothing- not even the slightest chance to visit our abode to collect my gains from the thrift collector. I was restricted from going anywhere, including my school. They said I needed time to get over all my sufferings –needed counseling to reform my mind. I obeyed all instructions, appreciated that I wasn't chastised in my home again for my wrong deeds. With the support of Mr Bangwe, I was orientated on the need to be satisfied with all things I have: with my family, shelter, food, and clothing. For all things in life has a time. He also taught me the value of a good name over fortunes. I learnt a lot from him, changed my thinking.

Mr Khama didn't return until after two months. I was peeling cassava with Ntatemogholo one morning and I caught sight of him from a few steps away.

He had a plump sack in one hand and a long folder under his armpit. Obviously, he was returning from work with the objective to stop by and see me after his grievance with my grandma. Seeing him, I dropped the knife I was working with, beamed with delight and ran towards him happily. I had waited for that day to come.

'Welcome sir. *Ngiya kwemukela!*' I took the bag from him and rushed to get him a wooden bench near our hut. If at all he was responsible for my scolding, I had long forgiven him. I had wanted to see him for his contribution to my victorious return to my family. Had it not been for him, I would have remained a fugitive in a negligible environment.

'Welcome to our humble abode', Ntatemogholo looked from him to me, motioning for his introduction. He had only heard of him but didn't know him. Nkuku spoke extensively about him- about how much she hated him and not needing to see his face again.

'He is the man that took me to the police. Mr. Khama'.

'Oh – you are welcome. How is your family?' Ntatemogholo was a man full of wisdom. He didn't show any sign of hearing much about him. He concluded, within himself, on the day he was discussed, that he was a rare gem. Hardly would you find a man so kind to surface and help the helpless after claiming his right. He actually appreciated him and showed this to him.

'*Dumela*. I really appreciate your support. Thanks a million times. God bless you'.

'Don't mention sir', he slipped the folder under his armpit again and sat on the bench gently, opposite him. I stood beside my grandpa, folding my arms behind me obediently.

'Come here. You have really changed now. You can see how fresh you are under the care of your guardians. You have no reason to run away from your family', he patted my bare back, smiling up at me. I smiled back shyly, covering my face with my palm. Ntatemogholo laughed from ear to ear and added saying, 'it is difficult for one to run away from poverty but very easy for poverty to depart from someone. But these little ones do not know that what an elder saw that sank his eyes like a pit will blind them like a bat. If a child has garments like an elder he cannot have rags like that elder'.

'Hun – you're so full of thoughts. You are really intelligent and wise. May your days be long on earth', he bowed in veneration for him, and looked up at him again in great admiration of his thoughtfulness. He spoke to him like his deceased father, reminded him of their days together. He used to advise him in parables and each time he remembered, he knew the child of whom he is.

'Please, forgive my wife for over reacting the first time she met you at the station. She thought you told the hooligans to punish him for taking your watch. And the boy told us he didn't steal it'.

'No – sir, I have my children too. My plan was to take him away from there and return him home. I have seen him a couple of times running after vehicles. I knew he wouldn't listen to me if I told him to return home, so, I dropped my watch and returned for it. I also trusted him when he said he didn't steal it. I –' he paused for him to speak as he waved his hand feebly. It's not respectful to deny an elder a chance to talk.

'It is over. Don't say anything again. Let's glorify God for using you to return the boy home. *Umusa khakulu*', he smiled broadly, uncovering his lost teeth. Five of them had fallen out in ten years and he never minded. He often told me they had tried and he had nothing to show off anymore.

'Thank you very much sir. *Dumela*', Khama prostrated and I marveled at much respect he portrayed within the twenty minutes he met my grandpa. He was indeed, a respectful and easy- going man – a man with countless human values.

'Next time you want to help a child out of trouble, don't entwine him in more trouble', Nkuku interrupted, bursting out from our hut.

She had a bowl of water in her hand. She had kept mute all the while to eaves drop on all their conversation.

'Here, this water is for you', she pointed the bowl at him but Mr Khama looked scared. He took a second look at it and smiled saying, 'no, I don't drink unrefined water. I fall sick easily. I'm sorry'.

Nkuku, who knew he rejected it on the ground of pollution or lack of trust, poured the water away very close to his legs. A pack of sand splashed on his trousers. Nonetheless he didn't worry that much for he already understood her complicated nature. What on the planet earth would make him drink from such a woman? He sneaked a look at her then stooped to brush his trousers, his mind occupied with my exact encounter with her and my mindless decision. She could partly be responsible. She owed him no apology with her countenance.

She handed the bowl to me then began a fresh topic with her husband.

'*Angizwa!* Why do you think Tchieu is keeping this long?'

'Sorry about that. I can send for sachet water if you don't mind', Ntatemogholo rather apologized on her behalf and she didn't appreciate this. She took that out on him.

'Why are you here again? The boy is doing fine and-' she asked bluntly and he felt anger cropping up in him. He gathered himself together then focused on his mission. He didn't know for how long he could put up with her harshness.

'I brought everything here for my new little friend', he disclosed unabashed, paying less attention to Nkuku.

'Thank you sir', my eyes travelled to the sack. Its tummy budged with enough stuff for me. Was that for only me?

'Thank you', Nkuku offered a forced gratitude. And he was surprised.

'I spoke with Kenosi before you came on that day and he told me all about himself. How he lost his dad as a child, his mother's situation- and everything', he refrained from saying anything about lack of food in their home. That, he deemed would amount to another page of trouble.

'Hun- everything a child shouldn't say to a stranger. He's just a foolish boy. Did he say all we have suffered to raise him after he moved here?' Nkuku gave him an evil eye.

'Yes, everything ma. And I have been watching him with the other fugitives. I saw what he experienced there and I was moved to offer him a support', he professed finally. Nkuku sat up enthralled. It is true that a white meal can emerge from the blackest pot. My two old grandparents listened to his plan conscientiously.

'I intend to sponsor his education from now till he graduates and provide all his needs till he grows big enough to look after himself, beginning from today. Actually, I wish to adopt him as my son', he touched his chest confidently. Nkuku shifted in her seat, Ntatemogholo nodded, smiling. I rushed to him and hugged him broadly.

'It's okay. God is with us – God has done it', he patted me fondly.

'God will bless you. Thank you very much. Thank you but we have to inform his mother first about your proposition. And his grand ma - here too will tell you what she feels about that', Ntatemogholo chose his words carefully to avoid being attacked in front of a visitor. He had experienced that numerous times.

'No – it's okay. We will inform his mother about it and see what we are going to do. We sincerely appreciate your plans for him. May God remember you too. *Dumela*', Nkuku appreciated him for the first time, without a smile.

'Amen, thank you very much ma. I also have two boys. One is exactly his age and the other is seventeen years old. I've also been through hardship when I was growing up like him and I know how it feels to –',

'He's not in any hardship. Did he tell you he was in hardship? No, he wasn't. He only had eyes bigger than his wild belly. We do all we can to please them', Nkuku cut in abruptly. She didn't like to lose her integrity for any reason. She would always defend herself when all is said and done. Admitting to that means she failed as my guardian and that would remain in my history.

Khama admitted with a nod. Nothing should cause a problem

between them again. After all, he was only doing me a favor. He could choose to leave and forget me forever. But he was nicer than that.

'I understand ma – these kids are very greedy. They want everything we can't afford', he played along with her, swallowing his actual supposition. This gladdened her.

'Ehn – now you just said the truth. Say the truth and you shall be set free. I like you now', she managed to smile and Khama liked that too. She looked more likable when she smiled.

'Thank you ma'.

'You are such a nice man. God will always replenish all you're spending. You are a giver; you will never turn a beggar *in sha Allah*'.

'Amin', he rubbed his palms together, receiving my grandpa's blessing. And Nkuku prayed for him too.

'May you not suffer any form of hardship in your life. Thank you very much'.

'Amin – thank you ma', he rose up from the chair then sank his hand in his pocket. He brought out some money and gave it to Ntatemogholo.

'Oh thank you. God will bless you more and more and more', he stretched the note appreciably. Khama turned to Nkuku and gave her the same amount of money.

'For me too? God will always be with you and your family', she smiled wholeheartedly for the first time. This gladdened Khama. He told them the next time he would visit and left.

Mma was glad to receive the message from him. What a huge favor and relief he was about to offer after my father's death! Nkuku suggested she still kept me in her custody but getting his support and they were okay with it. Was I happy with the new development? Choosing to be with Khama would have been better for me because he was about my father's age. He would have been able to nurture me better than my old grandparents if not for their mistrust for him. To them, some helpers take advantage of unfortunate kids in my situation and use them for evil works. They did what they could to protect me, although his actual intention wasn't known.

Khama didn't dispute their wishes. He gave all his support even if

I was still with my family. He changed my school to a commendable private school, provided enough food often, and reimbursed me when I hadn't enough to spend. Sometimes he requested for my list of needs and bought everything I wanted for me. Like a miracle, I had a foster father, mentoring me and leading me the right way and in all ways responding to all my supplication. I derived all I was deprived of back in a short time. Such is life – for good and bad.

I am thirty years Kenosi – the strong, brave and privileged son of Nayna. I came, I saw and conquered. Now a graduate of engineering, I was empowered to end our suffering. I am now playing the role of my father in my family- the backbone of my family. With my earning, I could meet everybody's need and sponsor member's education. It is the shout of Kenosi here and there. Thank God for my old helper, Khama. I wouldn't have been anything today without his support. As we are grateful to God for giving us a good life, I worship him at all times and always praise him for my attainment.

Whenever I flash back to my trying times, do I regret taking such steps? Yes, I do. Life is worth negotiating at the right time, not in childhood.

I considerably revolutionized my thinking, as an adult, that my luck to evade deprivation lies not in my hands but in the hands of time. It's only a matter of time; the deprived will become the endowed. Denial lies in all facets of life and appears in all forms- at different times. It emerges monstrously like a thief in the night, needless of your watchfulness. Notwithstanding, there are subjugators and durable victims that never work with time.

7

Zinyoro

...it is the silent and calm water that drowns a man.

Nature is beautiful. It is one of the awe-inspiring outputs of mysticism-refreshing, enchanting and incandescent. Some emerge the wonders of the world and a number of them the features we see around us daily. A tree erects, stretching out ranges of leaves and its acclimatizing branches for other creatures to nestle on and ease off environmental starkness. The sun awakens in the morning, peers through the azure sky above in admiration of more fascinating creatures. What about the clouds? They travel and float along the hands of time also gaping at the efforts of man, reaching for their great height and brushing through them like their treasured wind. Each day passes with new innovation, new idea. Animals of all variations also roam the earth - in the land, water, air and inside the ground at different times. The earth itself is unearthing uneven landforms: the hill, mountain, plateau, canyon, valley, and the shoreline. So wonderful, so beautiful. The night surely arrives with all its usual celestial objects, including the stars, planets, and the moon, existing with certain animals that mostly appear only at dusk. The day was never friendly to them. Man, himself, is a wonderful creature, mastering the kingdom of nature. What a wonderful world!

As lovely as nature is, what lies within is unbelievable. We see a lovely fish, ensnaring with scintillating colors and yet no one eats or touches it. Or a colorful snake crammed with poison and ready to attack, yet enthralling. Or a shady tree but feverish in nature. And a gorgeous human so terrible on the inside. Such is nature, such is life. For good or bad, for the deprived and derived.

Zinyoro pulled a long breath, took a second look at his parrot, and unleashed its cage to set it free. He shooed her out for freedom but she wouldn't budge. The budgie poked her curved bill and stretched her strong legs. She joggled her brightly colored feathers then returned to the interior of her long metal cage.

'Mazomba, it's time to leave. You are free now – go –and be free forever', he guided her back to the door of her cage but she returned inside, screaming and squawking.

'Diwai is wicked, Diwai will kill me', she elucidated discernibly. He heard what she said. He had always heard her for the past twenty years she had been with him. He loved and taught her all she could say today when they were just together - no intruder or hater-just the two of them. Things have changed. She could barely voice out to be heard except he's there. It was the yell of shush or 'gerraway' here and there. She turned a sickening bird and Diwai turned a wicked being.

'That is why you must leave. Diwai isn't around now, you may leave and be free', he brought her out of the cage. She made her usual kissing sound then struggled to get off his grasp and walk on the ground. He understood all her needs, and made out all her sounds. They were good friends, understanding partners.

'I won't leave for Diwai, I came before her', she emphasized, twisting her rounded nape, squawking. And he understood her pain. Despite her dissimilar nature, he knew her before his wife, appreciated her and cherished their moments before the coming of Chindori and his family. His attention drifted to his second pet and he asked, 'have you seen Chindori today?'

'Your wife drove him out with a ladle this morning. He ran away.

Chindori ran away'. He was perplexed, gathering disheartening information about his innocent dog. He loved pets and had kept them before meeting his wife. She knew them before she moved in. What went wrong? Did she suddenly hate them for a reason?

'You – get back here inside this cage and let me look around for Chindori. He may not return home now', he stooped to carry the parrot back to her cage. She crept back obediently, whistling and drawing attention to her empty food cup. She gave it a kick with her sharp clawed feet and the metal dropped noisily.

'I just put some food here in the morning', he marveled at the promptness of her intake, peering into the cup. Was she about to double in size? He put the food there barely two hours before. But thank God she could speak for herself.

'Diwai threw my food away and threw the tin back at me. Diwai is wicked. She is evil', she cocked an eye at him.

'Oh God, I am so sorry. I will get you another food right away', he hurried back in their kitchen to re fill the cup but met a big surprising label pinned down with a ladle on the pot. It was an instruction he had to read before taking further steps. He leaned forward and read, 'food not for animals'. His wife again! Ignoring her mindless instruction, he flung the pot open and filled the cup to the brim. It would sustain the bird for the whole day. What precisely she held against his friendly pets was yet undisclosed. She definitely wanted them to leave or cease to exist. It was always the report of pets. He could recollect all the calls he had received at work to report or reprimand a pet – the shout of Mazomba and Chindori day in - day out.

After feeding Mazomba, he set out to find Chindori. It was a Sunday so; he wouldn't have gone far away from home. He knew his locations: either with the other dogs in the neighborhood or on the trash, searching for something to eat. It was all Diwai's fault for he gave him everything to keep him away from danger. Dangers from the busy road preceding crazy drivers, and all sort of self -controlled vehicles or judicious mouths watering for fleshy dogs. Most of his friends had lost their pets in either of the ways. He would do all he could to protect his five –year- old dog, considering that it was more susceptible to trouble than Mazomba who spent all her time inside the house.

'*Ee yebo*-Bukhosi', he walked into his friend's compound tiredly. He also has a pet who was Chindori's good buddy. He had looked around for over three hours and hadn't seen him.

'*Aa muzaya. Salibonani* – I just saw your wife and your son. They passed here like four minutes ago', he squinted his eyes to recollect the time. Was he right? He wasn't sure. He stood up from his seat to exchange proper pleasantries with him.

'Oh – that's fine. How is your family? *O o nhia*?' he hugged him amiably. They both patted their back, smiling broadly. Their twelve years friendship had accustomed them to traditions they must display on every meeting.

'Where are you going in this hot sun?', he blocked himself from the severity of the radiation with his palm, grimacing and revealing his front teeth.

'It's my dog again. He left home this morning and had since not returned. I'm looking around for him', he looked over his shoulders and back westward.

'You will find him. He visited Yamurai this morning – and they were together for some time. He followed another friend towards - that way. A new buddy he met here yesterday', he pointed in direction of the high way connecting their major cities. And showing his true compassion for his pet, he clasped his hands above his head. That was the same route he had restricted him from going. What was about to befall him for going back there?

'I have to hurry now – before something bad happens to my friend', he shook hands with him, laughing heartily. He laughed too and watched him make his way towards the main road.

'Remember to check your mother's house too. You know he knows there', he shouted after him and he nodded, still waving back. Did he hear him clearly? Chindori wouldn't be there after what he went through when they popped in together. He entered her living room unpermitted and got a whack on his head. It was spicy enough to send him away forever. So, what would he be doing there? Poor Chindori.

His sense of clemency had set in unknowingly. He folded his arms behind him as he stood facing the two lane highway.

It was a busy Sunday. Both sides of the road lodged mounds of garbage radiating repulsive smell – bad enough to infect the nostrils. He tweaked his nose and crossed to the opposite side with two other pedestrians. Vagrants sat alongside the road, faces shielded with raffia caps. The atmosphere wasn't fair on them. It wafted its severity through unfitting caps, hit and burnt horridly. Hordes of people also stood by the road, waiting for vehicles to convey them to dissimilar locations.

Sellers weren't too far from the penetratingly smelling refuse. They warded off maddening flies, snuggling on their fried potatoes and chicken, Sadzan and Nyama. Aroma battled with stench and dragged for influence in the desolately searing air. Shops were still opened, amblers were numerous. The bustling wasn't yet over until 12am.

He remained silent, only craned his eyes around for him. It was too noisy you had to pay attention to pick a word out from the scene. Marketers, commuters, pedestrians, preachers, gossipers, musicians and even vehicles struggled to communicate at the same time. Except Chindori spotted him or caught sight of him first, they wouldn't meet there. He lost hope and began to walk home sadly, his head dropped.

He arrived home at 7pm, meeting Chindori crouched to the ground, tail tucked. Seeing him through the main entrance gate, he jumped on his feet and sped to his beloved, wagging his hairy tail, his tongue sticking out. He flung himself before his feet and rolled from side to side, showing his belly, anxiously waiting for his belly- rub. He was also very happy to see him. He bent to stroke him. His hand travelled from his hairy neck down a plain soft belly, more filled with excitement than what he perceived afterwards. It looked emptier, too flat like he hadn't eaten for days. He straightened up instantly, knowing that he needed food. Chindori hopped at him, touched his leg with his fore foot, calling for more attention. He turned to him again and gave a gentle head rub. His hand caressed his head back and forth affectionately, his eyes closing gently and paws curled up in great delight.

'Papa', his four- year- old son came around him with a hug. He didn't ignore the dog. Still giving him attention, he pulled his boy closer with his second hand. He had a pencil in his hand. He leaned over his father's shoulder and flogged Chindori's ear.

'Ahn! Don't flog the dog again. That's unfair. He didn't touch you, did he?' he corrected him, a tinge of anger in his tone. He hadn't yet gotten over his pressure to find him. And he wasn't happy that the child had possibly been inured to ill-treat his pet by his mother.

'Go ahead and flog the child for the miserable animals you gathered all over the house. Go on', Diwai walked up to him enraged.

Like a lightning flash, she ejected the child from his side. He was neither worked up nor astounded. She had long changed since he married her and had a child. The best side of her was only enjoyed at their pre- marital stage –only courtship. The rest exist in nightmare.

'If you were a normal man, shouldn't you welcome a child before a filthy and hopeless animal? This useless thing that has consumed all the faeces in the whole street today. Senseless master, useless pets', she cleaned her son unnecessarily. Zinyoro wasn't prepared for a shameful squabble. He didn't utter a word. He walked past her to get Chindori some food. And he tried to follow his master inside their living room.

'If you dare enter this place, you will be buried alive by your master today. I will destroy the most vital part of you and he- he – will hate you forever', she turned the dog off the road, gnashing her teeth in frenzy.

He turned back instantly and signaled to the dog to wait outside. He concurred, sat back in his restricted location. Each time he met a bad eye, he looked away, then looked at her again, tail still wagging behind him.

'Chindori, sit down. Diwai is wild – Diwai is wild', Mazomba whispered and screeched from her cage, her notched bill swivelling along her flanks for an insect.

'Shoo – stupid things. God knows I hate you both and my prayer will soon be answered'.

Zinyoro returned with a full plate of rice and chicken. He walked past her again, looking around for Chindori's plate. He jumped up enthusiastically, followed him everywhere he went, tail wagging, mouth watering.

'You dare not give it the food I cooked. Do you think cooking is easy? How dare you serve it my food without asking?' she struggled to snatch the food from him.

'What is wrong with you? What is your problem? Why do you hate my pets this much? Don't push me to do anything stupid. Stay away from me', he guided the food, prevented her from getting it.

'I don't care whatever you do. Give me my food back', she held his muscular hand, shoved and forced it down to get the food desperately.

'Okay – make this my dinner. I don't want any dinner tonight'.

'No way! We always eat together, have you forgotten? What if this is for both of us?'

'Honey – I saw lot of food there. That food can fill six more plates and I give money for food. I'm not complaining, am I?'

'Go and announce on CNN. Tell the whole world you give your wife money to cook for you'.

'To cook for all of us, including my pets'.

'What pets?' she got hold of the plate and poured the food away successfully. Hungry Chindori didn't mind. He scurried to the spot and devoured it on the grimy ground. A beggar has no choice to dictate his needs. He screamed in pain as Diwai kicked his belly before heading inside.

'Eat. Eat in pain, you filth. I hate you, ugly thing'. She shut the door behind her.

Zinyoro stood still, breathing heavily, his hands on his waist, head raised to the sky in deep regret. Why did he marry Diwai? Why didn't he wait long enough to understand her personality? Why did he allow her to fool him with her fake simplicity? False calmness – a sheep on the outside, a complete wolf within. Precisely what his friend said about her. She was trouble itself in disguise when he first met her three years back- all glossed with impeccable nature. Their courtship was merely six months of a quiet relationship – a time short enough to feign a true feeling. Was it just about his pets alone? Their problem spanned on lot of issues: from his late night arrival to unwanted friendship and heated argument that last for weeks. Sometimes he was saddened with the thought of returning home to resume a waiting and an unfinished argument or a fight he dropped off on his departure. Home was war, work was relaxing.

He walked slowly to a rock near his pet and sat down quietly. Chindori snuggled close. He got his hand on his belly and caressed it gently. He wished he was still a bachelor with his pets. They gave him peace and unperturbed friendship.

Undeniably, they were the best of his friends. His mind skidded to man's utmost need to find a feminine companion he calls a wife and the mother of his children. It works for most men so perfectly that they never complained. For him, he was already tired, for he hates regretting his actions. This was his biggest regret ever.

Night met him there, still seated next to his dog, head now buried between his legs morosely. Chindori had fallen asleep; limbs aligned and belly heaving in the middle. It was obvious Mazomba had also slept as there was no sound from her cage. What about Diwai and her son? There was no trace of them near him. They must have gone to bed too. If his wife gives him no joy, and didn't care for him, then who should? She never brought herself first in admission to guilt except he approached her and begged for it. Even so, he didn't want all of that at the moment. He hoped for peace in his lifetime. He wanted not to be robbed of pleasure, compassion and progress for having a family.

By the time he raised his face, it was twelve. Everywhere was dead silent and dark. He straightened up and stomped into his living room where he spent the rest of the new day. The rest wasn't uninterrupted or as sweet as he expected it to be. He was awoken by unsettled mind and riven attention in between his sleep.

He knew it - that he had long sold his heart to the wrong one and getting it back would be tougher than he envisioned. Engrossed with possible ways to reconcile with her, he tossed from side to side. But recalling his mother's doctrine about the strength of a real man, he kept back. She mistreated him and his pets, she had to apologize. He inferred as he fell into a deep sleep till the crack of dawn.

Chindori's energetic barking terminated his sleep at 8:30am. He sprang on his feet and gazed through his window silently, his heart racing in his chest. Did he see a stranger or was provoked by someone? He rubbed a load of sleep off his eyes, flickered his eyelid. His inquisitive sight raced from the busy dog to an empty surrounding and back to the dog to locate his direction. He focused on the entrance gate, rooted to the same spot, tail erected, jaw primed and mouth gawkily opened. He slipped on his shoes and walked to the yard stealthily. There, he met his mother standing beside the gate, afraid to enter his house. His face cracked into a welcoming smile as he walked up to her.

'*Ee unofara*? Did you see what this miserable thing did to me again?' she reported not stirring. When he saw his master, he built up more confidence to edge nearer and pestered more for her motive for visiting. You can't exchange peace for war or war for peace. He still boiled on her unfair treatment, maybe. Now, he claimed his territory.

'Will you back off or you will leave this house. What is this?' she flogged him with her scarf, her face noticeably wrapping up in rage.

'Hey! Chindori – sit down. That's enough, she's my mum. Don't you recognize her again?' he watched him return to his kennel.

'No – go ahead and take permission from it before I enter here. He's one of the reasons I am here this morning. Chindori cannot take over this house. No way, you have to put your family first. Why should you give him a chance to cause a rift between you and your wife?'

'Okay mum. Let's go inside then'.

'Your mother is here. Zinyoro, your mother is here', Mazomba reiterated from her cage.

'How are you Mazomba?' Zinyoro waved at her and she seized the opportunity to tell him what he should know.

'Your wife has left with her son this morning. She threw my food away and flogged Chindori. She is mean – she is mean. Diwai is wicked, sqwwwwwk-', she whispered. His mother ignored her, left him with his pets and entered the living room to wait for him. Zinyoro followed her instantly.

'Mother, what brought you here this early morning?'

'First, let me ask you what you are doing with these animals around you? What do you need them for? Now, you have a family. Let them go to where they belong.' she looked at him squarely, an earnest expression on her bold face. He noticed a little bruise on her face and instead asked a different question, knowing what her intention was.

'Are you still frying fish? Look at a bruise on your face', he pointed at the spot and she cut him short abruptly.

'Look – I'm not here for that. I want you to tell me why you're frustrating your family with these animals around you. Why should you give animals upper hands in your matrimony?' she emphasized and he got her right. Diwai had reported him to his mother as usual even though she was wrong.

He rose to his six feet and paced around the room, his hand on his side. Couldn't she correct her before visiting to ask questions? Why wrong upon another wrong and she overlooked it? After all, she raised him and she never saw her behave in that manner. She was always respectful to his father.

'Mother, I must confess to you that I am tired of marriage'.

'Why? What are you talking about? I don't understand you'.

'Mother, you raised me and you know me very well - that I am cool and well mannered. It's the way you raised me and you know it', he sat on the table in front of her sulkily. She adjusted in her seat, giving all her attention.

'Diwai has changed. She troubles me all the time. If she didn't report me to you, you wouldn't have heard anything. You know?'

'Yes, what really happened?'

'I don't know why she hates my pets and troubles us every time'.

'Us? Did you just say us? Since when did you start identifying with animals? This is shocking! Well, she told me you have to choose from those animals or her'.

'Mother – no – I can't drive them for any reason. I love my pets and she met us living together. If she can't beat us, she has to join us', he rose from his seat and walked to the door. Reasoning with him, she kept mute, merely staring at his full physique blocking the inflow of ray and brightness.

'Mother, I am a man, don't I have the right to enjoy my life and do the things I like to do again? All because of marriage? If her love is true, she should love the things that I love. They are not weapons, they are mere animals. I love my pets. What have I done wrong?' he turned his back at her and she felt pity for him- felt sorry for his overmuch love for animals. If only he could put them where they belong, peace would reign in his home.

She was the second of his father's three wives. Life was sincerely different with them – no complaint about his wishes or displeasure even though they were unhappy. No one had the nerve to raise a brow against his wish. Everything they had was embraced in good faith and intermittent gratitude. Everything has changed now, life itself has changed. Wives control and rule the homes now. She wished she had seen that earlier in her and discouraged her son from marrying her. A controlling wife is a lot of trouble. She thought silently, remained quiet. However, she mustn't show that to him or break their home.

'Mother, tell me how I am wrong. She deprived me of every right because of my pets. I can't play with my son because I have pets. I slept without eating last night. I should be in my office now but I can't because I woke up late'.

'You can still go. It's your business.'

'Diwai is wicked – she is wicked', Mazomba screamed, squawked and whistled to draw his attention but he had no time for her at the moment. His mother smiled secretly, understanding the parrot's message clearly.

'You have to caution the parrot to watch its mouth. That's demeaning to your wife, you know? An animal criticizing a human! What is this? You don't allow them to affront her. That parrot is rude, It has to stop', she pointed at her cage furiously.

'Mother, please advise her or we will leave here for her', he warned seriously. And she repudiated his plan.

'Leave for where? A man is always a man. Your father was a brave man'.

'I am not like him. I choose to be serene, not tough'.

'That is why you can't rule your home. Be a man, talk to your wife'.

'How?'

'Can't you talk to your own wife? Did I get her for you?' she questioned in a somewhat harsh tone, her brow furrowed. Her second son never sought her idea. He was happily married without sickening reports about bird and dog.

Despite knowing her flaws, she wasn't prepared to criticize Diwai for him. Come what may, he can't replace his fellow humans with animals except he is sick.

'Okay -mother, I will talk to her. I will talk to her'. He closed the topic as he became conscious of the time and all the works he left undone in his office two days ago. There were also two visitors waiting to see him on that day for the supply of cement in their new site.

'Mother - wait for me. We will leave at the same time. I have to hurry to work right now'. He began his preparation immediately while she reflected on his situation. Was it anything serious that needed immediate attention? With a shrug, she ignored the idea, waved the thought aside. She saw a fully grown man who could handle his affair independent of anyone, just like his brother – if only he could shut his wife up.

Later on, on the same day, he spoke to Diwai and eventually entreated her to maintain a stay for his helpless pets. She laid down certain unacceptable rules he found pretty difficult to admit: both of them should never roam the yard or eat from the food she cooked, and there shall be no more fondling of pets around the house. Also, the parrot wasn't allowed to talk in her presence anymore. He accepted. Provided they were still around him, he accepted her offensive rules. It was sorely painful for both of them to adhere to her rules that, he began to think of a new idea.

'Where did this dog get its bone from?' Diwai peered into Chindori's plate on her arrival from the market on a bright day.

'I don't know. It's a dog, it can get its food from anywhere if you fail to look after it', Zinyoro retorted, not looking up at her. He continued fixing the wheel of his motorcycle, secretly raging within. Whatever she was up to, he clearly understood.

'Are you sure this is not a human bone it brought home?' she used a stick to stir the bone, examined it carefully. Chindori stretched his body and drew closer to her. He smelled her body, kept sniffing for something. She took two sharp steps backward, pointing the stick at his face.

'Go back now! Dirty thing'. She sneaked a quick look at her husband to read his reactions but he wasn't, at all, paying attention to them. He was engrossed with the repair, deliberately avoiding her annoying line of attack.

'Did you not hear what I just said? That there is something strange in its plate', she reiterated angrily, her voice rising.

'Zinyoro bought our food. It is our food and it's nice', Mazomba screamed.

'Shoo! No more parrot talking to me. This is so strange. An animal interrupting a conversation. Zinyoro, I'm talking to you!' she yelled and Chindori ran away from her side.

'Why are you this difficult? If I saw all these in you, I wouldn't have been your wife. This is really humiliating'. She threw the stick at the dog then dashed back into the house disappointed. Zinyoro didn't move from his position or say anything. He unbolted a wheel, and disconnected its parts on the ground. Still staring blindly into the expanse of the compound, he pulled out a handkerchief to wipe the sweat towing down his face and jaw. Then, he looked over his shoulder and gave the space a bad eye. Wherever she went, it was meant for her - for her disturbance and narrow-mindedness. He had a lot on his mind; his pre - occupation would not be hers no matter what. In less than twenty minutes, he had to put the bike in proper shape if he would still supply his customers with cement as ordered. There were some of other competitors in the business, so punctuality is the soul of any surviving business. If he failed, she would also fail for no one would shoulder his responsibilities.

He pushed the thought aside and struggled to keep to time. Machines fail sometimes due to inadequate maintenance. He had assembled the parts and was fixing the wheel back. Chindori was asleep as usual, only Mazomba's sounds filled the silent environment. She whistled continuously for attention but he was too busy and mindful of time. He allowed his eyes to travel to his watch each time he worked. The smudge of oil on his palm got too disturbing and he wiped with a napkin in his bike. Diwai appeared from behind him with a new form of denigration. He sighed wearily.

'Can't you shush this horrible bird? I can't sleep inside the house – it keeps making this stupid noise. Should I leave this house for you?' she ranted, throwing her hands in the air. He dropped the spanner he had in his hand and pleaded.

'Diwai, please – forgive them for offending you. They are with me and I am very sorry for causing you this discomfort'.

He resumed his work. And to his greatest surprise, the parrot's cage he hanged on the wall for the past twenty years landed in front of him. The bird screeched and struggled for safety beneath the weight of a metal enclosure. She was badly injured: her flank ripped open and she had a broken crown, streaking blood down its lustrous feathers. Chindori sped to the spot either for good or bad. And perplexed Zinyoro rushed to save her life before he did anything stupid. He raised her to his face, watching her dilating eyes. Straining for breath, her mouth gaped open partly. She twitched her legs, twirled her nape, and battled for survival. With a start, he turned back at Diwai.

'If Mazomba should die, it will be a serious war between you and I in this house. You will see that you have finally broken my silence and you have freed the beast in me'.

He dropped the bird and tried to start his bike. He needed a ride to get to a veterinary clinic fast. The closest to them was almost a mile away.

'It will never survive. It is the dog's turn now. Its plan is very easy. It's a glutton', she hissed and returned inside the house.

The bike refused to work- work to at least, save Mazomba. His eyes didn't wander off her till she began to close her eyes gradually.

She finally drew her last breath and died five steps away from his struggling feet, her feather in the pool of her blood.

'Oh Mazomba – no, stay with me', he knelt beside her lifeless body, and cried like a baby. As if sensing the gravity of his situation, Chindori returned to sniff the bird and lolloped to his position quietly.

'I love you. I want you around me. You are my best friend – my true companion', he whispered in her ears, now holding her in his arms. But she was gone.

Everything changed after deliberately killing Mazomba. Diwai gave her husband the space she felt he deserved after the incidence. He turned the quietest and most reserved in the house. Again, she had wronged him but this time, she didn't visit his mother to report herself or the bird she killed. She kept the matter within the confine of their home. However, it got worse when he rejected her meals, returned home so late every day and spoke to only Chindori in the house. Was she pleased with the new development? She hadn't been able to figure out what to do to gain his attention like before even though she had apologized twice. He was still unforgiving.

When he returned on the fourth day, he was with the food he bought for him and Chindori. He entered the house quietly to get the cutleries he needed and returned to his ever waiting dog. He exulted, his tail shaking his body here and there. He pounced everywhere, salivating at the aroma of his meal. It was obvious he hadn't eaten any food after the breakfast he served him in the morning.

'Calm down – it's enough for both of us. I got you a big and chewy bone too. Here – enjoy it'. He watched him gobble up the fried rice and beef even before it was all emptied in his bowl.

'Take it easy. I still have more for you'. He washed his hands then settled on a bench to take his meal. Flies followed him everywhere – from the dog to him and back to the bench. They must also have a taste of his kindness. The scene wasn't pleasant enough for dining but for Diwai's trouble, he preferred to be there. Not knowing she stood at the window, spying on them, he guzzled the content in a bottled soft drink as soon as he finished eating. Poor man. She said to herself, dropping her gaze from the window. A mere look at him illuminated how starving he had been all day– a man deprived of love and care. A foolish man suffering for a worthless bird. She calculated, walking her son back into their room. She wouldn't release him to get infected by either of them, even though he didn't mind being with them. She needed just him: no animal around him. As long as Chindori was in their way, she knew there would be a solution one day.

By the time she returned to peer through the same window, he had fallen asleep on the bench. He snored piercingly, his head pillowed with his entwined fingers. Is this the man she married? She stood still just gazing at him: the charming look that invited her first, then his placid nature. Of all the six men she knew at the same time they met, he stood out in his appearance, conduct and wisdom. On top of that, he loved her with all his heart. It was the perfect love she craved for before he finally surfaced. She acknowledged that she loved him too, more than anyone on earth.

Their only problem stemmed from the two pets he intractably retained to devastate their love life. She bit her lips, reflecting on the effect of Mazomba's death on him. Did she kill her on purpose? No, she shook her head, conflicting with the idea. She only took his negligence out on the guiltless bird. He should put her first before anything else. Not even his son should replace her position in his heart. If only he could love only her and give unbroken attention, there would be peace forever. It was all she wanted.

He coughed and sneezed, hurtling a worrying fly away from his nostril. Diwai hid her face as his eyes flicked open. His long lashes descended tenderly again and he resumed his sleep. Warm air drifted through his pencil mustache, away from a rounded but well-ordered mouth. His fair complexion had metamorphosed from sun-burn, all dark patches around his face. She felt he worked too much – much more than necessary. It was another reason he maddened her. In their courtship, he often closed earlier to spend impressive and pleasant moments with her. After marriage, he was different. He turned a tough workaholic, hardly having time for his family.

She was still there when he awoke from his slumber in a sweat. He sat up on the seat and coughed continuously, until tears appeared on his lids. He rubbed it away with the tip of his shirt then fell into a deep thought. His eyes roamed from the cage back to sleeping Chindori. It was obvious he was missing the usual sounds from the bird and their rapport. Would he ever train another parrot to be as brave and smart as that? How would he get a new parrot? And if he did, would he ever have a chance to love a parrot again? He gazed straight at the window, thinking of his uncultured wife and caught her standing there. He hurled his attention away from her instantly. Surprisingly, she walked up to him and sat beside him on the bench.

'You have been sleeping and I waited there to discuss –'

'What do you want?' he demanded, breaking her off, a deep frown on his face. She sized him up then shifted away from him, unable to control her rising temper.

'Zinyoro, what is it? We beg God almighty and He forgives us. What else do you want - to - accept my apology?'

'My bird! Nothing else. Get me my parrot back and I will love you again'.

'What bird? The dead one? Zinyoro, you are a sick man. How could I get a dead bird back? ' she bawled at him, looking more horrified than surprised.

'*Eee!* Diwai – leave me alone, or I will have to leave you alone. I want my bird and that is all', he began to rise from the bench and she tugged him down aggressively.

'Where do you think you are going? This matter will be resolved today or you go nowhere!' He shook his head, looking up at her short stout body subduing him. Did she have the power to hold him if he desired to leave or could she command him around the house? Or worse still, stop him from seeing another woman? Never. Nonetheless, he chose to be calm. Be a controlled man.

'Look – I can see you are taking my quietness for stupidity. You have to be very careful', he pointed his warning finger at her.

'Else what? What can you do?'

'What can I do?'

'Yes – tell me what you can do!'

'Who knows what you did with that bird? From the way you

mourn it; it is obvious you tied your destiny to it. If not, what are you doing with a bird for twenty years? You are forty two years now and you have spent twenty years of your life with it. What makes it special?' she scowled and he hated her ugly angry face.

'You are so unrefined. A parrot is a special bird and that's the reason I loved it. Have you seen any other talking bird in your life?'

'What for? Sheer evil – evilly controlled bird living with an evil man. You need deliverance!' she ranted over his head. He wiped off her splattering spittle from his thick and curly hair. He tried as much as possible to put all things under control, even when she began to curse.

'You can't take my glory from me. If you used that bird or this demonic dog against me, you have failed'.

'Diwai, you killed an innocent bird and you are still unrepentant. You are not a good wife. I regret marrying you'.

He stood to leave the spot and avoid any unforeseen incidence. He discerned it would soon escalate into a fight if he remained there.

'You are going nowhere. You have to explain why I must find your dead bird for you', she knotted his shirt on his chest, and held him with it.

'Diwai, leave me alone. Let me go my way'. He spoke in a cool tone, tried to cool off her heated anger. She had once again derailed from his expectation. What he anticipated was another form of apology, following how much he missed his pet. But she had no regard for the pet, since she had no rethink. To her, it was a mere occurrence losing an ordinary bird. To him, it was much more than that.

Chindori and their son were their witnesses. Lungani stood just staring at his parents. He had no clue why they quarreled every time. He only watched and learnt to practice the same act.

'Do you see your son? Don't give him the impression that fighting is good. You have to stop this now', he whispered to her and she pushed him away. He shook his head as he fell back on the seat. Chindori stretched his body then walked to her. He shot his mouth at her then sniffed her body.

'Get away from me now!' he kicked at him but he missed. Dogs are smarter than birds. She thought finally before disappearing into the bosom of their bedroom disillusioned. Zinyoro gathered himself from the bench and left the house the moment she was out of sight.

He had seen, yet a new misdemeanor in his beloved wife. How much more would she unravel from her hidden characters? From all indication, she had proven to him that she was a fake. That she pretended to lure him into marriage. He shook his head as he made a sharp turn towards his brother's house. It was about forty minutes trek to his destination. He looked down at his watch and changed his mind. What precisely was he going to discuss with him? He just saw him the previous day and if he should reach there, he knew he would be forced to relate his hidden problem to him. He changed his route and discovered Chindori behind him. He had crept after him when he stormed out of the house. And he hated being followed to a far distance by him. It wasn't safe enough.

'Hey, buddy – you have to return home. You can't follow me to where I'm going. Go home and wait for me. I'm coming back', he rubbed his head then waited for him to leave but he didn't. He sat close to his foot, waving his tail, his floppy ears erected. Now considering his safety, he led him half way back home then commanded him.

'Go back now!' he bawled. He had familiarized with his angry face, knew when he was displeased. With that, he turned back obediently. He stood watching him hurry home before leaving, finally.

He drew a long - long breath when he started his journey afresh. He began to saunter down the long street. Luckily for him, he didn't come across any known face. He wasn't in the right mood to talk to anyone, so he headed straight to his mother's house. There, he knew he would have enough rest.

'Mother- Mother, *Salibonani*'. He moved around the whole house, calling her but no response. Remembering it was the general market day, he went out of the bungalow, eyes smoldered with depression. She wouldn't be back until 11pm; however she was his only solace. No one else could pacify or strengthen him like her. From childhood, she had been his crucial mentor, unburdening his heart at times like that.

'Oh God – almighty'. He waited in front of the house for the next five minutes then decided to leave, possibly search for a cool spot to reel away the hours.

It was 7:30pm and her customers were just arriving, including Zinyoro, one of her old friends. Her mouth dropped open at the sight of him. The last time he was there, he brought someone he introduced as his wife. That night, they ordered for a plate of spiced soup with soft drinks. And she could recollect the way she glued her eyes on them jealously. Zinyoro had been her heart desire from their childhood together, even though he never looked her way. Her attempt at getting him was like wetting a fruitless garden and she had to give up on him. Her vainly effort melted away on the same day his wife was brought forward and introduced by him in the same restaurant. What more could be that devastating? Would he have said that he didn't understand all her advances? He did and it was for that reason he brought his woman dauntingly.

She flinched then carried on with her table setting, ignoring his table. He had his head in his hand, looked unhappy. What would a married man be doing there alone at that time? She had done the work for ten years and understood every situation leading a married man there- for all her customers were men. It's either he had trouble staying with his wife or he just had a broken home. If a man doesn't chase something, something is definitely chasing him. His home must have broken recently from the look on his face. She imagined as she returned to their kitchen to check her cooking.

'Anerudo, go and ask that man what he wants to take? Tell him all we have'. She sent one of her waitresses to him. She stood and watched all his reactions. He looked up at her, and then rose from the chair to leave. She realized she had to take advantage of his unsuspected visit and approach him herself, else she wouldn't see him there again.

'Zinny! Zinny!!' she called after him, wiping her hands with her apron. She bit the gum between her teeth noisily, walking up to him. Did he remember she was there? Not really, he was too occupied with whatever she felt was bothering him.

'Hey – quite some time', he rubbed his eyes to conceal any feeling written there – anything at all she could read on his face and link to his situation.

'How is your wife?' she read him closely and he understood why. It's undeniable he saw all her advances earlier but every man has a choice. She wasn't his choice.

'My wife is fine. She is fine and you?' he asked sadly with a wobbly voice. She noticed that, got more concerned.

'I'm fine too. I can see you are about to leave. Is there a problem?' She smiled seductively, rolled her eyes, and stretched her chest. But none attracted him. He rather looked around the spot confusedly then sat in the chair, arms folded around him, head lowered. He was apparently undecided. Something keeps pushing him in that state of indecision: should he stay or leave? He scratched his head, thinking of what to order.

'We have your favorite soup and chilly soft drinks', she pulled back the chair opposite him and joined him.

He was strait- faced when he looked up. This was so strange to her. He was a very lively and friendly man.

'I'm also hungry. Anerudo! Come and serve our food'. The waitress patiently listened to their requests and hurried back in the kitchen. It was her business. If she liked, she could spend the whole night just sitting there with him. And for him, she could sacrifice anything. She smiled, looking straight in his eyes.

'I will soon leave here for – I think - em my mother should be back early'.

'Your mother? What about your wife?'

'That reminds me. I have to get going now. She is expecting me at home and-', he gave a sardonic smile, rising from the chair.

'I just told the waitress to serve our food'.

'Our food? No, my meal is ready at home. I have to leave right away'.

'Zinny? Are you alright? Why are you here then?' She leveled up with him, the evenness of their height quite obvious.

'Yes – I will be back another time. Today, I have to go. I'm sorry for – ', he brought out some money to pay for the food.

'No, you may leave. Don't bother to pay. Bye'. She pushed at the chairs, re –arranging the spot regretfully. He remained same as ever. She had her mind made up not to approach him again.

Zinyoro hit the road again, not knowing where else to go. He had long broken up with his best friend after Diwai accused him of instigating their recurring discords. The last day he visited was when she walked him out of their house – in front of him. He's a man of his words. He never returned there again as he vowed. No one seemed right to her, except her mother-in-law.

By the time he reached the junction leading to either his house or his mother's, he slowed down, contemplating on where to go. Heading home means continuity of what he dropped off before leaving while sleeping over in his mother's home meant much more trouble. Where precisely should he go? He cogitated for another ten minutes just standing and watching the passersby.

When he reached a decision, he sighed then took his steps leisurely. Since nothing interesting awaited him where he was heading, he felt no urge to hurry. Men hurry home to meet a pleasant or welcoming wife – to end a hectic day and commence an amorous night. Contrariwise, he began with trouble and ended with isolation. He wished he waited much longer with his pets before marrying a wife.

It was precisely 9:45pm when he stepped into his house. He rubbed worries off his face and bent over Chindori's kennel to find him. He wasn't there. His mind raced back to the moment he returned him to their street, then where he could possibly be at that hour. He never slept outside – his return time was always 7pm. He moved from edge to edge, calling him but he was nowhere around the house. It would be unwise to find him at that time, especially when he was so tired. He strode back inside quietly.

The bench he used in the day still stood there, including the cutleries he used to eat. If she didn't care about him, he didn't care too. He packed them aside to create room for stretching his body – and enjoying the display of nocturnal nature branching out above his head. His eyes could journey round the sky; make contact with the huge but tiny stars glittering in the dark. And the countless birds hovering round sonorously, rejoicing in the coming of yet another time to congregate, explore, and relish the vastness of their blessing. What more could be as exhilarating as having a space to share in oneness and understanding? In the moonless sky and its flourishing star lights, he visualized his future with a different woman: not so beautiful but kind and peaceful. A motherly spouse bordering him with love as numerous as the stars he viewed in the sky. The unique one he had dreamt of countless times in his bachelorhood. From experience, he had learnt that a woman's virtues surpass her beauty – that her look is merely a plus to her uprightness. However in the heart of his dilemma, he still believed in his dreams and early actualization. He never could tell for how much longer he could bear the pain of being ill-treated by his own wife.

He looked in the direction of her room wonderingly. Could she have gone to sleep without him? Definitely. He dropped his legs from the bench and sneaked into the room. There, he met her wide awake but in the middle of a telephone conversation with someone. She saw him clearly and carried on with her chat. This infuriated him so much that he couldn't help but ask.

'Diwai! Diwai! Does what go around come back around?' He carried his pillow in inclination to sleep alone in their living room. He wouldn't sleep where he would be rejected till day break. Never but she didn't care.

'Sorry, I'll call you back', she ended the call quickly and dropped the phone. She followed him into the living room to respond to his seemingly foolish question.

'Excuse me- this man, what do you mean by that question? Tell me what that means to you. You are so verbally abusive. Why are you like this?' she ranted, pointing at his face. She had mastered the home so well – she was the master of the house. She tensed her muscle, slammed into him in high spirit of assertion – like a car out of control. He stepped back, still holding his pillow.

'Remember you were not up to my standard. I just accepted you – I mean – managed you and look at you now. You are my biggest frustration. You are so annoying that I can't stand you for a whole day'.

'Diwai, I want to sleep. Please I have a lot to do tomorrow'.

'Then shush! Shut your mouth and spare me! Spare me!'

'Diwai, I have spared you. Excuse me, I want to sleep', he coiled in the settee and padded his head with the pillow. It looked like he had acted maturely enough to send her back to her room. But it wasn't over.

'You called me a bad wife. No man ever condemned me in my life except you – '. She cursed, stood still. He didn't reply. He only awaited a sound sleep. He had tons of supplies awaiting him the following day. If she chose to rant on, then it was her preference and she owned her mouth. He closed his eyes in pretense.

The house sooner became a ghost abode than expected. For the past two weeks, no one spoke to anyone, even when they brushed themselves anywhere within. Diwai had decided to hold grudges against her hubby until he came forward to apologize first. Nothing would push her to him first, following the advice from her many friends. Zinyoro, on the other hand, spent more time away than with her. Some of his favorite spots were Buhle's restaurant, his old friend's house and his brother's villa. They strengthened him, brought out the real man in him. With them, he was a happy man. He felt wanted, loved and respected. In no time, he stopped sleeping in his house to avoid every night trouble and insult.

He could recollect promising his mother not to hit a woman, no matter what - after he caught his father bantering her one day. It was indeed unforgiving and unforgettable each time he pictured her writhing and crying on the ground, in his father's compound with more bruises than usual. She had those marks on her, even after his death. Their problem arose from her request for a separate home to avert nagging from his two other wives. He pounced on her like a lion on a prey and lashed at her with his belt. With pain, she ran out of her room, forgetting to pick her wrapper. He was the same one that cladded her from shame and mockery surrounding her. Seeing this, he felt all her pains as he was the only one consoling her - the closest to her. Nonetheless, he vowed not to treat his wife the same way. It is surprising to him that Diwai wouldn't appreciate his serenity.

'Are we set to go home?' Buhle brought his attention to her restaurant, smiling broadly. Her dimpled cheeks glowed in the bright light. He had waited for her to close from work, then together they would walk home.

'Come here ', he beckoned to her, smiling back. He watched her glue her shapely ear to his mouth. 'Are you sure you are ready to close?' turning to face him, she whispered with seduction, 'anything for your joy. It is you now. It's been business since in the morning. If you don't want me to open tomorrow, it's alright'.

'I love you', he whispered back.

'You know I love you more', she pulled him up from the chair playfully, then led the way.

'I will see you all tomorrow', she waved at her waitresses before exiting with her newly -found love. At last, it was a happy landing for her after much trial. What someone owned and had no value for was her most esteemed and wanted. She knew how difficult it had been for her to get a good man like him and she was determined not to let go, even though Diwai changed her mind and came back for him.

'You know what I just remembered?' he asked holding her hand as they walked down a long busy street slowly.

'What did you remember, honey?' she squeezed his hand in hers with much adoration. She wanted to listen to him, wanted to talk to him all the time. He was her soul mate.

'That day in our primary school, when it rained heavily and our classroom was flooded. Remember we were all sent back home?' he recounted joyfully, his vigor and aura of companionship all emerging and making him feel ten years younger than his exact age. He liked such a feeling he hadn't had for the past five years he was in his marriage bondage. He wanted that forever.

'Yes – yes, I remember. We bathed in the rain and felt so happy', she completed the story, laughing really hard. They were best friends up till the age of thirty. To Zinny, they were just friends; to her they were more than friends. They were inseparable, bonded forever.

'What drifted your mind to that now?' she stopped walking, crossed to his side and just stood, facing him - an expression of love all over her. He broke into a cool smile, standing akimbo.

'You know something? Buhle, you are more than my friend. You mean the whole world to me. And do you see the sky now?' he pointed up and she also looked up.

'It looks like rain, we have to hasten up, hurry –let's go home', she dragged him along laughing. And they both played like kids – like the old times.

'We are not going to part and go to our parents tonight. We shall be together forever', Buhle added still jogging beside him. Each time, she paused and gave him a side- kick playfully.

'Remember that? Pinch and run game'.

'Yes, like this and run', he pinched her again and she laughed. Passersby slowed down to watch both grown love birds. But they didn't care about who was watching. They were both having a great time together.

Three weeks after Diwai stopped seeing her husband, she got so worried. She got obsessed with how she was going to bring him back to the house. It was obvious he left to avoid her trouble. She sat up on her bed late that night, contemplating on the next move to make. Throughout the previous week, he visited his mother –in –law who didn't sound like she hadn't heard any information about their dispute. Even so she admitted to knowing his whereabouts, she refused to inform her. She only promised to talk him into returning home and nothing had happened since then. His brother had shown his dislike for her from the beginning of their relationship, so she didn't bother visiting. In his office, he had a representative now. He scarcely visited, except he had much more supply around the environment. Her only hope should have been his phone but he rejected her calls often. What was she going to do next?

She rose from her bed, began to pace round her little room. There had been no sleep for her in the past two weeks. No sleep until he returned home. She shrugged sadly, mindless of whatever wrong she must have done or his motive for staying away. As advised by his mother, she was prepared to apologize to him and live in peace, since the pets causing their problem had both disappeared. It would be only him and his family now –just as she wanted. No Chindori or Mazomba.

Her eyes fell on her sleeping son for a moment then drifted to their traditional wedding picture hanging on the wall. Has he left her? Never! She refuted the thought of not seeing him around again. She was just twenty eight with a kid. The thought of being alone with the boy sickened her because he already started demanding for him. Daddy this – daddy that. When shushed, he obeyed for only about two hours then he spoke about him again and again.

Concluding that she had to find him the next day, she pulled a long breath. She sank in her bed sadly, still gazing at their wedding picture. Whether good or bad, she was prepared to accept him, after having a taste of loneliness and separation. It was the most difficult time of her life as she imagined him with someone else, probably a better woman. The hurtful feeling ate deep into her heart. And she began to cry.

As usual, Zinyoro visited his mother on Tuesdays to avoid running into Diwai who had a board meeting on the same day in her office. He knew all her schedules and did all he could not to see her. Buhle wasn't a stranger to his mother. They grew up in the same neighborhood and their mothers were friends too. In their childhood, Buhle would visit and spend a whole day in their house and he would do the same on the following day. They were like the same family.

When she was re- introduced to her on that free Tuesday, she was astonished for two reasons. One, he was a married man and two, Buhle was like her sister. However, he convinced her that nothing is new under the sun.

'Mother, Diwai showed me hell in that house. I can't continue living that way'. He walked in to get Buhle a seat and returned in a jiffy. 'Here, sit here and relax. Everything is fine, okay?' Buhle nodded, smiling. His mother did not smile. She wasn't pleased with his new idea.

'No, you have to be sincere to her if you truly love her as your sister', his mother corrected his wrong insinuation, looking very serious.

'Sincere about what, mother?' he asked in a very serious tone.

'About your marriage, Zinyoro. Your marriage. Buhle, your friend is happily married', she declared seriously and she kept smiling, certain about something she didn't know. She shone with much confidence.

'Mother, I am not happily married. I am out of that marriage and I am going to marry Buhle. That's why we are here'.

'It's too early my son and I won't concede to that now. Buhle, I'm sorry, I need to see your mother about this. My son is deceiving you'.

'Oh mother, stop it! Stop killing my joy. This is very serious, more serious than you imagine', he lost his temper, forgetting all the respect he gave to her. She studied his seriousness and fell silent sadly. He had not been so badly treated in his life.

He sounded more emotionally disturbed than he used to explain to her. To her, there could be more to the matter than what she heard and saw.

'Mother, you didn't live with us for five years, did you? Those years were like dining with my enemy in hell. I felt emotionally disturbed. I was torn apart. Imagine not smiling for a whole week. Mother, it was like that and I am out of it for good'.

He stopped talking and nobody spoke. Three faces showed different impressions, communicated with one another in the silent yard. His mother sighed again. Without lying, she understood all he had been through. He was a very reserved man, choosing to keep his secret buried. But unknown to him, she used to read the emotions hovering around him. Sometimes he would look drawn and lifeless – at another time, he would be sad or emotionally troubled. She knew it would bore down to separation and it had happened finally –despite all her advice to her stubborn daughter- in- law.

'Mother, Diwai didn't trouble me alone. She punished my son, blocked him from reaching me in that same house. She also punished my pets. She killed my parrot before my eyes and drove my dog away. Why was she that awful if she wanted this marriage?'

'Zinyoro, that's okay. People have problems in their homes, settle and carry on. Yours is not the first. I'm sure she has learnt from her mistake', she tried to repudiate his self-determination in front of a new woman. It wasn't ideal enough. She spoke to him convincingly but he already came to a decision about it. He gave no reply, after he said all he had to say. He turned to Buhle and began a new topic with her.

'That man on the site is very funny. Did you see the way he held my money? I like the way you spoke to him in a gentle manner. He had no choice than to pay me and just leave. Trouble maker'. They both laughed, ignoring his aged mother. When their discussion continued for the next two minutes, she cleared her throat to draw his attention.

'Sorry, mother. What do you want Buhle to do for you before we leave?' Hearing this, Buhle stood up instantly, preparedly.

'No –I have finished all my works. I was about going back inside when you came'.

'We will soon leave too. We still have a movie to watch by 7:30pm', he checked his time.

'Movie? When was the last time you saw your son?' she demanded, distracting him again. He got tired of her endless proposition and stood up to leave.

'Buhle, let's go now. The movie begins in twenty minutes ', he pulled her up from her seat. She understood they both had to leave if the issue about his ex-wife must end. It wasn't what she liked to hear too.

'Goodbye ma. I am always around you. I can come back any time soon', Buhle said softly, her dimples appearing and deepening as she smiled.

'Okay –my regards to your mother', she replied with mixed feelings: sad and happy. Neither Buhle nor Zinny cared. They walked away from the house holding hands and knocking heads in laughter. For them, it was the beginning of a flawless love life: an affair so full of respect and understanding. Whatever his mother wanted or felt didn't matter to him. She could advice or beg all she wanted; he wouldn't live with Diwai again. He had pursued marriage and family to no avail and now he pursued true love and happiness.

Now alone in the yard, Edzai, Zinny's mother kept her eyes glued to the gate absently. She still didn't believe what she saw. It seemed like a dream. Was he really going to leave his wife and marry another woman? She wondered. The Zinyoro she knew had transformed from a caring and patient man into a determined and unyielding man. What became of all his virtues of consideration and simplicity? His patience and calmness? And the perseverance she taught him? Did they all melt away at the time he should return to his family for continuity? She wasn't quite sure if he wouldn't end up with both of them. Yes, with both Diwai and Buhle, he would build a polygamous home like hers. And there would be trouble upon a new trouble each day of his life. What about Buhle? Did he really know her? What she prayed against everyday would eventually befall her loving son. She heaved a deep sigh, and concluded that, be that as it may, Diwai changed him. She put all the blame on her.

At the time she rose to walk back into the lonely bosom of her bedroom, her main gate oscillated forcibly and Diwai herself walked in, hauling her crying son after her. He retracted obstinately, his second foot gummed to the ground with all his strength. She went around him, slapped his buttocks and unstuck the foot from the ground for a quick drive and of course, obedience. He cried out louder. Sick of all their day- long drama, Edzai took the boy from her.

'He needs to be taught a good lesson. Like father like son', Diwai said throwing his school bag at him. Her overreaction was uncalled for. Her mother –in –law thought it was a transfer of aggression and instantly gave a suggestion.

'Why not leave him here with me? Maybe he's tired of being with only you all the time', she wiped his face with her scarf.

'I'm just tired of everything. I've not seen Zin for the past three months now. I don't know what else I'm going to do', she declared almost crying. Edzai took one long hard look at her pitiful face then decided to open up to her to help save her fallen marriage.

'He was here. He just left with a new wife. He wants to marry another wife'.

'What?' Diwai got paralyzed by her mind-numbing information. She dropped her handbag with all the stuffs she got from the market for cooking. In the course, her raw sliced fish slipped, poured in the sand.

'Don't ruin this fish. It's very costly now', she stooped to pick them for her. From the look on her face, she didn't care about anything but her marriage. She remained flabbergasted, merely watched all her moves vaguely. Tears appeared beneath her eyelids.

'Oh my God, God sees my heart. I've said all I should today to dissuade him from his unanticipated act but he refused', Edzai recounted feelingly. She dropped the fish aside then wiped her tears for her. Her little son stood watching her, wondering why she was also crying. He sped to her and gave her a hug.

'Mummy – sorry', he said rubbing her face. Edzai carried the child away from her - away from her pathetic mood. She served him some food and returned to his sad mother.

'Diwai- I'm sorry, you are responsible for this separation. I took you as my daughter, shared my feelings and experiences in marriage with you to help you build your home but you didn't listen. Now, look at what is about to happen. I warned you, remember?' she recollected. She didn't raise her face to her. She kept dripping her tears on her skirt –the same one she planned to wear to the office the next day. She was hot and sweating all over.

'Diwai, why did you kill his pets? I think you went too far'.

'I didn't know the parrot would die but I didn't kill his dog', she forced her head up, crying loudly, her bloodshot eyes, in a pool of tears.

'Diwai, it's okay. We will see what we can do about it. But you know I can't force him to decide. He's a man. Let's be prayerful. It's okay. You can stay with me tonight, please. You can't go home now'.

It was saddening for Diwai, discovering that her beloved no longer had interest in her. Their marriage wasn't binding; he could leave anytime he wanted. He followed the path he desired and this embittered her. Would she have said that she didn't overreact or take advantage of his tranquility? No, she knew she depended on her friends' suggestion to drive him out of her life. He was like a drum succumbing to the direction of its stick. Whatever it commands, it does, even though it was time to be ruptured. He danced to her tune day and night but fled when she changed. She was prepared to become a changed woman and give her best in their matrimony. Just one chance was all she needed

Precisely four weeks after pleading to no avail, Edzai called a family meeting in her yard, to reconcile Diwai with her husband. The venue was tidy and roomy as all worthies from each family arrived- one after the other- exactly the way they appeared for their traditional wedding. Elaborate pleasantries were exchanged at the inception, remembering that they met last at their wedding six years ago. It was against the tradition to roam their matrimonial home after marriage, except there was a trouble as such. Nevertheless, they abandoned their schedules for that day- to gather and restore peace in their home. Diwai herself was punctual with her son. But only one important being was absent. Without him, there wouldn't be any issue to discuss on that day as the matter revolved around him.

'But you told us your son was informed about this meeting. How come he's not here yet?' Diwai's father pestered Edzai, anger burning through him. They had waited for about three hours after the appointed time. What was he up to? He kept staring back at the gate, expecting him, running out of patience.

'I'm sincerely sorry. He will soon be here.' She left the group and went to her second son for confirmation. He had stood apart from everyone since he arrived. Deep within him, he was delighted his brother had finally woken from his slumber and walked off the distressing marriage. What had he not witnessed in their home? Lot of eyesore – eyesore he wouldn't accept from his wife.

However, he was glad that he finally listened to his advice and became a free man. They both had an agreement and he wasn't expecting to see him there.

'Babanana –have you called your brother today? His phone is turned off and –'

'Mother, I have a business waiting for me at 6pm. Maybe we should all leave. It's his life anyway'.

'How am I going to say that? Diwai's father is very angry', she remarked nervously.

'Angry? Angry about what? The same anger his daughter couldn't control and now – mother, I want to leave', he controlled his surging irritation then left them waiting.

'Is this a good life? Is this the way you trained your sons to disrespect waiting elders? Look, what gives him much effrontery to keep us waiting here?' Diwai's father flew into a rage completely out of control. He stood up from his chair and prepared to leave. His wife followed suit grumbling, and another elder stood, followed by all of Diwai's family. They all gave vent to their resentment at the same time. The whole yard turned noisy and chaos slipped into the quiet street. Edzai knelt down begging for forgiveness.

'You don't have to beg them to wait. Get up! If Zin is not here, he has passed a message to us', the head of Zin's family interrupted. Zin had earlier explained to him how he felt and why he wouldn't be there. He wasn't surprised too.

'What message', four of Diwai's members chorused arguably.

'The marriage is over'.

'You are a miserable man. I can't blame you. I put the blame on oranges that bring forth trouble to its tree. Diwai - leave with us right now. I'm not here to challenge poverty and impossibility. Out of here now!', Diwai's father ordered and they all left noisily, rubbing minds, expressing feelings and finally hurling all the blame on her for choosing an undesirable man. As flies only support a diseased wound, every member skipped her faults, even overlooked the innocent pets she ill-treated and called Zin several bad names. They tagged him the worst man in his generation.

The tribulation that fidgets or faces a man sometimes turns its back against another man, scarcely remembered him and never knew the route to his house. As Diwai wept over her lost love, Buhle basked in a happy relationship. Their new home was opened with all pets of their dream – a new dog and parrot plus the cat that Buhle cherished. They both built a harmonious home three months after he wedded her. It was like life and its continuity when both hearts agreed as one, shared the same feeling and enjoyed wishes in common.

The night awaits both lovers, strolling out hand in hand and admiring the beauty of nature. The day impatiently waits to commence a new day. It was a happy life any good love could wish for. A happy life devoid of danger, verbal attacks, fear, hatred, malice and uncertainty. Everything succumbs to the power of love. The future was vividly present. It lived with them, played along and prepared for the dismissal of every new day. The atmosphere was cool, friendly and so full of freedom. Understanding got control over the two. And they lived happily ever after.

Glossary

RUQAYAH- Hausa language from Nigeria

Na iya bayanna mini cewa- I can explain that
Ina zuwa- wait
Me na wannan? - What is this?
Agbada- a male traditional wear, a piece of overflowing material always covering down to the knee.
Da ita- I can think about it
Baba- father
Nagode-thank you
Amin- amen
Muka fahimitaa da-we understand that
Wallahi- I swear in the name of Allah
Allah-God
Mi ni ni?-what is it?
Kanji ko?-
Jalabia-A long Muslim dress worn by both male and female
Tesbiy- a Muslim rosary for prayer
Hijab-a Muslim veil
Nawa ne- what time is it?
Da ni- with me
Kente- a traditional tie- and-dye material
Mun ki yarda da- we disagree about that
Ina ya ke? - Where is he?
Subhana llahi- God is perfect
Alhamdulillah- praise to God

Alakia eh- God forbid
Kanji ko?- do you understand
Mi ni ni?- What is it?
Nikkai- Islamic traditional wedding
Mallam- Islamic clerics

NANA-Ghanaian language.

Adjei- an expression of severe pain or bad news.
Adua bie- a kind of bean soup
Abolo- cassava bread
Akwaaba-welcome
Maa ha- good afternoon
Me ho ye- I'm fine
Kwatta- nothing at all
Chale- you know?
Ayekoo- well done
Ma a duo- good evening
Yaa- nua- responding to greeting
Akpate shie - home- distilled gin
Akuffo- small sized club bear
Kabako- we have a big problem
Yamin pengu- God forbid
Kenke- corn meal
Lasi- lasi- back-biting
Wa ami awu! - Shame on you!
Akosombo- electricity

DO THI NGOC- Burundi language.

Bangwe! - stop!
Urakoze cane- thank you very much
Kuki?- why
Urakomeye- how are you?
Bwakeye-hello

Amakuru?-what's new?
Ego- yes
Kira- bless you
Turabonaye- see you later
Amahoro- peace
Ubuyene- right now
Sindabizi- I don't know

DAFINA-Swahili language spoken in Kenya

Habari- how are you?
Hatari- danger
Pole- sorry for your misfortune
Sijambo- I am fine
Kwaheri-goodbye
Mambo- what's up
Asante- thank you
Tafadhali- please
Pole sana- please
Hakuna matata- no worries
Karibu-welcome
Samahani- excuse me
Nini? –what?

KENOSI-Botswana language

Dumela- thank you
Hamba kahle- bye
Uku buya- come back
Ukuqala-firstly
Ngiya kwemukela! - welcome!
Sala kahle!-goodbye (to people staying)
Hamba kahle-goodbye (to a person leaving)
Woza name- come with me
Umunz?-Mr.?

Umuza kakhulu- you're very kind
Angizwa! - I don't understand!
Angazi- I don't know
Ngilambile-I'm hungry

SENAMI-Egun Language from Republic du Benin.

Mi fon dagbe? - How are you this morning?
E yan gaji- it's very nice
Mawu- God
Mi wa yi wegbe- come and go home
Mi se- do you understand?
Mi ku dowe?- How are you today?
E yan- it is well
Mijale- please
Ato gblaja- large ears
Mawu tin- there's God.
Asu che- my husband
Iya che- my mother
Soeurs- sister

ZINYORO-Shona language from Zimbabwe.

Salibonani-how are you?
Ee yebo- hello
Ee unofara-how are you?
O o nhia- how is life?
Eee- yes
Aa muzaya! - friend!

Printed in the United States
by Baker & Taylor Publisher Services